"Nate, hurry. Kiss her. Kiss her now."

Ellie's eyes popped open, and she stared at her grandmother in embarrassed horror. "Granny, are you cra—"

"Are we going for quick and chaste or down and dirty?" Nate asked, a teasing note in his voice.

Ellie opened her mouth to blurt *quick and chaste* when the rebellious streak that she mostly ignored took over. "Down and dirty."

"Totally not what I expected you to say," Nate murmured as he wrapped an arm around her waist, drawing her closer.

Maybe this wasn't such a good idea after all but it was too late to change her mind. His mouth was on hers, his lips surprisingly soft and gentle. She clutched his jacket, dizzy from the intensity of her feelings. She swore she heard violins.

Nate broke the kiss and stared at her.

"Good. You look relaxed and ravished, Ellie my girl. And you, laddie"—her grandmother grinned at Nate—"look stunned."

Praise for Debbie Mason and the Highland Falls Series

"Debbie Mason writes romance like none other."
—FreshFiction.com

"I've never met a Debbie Mason story that I didn't enjoy."
—KeeperBookshelf.com

"I'm telling you right now, if you haven't yet read a book by Debbie Mason you don't know what you're missing."
—RomancingtheReaders.blogspot.com

"It's not just romance. It's grief and mourning, guilt and truth, second chances and revelations."
—WrittenLoveReviews.blogspot.com

"Mason always makes me smile and touches my heart in the most unexpected and wonderful ways."
—HerdingCats-BurningSoup.com

"No one writes heartful small-town romance like Debbie Mason, and I always count the days until the next book!"
—TheManyFacesofRomance.blogspot.com

The Inn on Mirror Lake

The Inn on Mirror Lake

DEBBIE MASON

A Highland Falls Novel

FOREVER
New York   Boston

Copyright © 2022 by Debbie Mazzuca
Cover design by Daniela Medina
Cover art by Thomas Hallman
Cover images © iStock; © Depositphotos; © Shutterstock
Cover copyright © 2022 by Hachette Book Group, Inc.

Forever
Hachette Book Group
1290 Avenue of the Americas, New York, NY 10104
read-forever.com
twitter.com/readforeverpub

First Edition: February 2022

Forever is an imprint of Grand Central Publishing. The Forever name and logo are trademarks of Hachette Book Group, Inc.

The publisher is not responsible for websites (or their content) that are not owned by the publisher.

The Hachette Speakers Bureau provides a wide range of authors for speaking events. To find out more, go to www.hachettespeakersbureau.com or call (866) 376-6591.

ISBNs: 978-1-5387-2063-9 (mass market); 978-1-5387-2064-6 (ebook)

Printed in the United States of America

OPM

10 9 8 7 6 5 4 3 2 1

This book is dedicated with much love to my wonderful and supportive family, especially my husband, Perry, who has been my hero and my biggest cheerleader for more than forty years.

Acknowledgments

If you're reading this book, it's thanks to the dedicated team at Grand Central/Forever that works tirelessly to get my stories into the hands of readers. My sincere thanks and gratitude to the sales team, the art department for another gorgeous cover, the marketing team, and everyone in editorial, especially my incredibly talented editor, Alex Logan, who never fails to make each book better.

Thanks also to my agent, Pamela Harty, for her support and friendship these past twelve years.

And to you, dear reader, my heartfelt thanks for buying this book. I hope you enjoy your time with Nate and Ellie in Highland Falls. A special thank-you to reader group member Lorraine Shirlow for naming Toby.

The Inn on Mirror Lake

Chapter One

♥

Elliana MacLeod stood in the middle of the inn's sun-drenched dining room, surrounded by women devouring every item on the spring tea menu with delighted abandon. It was the first time since Ellie had arrived last August to help out her grandfather after his stroke that they'd had more than a handful of people dining at the inn. If it weren't all an act for her mother's benefit, Ellie would be doing a happy dance instead of wringing her hands.

"Are you okay? You look nervous." Ellie's cousin Sadie came to stand beside her, carrying a rose bone china teapot and a platter of fragrant iced scones on a silver tray. Her dark hair pulled back in a ponytail, Sadie had taken on the role of waitress, a position Ellie usually found herself in. Their one and only waitress had quit last month due to the lack of hours.

"Why don't you have a cup of white peony tea and a lavender cream scone?" Sadie suggested. "Spill the Tea and Bites of Bliss outdid themselves. Everything tastes as incredible as it smells."

Since the cook had left the same month and for the same reason as the waitress, Ellie had taken over kitchen duty. She couldn't have pulled off today's menu without the local tea shop and bakery pitching in.

"Thanks, but I couldn't eat another bite." Ellie had been stress eating since she got the phone call from her mother informing her of her intentions for the inn and Ellie's Grandpa Joe. "The scones look amazing though. Everything does," she said, glancing at the white linen–draped tables with their gorgeous spring floral arrangements.

The mayor had arrived earlier that morning with armfuls of pastel tulips and boxes of crystal vases to decorate the tables. "I don't know how I'll repay everyone."

Moments after Ellie told Sadie about her mother's phone call, her cousin had organized a meeting of the Sisterhood, a group of Highland Falls' most influential women, who then put out a call to their families and friends. Everyone had jumped on board with the plan to convince Ellie's mother that the inn was a going concern.

"No one expects you to repay them. They'd be offended if you offered. Mirror Lake Inn is as much a part of the town's heritage as it is yours." Sadie looked around the dining room with its faded red floral-printed wallpaper and stone fireplace. "Honestly, I think everyone's feeling bad that they haven't been more supportive of the inn."

"It's not like Grandpa Joe went out of his way

to attract business after Grandma Mary died, and I haven't been much better."

"Don't be so hard on yourself. You've been looking after Joe. With no help from your parents or sister and brother, I might add," Sadie said.

"It's not like Bri could take time away from her counseling practice, and Jace is halfway around the world." Her younger sister and brother had high-powered careers, something her mother pointed out to Ellie at every opportunity.

"I guess, but your parents don't have an excuse. They live five hours away."

Her parents worked at Duke University in Durham. Her mother was an administrator, and her father was a professor. "To be honest, I didn't exactly encourage them to come." In fact, she'd done her best to discourage them from visiting. At least in the beginning. One look at the state of the inn and Grandpa's Joe condition when Ellie had first arrived, and her mother would have put up a *For Sale* sign and stuck her father in a home.

At least Ellie had bought her grandfather time. She hoped that once her mother saw how well Joe was doing, she'd back off. And while Ellie wouldn't have been able to override her mother's decision last year, she had the means to do so now. She just hoped she didn't have to use them.

Ellie shut down thoughts of the upcoming meeting with her mother and smiled at her cousin. "Besides, I had you and Granny. I don't know what I would have done without you guys. Or Jonathan." Jonathan Knight was Sadie's grandfather by marriage and had been renting a room at the inn since last fall. The former superior court judge had been a godsend in more ways than one.

"Where is he, by the way?" Sadie asked. "I haven't seen him since I got here." Several women called out to Sadie, wanting their tea. "I'm coming," she told them, and then she said to Ellie, "Don't let your mother intimidate you. If she tries bullying you into agreeing with her, just remember how Joe looked when Aunt Miranda told him she planned to sell the inn and put him in a home."

That was one image Ellie wished she could wipe from her mind. But Sadie was right. For her grandfather's sake, Ellie had to stand up to her mother. She couldn't let her run roughshod over her like she always did.

As Sadie walked away, Ellie realized her cousin was right about something else. Jonathan was nowhere to be seen and neither was Grandpa Joe. An older woman waved her over to a table. "What's in this sandwich, dear? It's delicious."

Ellie had been up since four that morning making sandwiches—her only contribution to the tea. "I'm so glad you're enjoying them." She glanced at the filling in the dainty tea sandwich. "Chicken, cranberries, mayo, Dijon mustard, and watercress."

The woman hummed with pleasure. "You should do a tea every weekend. We'd book standing reservations, wouldn't we, ladies?" she said to her table companions.

"Then you'll be happy to hear that Ellie just told me the inn will be serving tea every Saturday and Sunday afternoon starting next week. So be sure to make your reservations before you leave," said Abby Mackenzie, who'd come to stand beside Ellie.

Abby was a social media celebrity. Her popular YouTube channel and podcast, *Abby Does Highland Falls*, had put their small North Carolina mountain town on the map. The petite redheaded dynamo had been responsible for turning around the fortunes of several local businesses. Despite having given birth to a baby girl a matter of weeks ago, she'd spearheaded today's event at the inn.

"Enjoy your tea, ladies. And thanks again for giving up your afternoon to support the inn and Joe," Abby said, looping her arm through Ellie's.

Ellie added her thanks, smiling when the women told her to call on them anytime.

"Remind me again when I agreed to offer an afternoon tea every Saturday and Sunday," Ellie whispered as Abby led her away from the table.

Abby grinned. "Don't worry, Babs and Bliss are onboard," she said, referring to the owners of Spill the Tea and Bites of Bliss, respectively. "It'll be great promotion for them, especially once people start booking the dining room for weddings, showers, and birthdays."

"I've been here eight months, and the only one who booked the dining room is my grandfather. For his poker parties."

"Trust me, once Sadie's finished the redesign of

the inn's website, you'll have more event bookings
than you can handle. Especially if we win our bid for
most romantic small town in America. People will be
flocking to Highland Falls and the inn."

A week before Christmas, Happy Ever After Entertainment, a movie production company, had opened
up a contest for the most romantic small town in
America. The company would film its next movie
in the winning town. As its name suggested, Happy
Ever After Entertainment was known for its romantic,
wholesome movies.

"I know it's not easy for you to lie to your mother
about the state of the inn's finances, but it's only a
matter of time before it's running in the black," Abby
continued. "Which reminds me, Mallory, the kids, and
I are in the two-bedroom suite. So between us and the
Sisterhood, there's no room at the inn. At least you
won't have to lie to your mother if they planned on
staying."

There were twelve guest rooms at the inn but
only nine were available for rent. Ellie, Joe, and
the judge occupied the other three. Mallory, Sadie
and Abby's best friend, could have filled the two-
bedroom suite with her family alone. Mallory and
her husband Gabe, the chief of police, had six chil-
dren between them—five boys and a six-month-old
daughter.

"It'll make it easier to lie to her, but it's still a
lie. It's not like you guys are staying all night," Ellie
said as she walked from the dining room into the
reception area.

"Who says? We're planning on celebrating with you and Joe after your parents—"

An alarm emanating from the pocket of Ellie's peacock-blue slacks interrupted Abby. A chorus of shrill beeps went off simultaneously in the dining room. Sadie had set up the group alert on their phones to warn of Ellie's parents' impending arrival. Members of the Sisterhood, who were stationed at the entrance to Highland Falls, had issued the warning.

Abby leaned back, calling into the dining room, "Fifteen minutes to showtime, ladies."

Ellie retrieved her phone and glanced at the text on her screen. "This isn't good. My mother brought reinforcements. My sister, Bri, and her husband are following behind in their SUV."

"Don't buy trouble. They might be on your side," Abby said.

"Maybe Bri, but not her husband. Richard is in lockstep with my mother about everything. Bri won't stand up to either one of them."

Bri had married Richard two years ago. Other than their wedding and a disastrous Christmas visit that same year, Ellie hadn't spent any time with the couple. She'd taken an almost instant dislike to the investment banker. Her parents, especially her mother, fawned all over the man. Even Ellie's brother, who was usually a good judge of character, seemed to like her sister's husband. But while they saw what Richard wanted them to see, Ellie saw what he tried to hide.

"If anything, my mother brought Bri to bolster her

case for putting Grandpa in a home." Ellie's sister was
a family therapist.

Ellie pushed her worries aside, smiling as she
approached the registration desk. Mallory's seventeen-
year-old stepson from her first marriage, Oliver, had
volunteered to staff the front desk for the afternoon.
He looked like British royal Prince William and had
the accent to go along with his good looks. "Oliver,
have you seen my grandfather?"

"He left with the judge about twenty minutes ago."

"Did they happen to say where they were going or
when they'd be back?" Ellie asked, a sinking feeling
coming over her at Oliver's head shake.

"I'll get Gabe to put out an alert. They couldn't have
gotten far," Abby said, head bent over her phone.

"You didn't do anything wrong, Oliver. I should
have kept a closer eye on my grandfather." She knew
how Joe felt about the upcoming confrontation with
her mother.

Oliver frowned, and Ellie briefly closed her eyes.
He hadn't voiced the thought out loud; she'd read his
mind. She was psychic. No one other than her mother
and Sadie knew of her abilities, and that's the way
she meant to keep it. Although her grandmother might
have an inkling since Ellie had inherited the gift—
curse—from her.

"I'll check if the truck's in the parking lot." Ellie
headed for the door. Her grandfather and the judge
used the inn's truck whenever they went into town.
But Jonathan knew how important today was. Surely
he wouldn't aid in her grandfather's escape.

As she opened the door, Ellie glanced back at Oliver and clearly saw an image of her grandfather with a bottle of beer and a cigar in his hands. Joe had sworn Oliver to secrecy. It wasn't something Ellie could ask about without revealing her own secret.

She stepped onto the wraparound front porch. The wooden rocking chairs were empty, the plaid woolen blankets folded neatly over the arms undisturbed. A quick scan of the packed parking lot on her right revealed the red truck was still in its spot.

She walked down the steps, taking the meandering cobblestone path bordered by rhododendrons. Come June, they'd be a sea of purple flowers. As she rounded the inn, the sweet scent from a cluster of mountain magnolia trees greeted her. She looked out over the rolling green lawn to the two empty Adirondack chairs on the dock. Not completely empty, she thought, spying a beer bottle and a cigar on the arm of a chair.

Making her way down the sloping lawn to the dock, she called, "Grandpa Joe! Judge!" Her voice echoed off the sapphire-blue lake. But other than three quacking ducks paddling through the lily pads on her left, no one responded to her calls.

She picked up the half-empty beer bottle and the cigar from the chair, wondering if, like a dog, her highly tuned sixth sense would twig to her grandfather's whereabouts with a sip of his beer or a puff on his cigar. At this point she was willing to try anything and stuck his half-smoked cigar between her lips. She took a deep pull, but other than a faint whiff of its sweet, peppery scent, she got nothing.

The rough rumble of an engine distracted her, and she turned. A man sat astride a black Harley wearing a leather jacket. His face obscured by a black-visored helmet, he looked big and bad, and her heart began to race. Not from nerves but from attraction. She knew who he was, and not because of her psychic abilities. Nate Black was the one person she couldn't read.

Focused on him as she was, it took a moment for her to realize he wasn't alone. A petite woman got off the back of the motorcycle. Ellie stared in shock when the Betty White look-alike removed the helmet from her head.

It was Agnes MacLeod, her grandmother. "Granny, what are you…" Nate removed his helmet, and Ellie instantly lost her train of thought. His wavy dark hair—longer than she remembered—brushed the collar of his leather jacket, his ruggedly handsome face half-hidden behind a beard. At the flash of his strong white teeth through that dark, heavy beard, she nearly tripped over her own two feet.

Way to play it cool, Ellie. She was acting like the thirteen-year-old geek she used to be if the coolest guy in high school had just smiled at her. His smile widened, fine lines crinkling the corners of his dark eyes, and she found herself smiling in return. Hopefully just a nice, friendly smile and not one that betrayed the *Oh my Lord, you are so flipping hot I want to kiss you* thought currently running through her brain.

"Hey, Ellie. How's it going?" he said, swinging a muscled, jean-clad leg over his motorbike.

Her knees went weak at the sound of his deep, sexy voice saying her name. She rolled her eyes at her reaction. She had to get a grip. And get out more. There was no way Nate Black should affect her like this. She was a mature, self-possessed woman, not some starry-eyed teenager in the throes of her first crush. She needed...to say something.

"Hi, Nate. It's nice to see you again." She offered her hand to the man now standing beside her grandmother, because that's what a composed thirty-three-year-old woman would do. "Oh," she said upon noticing the cigar between her fingers. She transferred it to her other hand, the one holding the half-empty beer bottle. "It's not what it looks like. I was just"—she couldn't say *trying to get a read on my grandfather's whereabouts*—"picking up after Joe."

Nate took her outstretched hand in his and smiled. "Don't worry, your secret's safe with me."

What was he talking about? Her secret crush on him or her secret psychic abilities? But the worry that he might have guessed either of her secrets vanished at the feel of his warm, strong hand enveloping hers.

"Why are you two being so formal? You should be hugging, not shaking hands," her grandmother said, pushing Ellie into Nate.

"Mrs. M," Nate muttered, releasing Ellie's hand to slide his arms around her. No doubt to steady her and not to comply with her grandmother's blatant attempt at matchmaking. Her grandmother loved Nate and didn't bother hiding the fact that she thought he and Ellie were a perfect match.

Ignoring how wonderful he smelled and how incredible it felt to be in his arms again, Ellie gave him a quick, friendly hug and then backed away.

"What?" her grandmother said. "You don't think it's odd my granddaughter doesn't give you a hug instead of a handshake when you spent the night of Sadie and Chase's wedding in each other's arms?"

"Granny! We danced. We didn't—"

Her grandmother frowned. "I know. That's what I just said."

Ellie's cheeks flamed with heat. "Right, of course. Don't mind me. I didn't get a lot of sleep last night." She held up the beer bottle and cigar. "And Grandpa Joe is missing."

Agnes held up her phone. "We got the alert. No one in town has seen him. But don't worry, Nate will find him."

"I'm sure Nate has better things to do, Granny. You can't just—"

"Ellie, it's fine. I don't mind." The three of them turned at the sound of two vehicles coming up the gravel road. Ellie closed her eyes and took a calming breath. Her family had arrived.

"Nate, hurry. Kiss her. Kiss her now."

Ellie's eyes popped open, and she stared at her grandmother in embarrassed horror. "Granny, are you cra—"

"It's not a big deal, Ellie. Mrs. M told me what's up. She figures your mother won't mess with you if she thinks you have someone like me backing you up."

"You mean, like a boyfriend? You're supposed to be my boyfriend?"

Nate shrugged. "Half the town is in on the act to save the inn and Joe. I don't mind doing my part." He stepped closer, smiling down at her as he tipped up her chin with his knuckle. "What do you say?"

"I don't know if this is a good idea. I—"

"Be quiet and kiss the man. They won't believe you're a couple if they don't see it with their own eyes."

Chapter Two

♥

Ellie looked from her grandmother to Nate. The poor man had no idea what he was getting himself into. He might be an agent with the North Carolina State Bureau of Investigation and incredibly good at his job, but Agnes MacLeod was as devious as any of the criminals he'd put away. She was also right, to a certain degree.

While Nate's act wouldn't deter her mother from trying to railroad her into going along with her plan, Ellie's fake in-a-relationship status might deter her mother from listing all the reasons she would never be in one again. It was one of her mother's favorite gaslighting tactics to throw Ellie off balance.

"What are you two waiting for? They're turning into the inn," her grandmother said.

Nate stepped back, lowering his hand from Ellie's chin. "Are you okay?"

She looked up at him and smiled. He might give off a dangerous bad-boy vibe, but he was an incredibly nice guy. And it wasn't as if Ellie hadn't thought about kissing him. She'd actually given it quite a bit of thought the night of her cousin's wedding. They might have already done the deed if he hadn't been called away in the middle of their last dance together that moonlit night in October.

"I'm good. Let's do this." She stepped in to Nate and placed a hand on his chest. The man was seriously built and gorgeous. His muscles...No. No thinking about his muscles or how handsome he was. They were simply playing a part for a few hours. She'd deal with her grandmother's off-the-wall expectations later. It wasn't as if Nate would be around for more than a day anyway. The man was married to his job.

"Are we going for quick and chaste or down and dirty?" he asked, a teasing note in his voice.

She blinked up at him. Heat spread through her body at his question and her grandmother's snort of laughter. Ellie opened her mouth to blurt *Quick and chaste* when she caught a glimpse of her mother's face as the black SUV drove by. The rebellious streak in Ellie that she mostly ignored took over. "Down and dirty."

"Totally not what I expected you to say," Nate murmured as he wrapped an arm around her waist, drawing her closer.

Maybe this wasn't such a good idea after all. Her body was practically humming with desire. But it was too late to change her mind. His mouth was on hers, his lips surprisingly soft and gentle. Their breaths mingled in a kiss that was more teasingly seductive than down and dirty.

There was no urgent plundering. It was a lush

exploration of her mouth by a man who knew exactly what he was doing, and he did it very, very well. He angled his head, and she followed, deepening the kiss. It was like a sensual dance, one they'd performed before. She clutched his leather jacket, dizzy from the intensity of her feelings. She swore she heard violins. The sound of car doors slamming interrupted the romantic soundtrack in her mind.

Nate broke the kiss and stared at her.

"Good. You look relaxed and ravished, Ellie my girl. A much better look on you than pale and stressed out. And you, laddie"—her grandmother grinned at Nate—"look stunned."

Nate's mouth flattened. "You and I need to have a chat, Mrs. M." He glanced over Ellie's head. "But it'll have to wait," he said. Then he reached for Ellie.

He wasn't going to kiss her again, was he? She didn't think her mind or body could take it. "Um, Nate, I don't think it's a good idea for you to kiss me again."

"You and me both," he said under his breath, and then he took the cigar and beer bottle from her hand. "I'll text you when I find Joe, and you can tell me how you want to play it."

She looked over her shoulder. Her parents were out of their car, waiting for her sister and Richard to join them. Ellie returned her attention to Nate, retrieving her phone from her pocket.

"I've got your number," he said without meeting her gaze. He lifted his chin. "What's across the lake?"

She glanced at the rooftops barely visible through

the trees. "Cabins. They're part of the inn, but my grandfather hasn't rented them out in years."

"Is there an access road?"

"I'm pretty sure there is, but we usually walked around the lake or took the boat." She looked to the right of the dock where the rowboat had been this morning. "It's gone."

"Probably faster if I go by boat. Do you have another one?"

She nodded, wondering what she'd done wrong. He wouldn't look at her. Had she offended him when she said she didn't think they should kiss again? He seemed to be on the same page as her, but—

"Elliana, what is going on?" Her mother's annoyed voice interrupted Ellie's thoughts about Nate and his reaction.

She turned. Her parents and Bri and Richard were standing on the path by the steps, glancing from her to Nate. They looked like lawyers in their expensive dark suits. Her father and Bri greeted her with wan smiles and finger-waves while her mother and Richard wore the same tight-lipped expression. Her mother's gaze narrowed on Agnes. They'd had a strained relationship for as long as Ellie could remember.

Forcing a smile and a cheery note to her voice, Ellie said, "Nothing's wrong." At Miranda's furrowed brow, Ellie realized that wasn't the correct response to her mother's question. It was also a lie. This whole thing was a lie, and Ellie didn't like to lie almost as much as she didn't like conflict. And conflict was the name of the game when dealing with her mother.

Obviously lying was too because she needed to come up with an excuse as to why Joe was MIA. "I was just asking Nate when he thought he'd be finished with Joe. Nate is Grandpa's...physiotherapist. They're working on the cabins as part of his therapy. But don't worry; they shouldn't be much longer."

Wow. She was getting really good at lying with a straight face. She was also pretty impressed with how quickly she'd come up with their cover, especially since she was still dazed by Nate's kiss and confused by his reaction. At least her legs were no longer weak. The best part was that she'd given Nate an out if he wanted it. He didn't have to say he was her boyfriend. She'd figure out an excuse for the kiss her family had witnessed. Or maybe she wouldn't. Maybe she'd let them draw their own conclusions. The rebel in her approved of that idea.

Her family glanced at Nate, who moved to Ellie's side, slinging an arm around her shoulders. "Don't make promises you might not be able to keep, babe. You know what Joe's like when he gets a hammer in his hand."

Okay, so they were obviously continuing the charade.

Nate smiled at her family, although it wasn't so much a smile as a baring of teeth.

Ellie wondered what Agnes had told him about her parents, specifically her mother. Nate loved her grandmother as much as she loved him. So Ellie couldn't see him being happy to learn how her mother treated Agnes.

Ellie introduced her family to Nate. Her father and

her sister offered him polite smiles while her mother and Richard offered curt nods.

"Hey there, folks. Sorry to delay your meeting but I'll do my best to get Joe back before you leave," Nate told her family.

"Do you usually drink and smoke when working with a client?" Richard asked with a pointed look at the beer bottle and cigar in Nate's hand.

Nate laughed. It wasn't an amused laugh. "Joe's more like family than a client. Ellie asked me to help out with his therapy, and there's nothing I wouldn't do to make my girl happy." His dark eyes narrowed at Richard. "Nothing."

This wasn't going to end well. "And you know how much I appreciate everything you've done for Grandpa, honey." She patted his chest and smiled up at him, widening her eyes in hopes of conveying an *I've got this* message. Which he ignored because he was still staring down Richard.

"You're welcome to join us, man. You look like you could use a workout. Hang on to these for me, babe." Nate handed her the beer bottle and cigar and then took off his leather jacket, revealing a black T-shirt that highlighted his gorgeous inked arms and amazing bod. He was built like the Rock. Without thinking, she took a swig of beer. It was warm.

Ellie glanced at her grandmother, who was grinning from ear to ear. Ellie wouldn't get any help from her. She was enjoying this way too much.

"Why don't you guys go ahead in? I'll be right with you." Her father and Richard seemed happy to leave, but her mother and sister stood there slack jawed, staring at Nate.

"Brianna," Richard snapped, grabbing her sister's arm.

Bri winced as her husband's fingers closed around her bicep. Ellie stiffened. She opened her mouth to say something but heard her sister's thoughts as clearly as if they were her own. *Please don't, Ellie. Please don't say anything.* Beside Ellie, Nate went to move, his expression hard. She placed a hand on his arm to keep him in place.

As though oblivious to the tension or the reason for it, her mother tapped her watch. "I expect my father to be here by three, Mr. Black. Elliana." She nodded at the door and then joined the rest of the family inside, obviously expecting Ellie to follow.

"What the hell?" Nate stared at the closed door with his hands fisted on his narrow hips. Then his gaze swung to her.

"I've tried to talk to her, Nate. She denies anything's wrong. To hear her, you'd think Richard was a saint." And that Ellie was overreacting.

His expression softened. "I'm not blaming you. Your sister obviously didn't want you to interfere. I just don't get why your parents didn't step in, especially your father."

"Miranda only sees what she wants to. And as brilliant as Bryan is, my son is clueless to what's going on around him. He also doesn't have the spine to stand up to his wife." Looking at the inn, her grandmother nodded. "But from what I've just seen, with not only your sister but you, Ellie, it's long past time for me to share a few truths with my son."

Ellie's heart raced, terrified at the secret her grandmother was about to share with her father. It would tear her family apart. She couldn't let her do it.

"Granny, I don't think this is the time. I know you're just trying to help me and Bri, but it won't. It'll make things worse. Maybe you should go with Nate." Ellie wasn't just trying to protect her mother and her sister; she was trying to protect her grandmother too.

"You don't need to worry about me, Ellie. Your mother's threats no longer scare me. It's not like she can stop me from seeing you and your sister and brother. You're all old enough to make up your own minds. But it's about time your father stood up for his daughters. I expect better from my son, and I plan to tell him so."

Her panic that Agnes was going to expose her mother's secret subsided. Maybe she'd been wrong, and her grandmother didn't even know what it was. Or maybe, like Ellie, she knew how disastrous the fallout would be should her father and sister find out.

"If you ladies need me, you've got my number." Nate tossed his leather jacket onto his Harley and headed for the dock.

Ellie was about to tell him she actually didn't have his number when her phone pinged. She took it out of her pocket and glanced at the screen. He'd sent a thumbs-up emoji. She didn't know what she'd expected but obviously something more if the twinge of disappointment in her chest was anything to go by.

Get a grip, she told herself. She was letting the feelings she'd experienced when he kissed her mess with her head. Nate obviously didn't have the same problem. Then again, he'd spent most of his law enforcement career working undercover, which meant he knew how to act. Good thing one of them did.

"The canoes are in the shed, Nate. If you'd like, I can give you a brief tutorial on the J-stroke. It makes it easier to paddle solo."

He shot her a raised-eyebrow look over his shoulder.

"Okay, then. Well, I really appreciate you doing this. I know you're busy, and all of this must seem pretty crazy to you, but—"

"Don't worry, you can make it up to him later." Her grandmother grinned, looping her arm through Ellie's. "Now let's go save the inn and Joe."

Fifteen minutes later, as Ellie sat across the desk from her mother, her sister, and Richard in the office, her hope that she could reason with her family was dwindling fast. So far, the only thing that had gone right was her father agreeing over his wife's objections to have tea with his mother. They'd left them in the dining room surrounded by women her father had gone to school with, reminiscing about the good old days. Her mother hadn't been happy about the turn of events and was taking her bad mood out on Ellie. She clearly blamed her for Agnes being there.

"No. I don't want tea or sandwiches." Her mother rejected the offer Ellie had just made with a dismissive wave of her hand. "This isn't a social call, Elliana. I'm here to speak to my father."

"I realize that, and Grandpa will be here soon. I just thought you might want something to eat while you wait." She glanced at her sister. "Bri, would you like—"

Richard cut her off. "No, she doesn't want anything to eat. She wants the same thing your mother wants. To get this meeting underway."

Shocked at the level of anger he'd directed at her, Ellie leaned back in the chair. She tried not to read people's thoughts. Not only did she consider it an invasion of their privacy, she'd found out the hard way that it was better not to know what people thought of you. Thankfully, she'd become exceptionally good at blocking them out. But when she was stressed or emotional, as she was now, her barriers went down. Richard wanted her gone. He was angry she was there. Afraid she'd blow the deal he'd put together.

But it was Bri shrinking in her chair in response to her husband's anger that caused Ellie to snap, "My sister can speak for herself, Richard."

"Elliana! Apologize to your brother-in-law this instant and then you can leave us. This has nothing to do with you," her mother said.

"Excuse me. It has nothing to do with me? I've been the one running the inn and looking after Grandpa since he had his stroke."

"You were here for one reason and one reason only. You needed a place to hide and to lick your wounds after Spencer left you at the altar," her mother said.

Despite what everyone believed, Ellie's fiancé, actor

Spencer Dale, hadn't left her at the altar. She didn't contradict them because the truth was worse.

"What you should have been doing instead of hiding out here is fighting to get Spencer back," her mother continued. "He was the best thing that ever happened to you. You actually showed some initiative and drive when you were with him."

"Contrary to what you seem to believe, Mom, I started Custom Concierge before I met Spencer." Her personal shopping business had barely been breaking even before she started dating Spencer, but it had nothing to do with a lack of initiative or drive.

It wasn't easy getting a business off the ground—many small companies failed in their first two years. Hers might have too if not for Spencer's connections and friends becoming her customers and promoting her services. But they hadn't been as loyal as she'd thought they were. They'd abandoned her not long after she and Spencer split up.

"I didn't realize you were still running your company while you've been here. That must be very difficult for you." Her mother glanced at Richard, who raised his eyebrows. Ellie didn't need to be psychic to know that they'd come prepared. They'd looked into Custom Concierge.

"I'm no longer taking on new clients. I have a stable of loyal customers I shop for online." She had twenty-five. Lucky for her they were very wealthy clients. Still, she barely made enough to pay the bills. She'd managed to keep the lights on at the inn and cover the property taxes without dipping into her limited savings, but it was getting harder to do the longer she was here.

"It's admirable you've been able to keep your company afloat under the circumstances. I'm sure you'll be able to attract new customers once you're back in New York."

A warm bubble of happiness expanded in Ellie's chest. She knew better than to take her mother's rare compliment at face value, but it seemed she couldn't keep herself from seeking her approval.

"I'm not moving back to New York," Ellie said, surprising herself. She'd planned on staying just long enough to get the inn and her grandfather back on their feet, but lately she'd had a change of heart. She enjoyed the slow pace and natural beauty of Highland Falls and loved the sense of community that came from living in a small town. But until that moment, she hadn't realized she'd made up her mind.

"You can't mean to stay in Highland Falls once the inn is sold and your grandfather is in a home?" Her mother's eyes narrowed. "This doesn't have anything to do with the vulgar display we witnessed when we arrived, does it? You're fooling yourself if you believe a man like that would want you for more than a—"

"It was a kiss, not a vulgar display. But Nate has nothing to do with the reason I'm staying." Because who would want to be with a woman who hears other people's thoughts in her head? Her mother had said it to her before; now she was just thinking it. At one time she'd convinced Ellie she was mentally unstable.

But Ellie was an adult now, and that tactic no longer worked on her. Nor would she allow her mother's thoughts at that moment to throw her off balance.

Her nails biting into her sweaty palms, Ellie forced herself to meet her mother's combative stare. "Grandpa asked me to stay and help him run the inn, and I've agreed."

"The inn is as good as sold, Elliana. There's nothing for you here. Go back to New York."

"Grandpa won't sell the inn, Mom. It's the only home he's ever known. It's been in his family, your family, for five generations. That might not mean something to you, but it does to him. And to me."

"This is your mother's decision, Elliana, not yours."

"Actually, Richard, it's my grandfather's decision. He's not selling the inn, and he isn't going into a home."

Richard looked ready to explode. Her sister rubbed his arm, her eyes pleading with Ellie as she said, "I know how much you love Grandpa, but this is the best decision for everyone involved. You've given up eight months of your life to take care of Grandpa and run the inn, and we're all grateful that you stepped in. But you've sacrificed enough."

"How is this the best decision for everyone involved? Grandpa is happy here, and so am I. As you can see, the inn is doing well, and once the new website is up and running, we'll be—"

Her mother slapped her palms on the arms of her chair. "Stop it right now, Elliana. We have an agreement in place with a development company who will be building high-end vacation homes on the property, and—"

"They're tearing down the inn?" Ellie said past the ball of emotion swelling in her throat.

"Of course they're tearing it down. Despite what you and your grandfather think, the inn's only real value is the land, for which the developer is willing to pay an obscene amount of money. And that's thanks to Richard. Without him, this deal wouldn't have—"

"A deal that Grandpa never authorized. You have no right to sign an agreement on his behalf. You have no right to sell the inn out from under him. I won't let you."

"You listen to me, young lady. This is my father we're talking about, not yours. I have every right to act on his behalf. He no longer has the mental capacity to make decisions that are in his best interest."

"Is that why you're here, Bri? To run some kind of test on Grandpa to prove he isn't of sound mind? Because if it is, you're wasting your time. He's as sharp as ever and fully recovered from his stroke. Something all of you would know if you'd bothered to come see him before now."

Ellie's cell phone vibrated on the desk. It was Nate. "I have to take this." Ignoring her mother and Richard calling her out for how she'd spoken to her sister, Ellie got up from her chair on shaky legs. She rounded the desk, brushing past Richard, who she was positive intentionally knocked his elbow against hers as she opened the office door. After stepping into the hall, she closed the door behind her and leaned against the wall. "Did you find him?" she whispered into the phone.

"I did, but we have a problem. He's in the middle of a poker game, and he's winning. I gather this is a once-in-a-lifetime experience for him, so unless you want me to drag him out of here kicking and screaming, you need to give me something to work with."

"Put him on the phone."

Nate laughed. "You're full of surprises, Ellie. Even I wouldn't mess with you when you use that tone of voice."

"I wish it worked on my mother. Let's hope it works on her father."

"Everything okay?"

"No. They can't be reasoned with, Nate. They're completely ignoring Grandpa's feelings and wishes. All they see is dollar signs."

"Hang on. Joe, your granddaughter needs you, so get your ass out of the chair and let's go."

Ellie smiled at Nate's take-no-prisoners voice, hoping it was enough to convince her grandfather to fold and come peacefully. In the background, other voices joined Joe's so she couldn't make out what was said. Then Nate came back on the line. "That didn't go as I expected." At the sound of a door closing, the muffled voices were replaced by the chirping of birds. "Unless you want me to carry him and his chair out of there, he's not leaving. He's as stubborn as Mrs. M. But I have a feeling what it comes down to is he's afraid he'll let you down, Ellie."

"Why? He's doing so well."

"He doesn't think your mother will agree. He's sure she'll test him and just as sure he'll fail. From what I just saw, he might be right, Ellie. His hand shook, and he was slurring his words. The stress seems to have aggravated his symptoms."

Her heart hurt for her grandfather, and in that moment she hated her mother for what she was doing. "Tell Grandpa it's okay and to enjoy his poker game. I'll handle my mother. I'm sorry I wasted your time, Nate. But at least I know he's all right. Thank you for tracking him down."

"It's not a big deal. But the judge implied you don't need Joe, Ellie. He said you have the means to stop your mother."

"I do. I'd just hoped it wouldn't come to this." Because she knew exactly what would happen when she informed her mother that Grandpa Joe had changed his will and given Ellie power of attorney.

Chapter Three

♥

Nate glanced at the inn across the lake, wondering if he should head back and act the part of Ellie's scary boyfriend. She'd sounded upset and maybe a little panicked. He didn't like thinking of her facing down her mother and brother-in-law on her own. But as he walked through the trees to the canoe he'd pulled up on the rocky shore, he imagined what his sisters would say.

He had five of them—all older and strong-minded. They were never shy about sharing their opinions with him. About anything and everything but mostly about women and his love life. No doubt they'd roll their eyes at the thought of him paddling to Ellie's rescue. Easy for them—they hadn't met her family. Still, Ellie hadn't asked for his help. She also didn't come across as a woman who needed rescuing.

Then again, he didn't know her all that well. They'd spent a grand total of eight hours in each other's company. Very enjoyable hours, he conceded, remembering his time with her at his best friend's wedding.

They'd had a lot of fun together, despite an attraction that had a neon stop sign flashing in his brain before the night was over.

While Ellie was head-turningly gorgeous, and she'd definitely turned his head with all that long dark hair and her big violet eyes, she was also Mrs. M's grand-daughter, which meant she was off-limits. Something he should have reminded himself of when Mrs. M had shared her fake-relationship plan with him. He might have if he hadn't been looking for a little normalcy and some lighthearted fun after spending months un-dercover tracking the men he held responsible for his childhood best friend's murder.

Nate had gotten a hell of a lot more than he'd bar-gained for when he'd kissed Ellie. Mrs. M hadn't been wrong when she'd said he looked stunned. He had been. He'd also been angry at himself for not cluing in to what Mrs. M was really up to. She didn't want him to play Ellie's fake boyfriend. She wanted him to take on the role for real.

Mrs. M had orchestrated that kiss between them for one reason and one reason only. To ensure that Nate did what he was doing right now—obsess about a kiss that had shaken him to his core. Obsess about a woman who'd turned his impression of her on its ear with one devastatingly passionate kiss. Under the sweet, unas-suming demeanor Ellie showed to the world was a sexy-as-hell woman with unexplored depths and desires.

And he was the idiot who'd put the down-and-dirty option on the table. But in his defense he'd been teasing Ellie, having a little fun with her. The joke was clearly on him. It was a good thing he didn't plan on sticking around for long, or he might be tempted to strip away those demure layers to the real woman beneath.

He returned to the cabin and sat on the front step, checking the messages on his phone. There were two from Gina, Brodie's widow. The three of them had grown up together. Gina was the reason Nate had stopped in to check on Mrs. M. He had time to kill before he met up with her tomorrow. He was about to respond to her latest message when he sensed a change in the air. He looked around for a sign of an incoming threat. Somewhere behind the cabin, trees rustled and a branch snapped. He went for the gun in his ankle holster, placing it beside him on the step. These days, he couldn't be too careful. He'd stirred up a lot of heat this past week.

The rustling got louder, and a male voice cursed. Nate relaxed. He knew that voice. "Watch where you step, Roberts. I saw a copperhead sunning himself on a rock not five minutes ago." He laughed when his former partner sprinted past the front of the cabin.

Chase glanced at him over his shoulder and nearly slammed into a tree, which made Nate laugh harder. The FBI agent called him a particularly foul name.

Nate grinned as Chase walked back to join him on the step. Chase Roberts was one of the finest agents he'd ever worked with. Their undercover op last summer to find Brodie's killer had gotten off to a rocky start. Chase was by the book, and Nate hadn't met a rule he hadn't tried to bend. Now Nate counted him as his closest friend.

"You're an ass."

"I missed you too," Nate said, pulling him in for a one-armed hug. That was another difference between them—Nate was affectionate and Chase wasn't. Or at least he hadn't been. Living with Sadie had changed him. For the better in Nate's opinion.

Chase returned his hug. "Yeah, you missed me so much you didn't call to let me know you were in town."

"I got waylaid by Mrs. M. Where's your sidekick?"

Chase's face lit up with a smile, the way it always did whenever he thought about his fifteen-month-old daughter. He'd adopted Sadie's little girl last year, but Chase had claimed her as his own the day they'd delivered her on the side of the road in the middle of a snowstorm.

"With Elijah. Sadie asked me to look for Joe." Elijah was Sadie's brother. He was also the reason they had been undercover last year. Elijah had been their primary suspect in Brodie's murder.

"How did you figure out Joe was here?" Nate asked.

"I made a couple of calls. Found out their poker buddies were missing and someone saw them heading in the direction of the inn over an hour ago. Their cars are parked on the side of the road, so I followed the path."

"Gotta love small-town gossip. But I could have saved you a trek through the woods and a potential run-in with a copperhead if you'd given me a call."

"Thought about it, but then I figured you might need backup. So just remember what I was willing to do for you next time I ask you to babysit Michaela."

Nate laughed. "Unlike you, I'm not afraid of snakes, and I think I can handle four poker-loving old men." Except he hadn't been able to convince Joe to leave with him.

"I wasn't talking about the snakes or the poker buddies. I was talking about Agnes." Chase gave him a raised-eyebrow look. "What were you thinking, making out with Ellie in front of the inn? Not to mention in front of Agnes."

"I wasn't making out with her. I just—" Chase held up his phone. On the screen was a picture of Nate kissing Ellie. "Who the hell sent you that?"

"Who do you think? Agnes sent it to Sadie, who sent it to me."

Nate hadn't even noticed her taking the picture, which proved how completely that kiss had rocked his world.

"I thought you were smarter than that, bro. Sadie warned you at the wedding that Agnes was trying to set you two up." Chase angled his head to study him. "Unless there's something you're not telling me?"

"What are you talking about?"

"Come on, it was obvious you were attracted to Ellie. You spent the entire reception together." Chase glanced at his phone. "And you look like you were into this kiss as much as Ellie. You haven't been dating her behind our backs, have you?"

Nate snorted. "I don't *date*. You know that."

"I do, which makes what you're doing with Ellie all the more confusing."

"I'm not doing anything." Chase once again held up

his phone. Nate wished he'd stop doing that. He was trying his best to get the kiss out of his head, which was why he snagged Chase's phone and deleted the photo. "Agnes asked me to help out Ellie by pretending to be her boyfriend. She figured Ellie's mother would think twice about messing with her if she thought she was dating"—he made air quotes—"'someone like me.'"

Chase laughed. "And you believed her?"

"What can I say? I'm sleep deprived. It's been a rough few months. I was up for a little fun."

The amusement left Chase's face. "I imagine it has been. I've been worried about you. Your one-word responses to my *Are you alive?* texts weren't very reassuring."

"Sorry about that. But you know what it's like when you're in deep cover." The only way to get out alive was to become the person you were playing. There was no room for mistakes, no room for the people you loved and had left behind.

He'd spent most of his career with the NCSBI undercover. He had no delusions as to why his boss chose him for the assignments ninety percent of the time. The role of motorcycle-riding gang member came naturally to him because, at one time, he'd been in the life.

"The only time I've been undercover was with you last summer, and we had each other's backs. So no, I don't really understand what it's like. But word is you got the guy who'd been supplying the Whiteside Mountain Gang with drugs. Something I had to hear from my boss and not you, by the way."

"When it comes to mothering me, my sisters have

you beat. I swear they've got someone at the field office feeding them information. The minute I pulled into the NCSBI parking lot, they started calling me. They didn't let up until I answered." Chase's boss was married to Nate's oldest sister, so he'd known his brother-in-law would pass along the information about the arrest. "I meant to call you after I debriefed my boss, but things went sideways fast, and I didn't get a chance."

The truth was, he'd been putting off this conversation with Chase. He wouldn't react well to Nate's news.

Chase's eyes narrowed. "What do you mean things went sideways during your debrief?"

"My boss and I had a slight disagreement on how to move forward with the case." "Slight" was an understatement. They'd nearly come to blows.

"You got the guy. It's over. Case closed."

"No, it's not. The guy I brought in isn't the one calling the shots. I won't rest until I bring the organization down."

"Let it go, Nate. We put Brodie's murderer and accomplices away. They won't ever see the light of day."

"I can't let it go. I won't stop until everyone connected to Brodie's murder has been charged and convicted."

"Do you hear yourself? You're obsessed. Your need for revenge at any cost is going to get you killed." Chase scrubbed his face. "I can't believe your boss is letting you go out there again."

"He's not. He put me on mandatory leave."

"Good. At least someone at the NCSBI is thinking straight."

"I quit."

"You what?"

He shrugged. "I owe it to Brodie to see this through. I owe it to his son. And I don't need to deal with the red tape and the bullshit. It'll be faster if I do it my way."

"Yeah, because God forbid you have to follow the rules. Rules that are in place to protect you. To keep you alive. So what's this? Your goodbye tour before you go out there again? You're so caught up in this, I'm surprised you even bothered."

Chase knew him a little too well. "Look, I get that you're angry that I can't let this go."

"Angry? I'm not angry. I'm terrified. Terrified that this obsession of yours, your need for revenge at any cost, is going to get you killed."

"I love you too, bro." Nate grinned and went to hug Chase but he shoved him away.

"Knock it off. I'm serious. This is your life we're talking about."

"That's the point, Chase. I won't be able to live with myself if I don't avenge Brodie's murder. I owe him. And just FYI, I don't do goodbye tours because I'm not planning to die. I came to check up on you guys and to touch base with Gina." He left *before I go undercover again* unsaid.

"Brodie's widow?"

"Yeah, she's having trouble with the kid. She asked if I'd talk to him. I don't know if it'll do any good, but she seems to think it'll help."

Chase studied him. Then he said quietly, "You have nothing to feel guilty about, you know."

He did, but that wasn't something he'd share with Chase. He'd just make excuses for him because that's what friends do, and Nate couldn't ask for a better one. He caught a flicker of movement out of the corner of his eye and looked out over the water. Ellie lay back in a red canoe in the middle of the lake.

Chase followed the direction of his gaze and frowned. "What's she doing?"

Nate smiled. "It looks like she's taking a nap."

"For someone you're supposedly fake-dating, you look pretty happy to see her."

Damn straight he was. He couldn't have asked for a better distraction from their conversation. Nate returned his gun to his ankle holster—ignoring Chase's raised eyebrow—and then leaned back to open the cabin door. "Joe, you better wrap up your game. Ellie's on her way over."

"No can do, son. The judge practically cleaned me out. I gotta win my money back. Three more hands should do it. I'm sure you can think of something to keep my granddaughter busy." He smirked.

Nate bowed his head. *Mrs. M strikes again.* "It's not what it looks like," he muttered.

"Whatever it was, keep doing it. We're just glad Agnes finally found our Ellie a man she likes, and she seems to really like you, son." Again with that smirk. "She sure didn't like any of the men we set her up with, did she, Judge?"

"No, and I'd had high hopes for the last one. He

seemed like such a nice young man," Chase's grand-father said.

"Not according to Ellie. She said he was a serial killer in the making, remember?"

"How could I forget? She threatened to make us cook for ourselves if we set her up again."

"What do you expect when you found her dates online? I told you to let me vet them first," said Colin Murphy. The former CIA agent was dating Mrs. M.

"They didn't want to lose their bet," said Ed, the fourth member of their poker party.

"No. The bet wasn't the issue," the judge objected. "We wanted to prove to Agnes and her friends that we know Ellie as well as they do and that we're perfectly capable of finding her a nice young man." The judge leaned back in his chair to give Nate an up-and-down look. "And I'm not convinced Mr. Black is the right man for our Ellie."

"On that we agree, Judge. So you'll be relieved to know we aren't dating. We were just going along with Agnes's plan to convince Ellie's parents she had someone like me looking out for her." Seriously. How could he have been so stupid? And why did it bother him that Joe and the judge had been setting Ellie up with other men? Because it sounded like they'd been setting her up with a bunch of asshats, he told himself. Ellie deserved better.

Colin and Ed laughed like the joke was on him, and Joe grinned. "Keep telling yourself that if it makes you feel better, son."

"I can see Agnes's point, but all Ellie needed was

the papers I drew up to put that mother of hers in her place." The judge winced. "Sorry, Joe. I shouldn't speak about your daughter that way."

"No need to apologize, Judge. I've said and thought a lot worse. I just hope me giving Ellie power of attorney is enough to stop this foolishness. Imagine, my own daughter turning on me like that." He shook his head. "I don't know what I did to deserve this." The words came out slurred, the cards trembling in Joe's shaking hand.

Colin and Ed shared a telling glance. They were clearly worried about their friend, and just as angry at Miranda MacLeod as Joe and the judge. As the three men comforted their old friend, Nate closed the cabin door and joined Chase at the foot of the steps.

Nate glanced at Ellie. The canoe had drifted closer, but she hadn't moved from her prone position. "I'm guessing the meeting with her mother didn't go well."

"That's an understatement from what Sadie just texted me. Everyone in the dining room heard Ellie's mother and brother-in-law yelling in the office. It got so bad that Ellie's father intervened, which I gather is a pretty big deal. They left five minutes ago with a threat that it wasn't over. Ellie was out of the inn and on her way over here before anyone had a chance to talk to her, so you're up."

"I'm up for what?" Nate asked distractedly, angry at himself for not following through with his earlier thought that he should head back to the inn.

"Boyfriend duty. Sadie and Agnes are counting on you to comfort Ellie."

Nate narrowed his eyes at the smile Chase tried to hide. "You know, it wasn't that long ago you warned me away from Ellie. I think your exact words were, 'Don't mess around with her. She's not your type.'"

"That's exactly what I said. The women you 'date'"—Chase made air quotes—"are exactly like you. They're up for a good time but not for a long time, and that's not Ellie."

"I'm glad we agree."

"You didn't let me finish. Ellie might not be your usual type, but she is exactly the kind of woman you need in your life. Don't roll your eyes. I have personal experience to draw on, and you don't. Take me and Sadie for example. Not only were we—still are, I guess—total opposites, never in a million years did I see myself leaving DC and giving up on my career aspirations for a woman. Yet it was the best decision I ever made. It took Sadie for me to realize I wasn't living my life. I was just going through the motions."

Nate sighed. "You've turned into one of them."

"One of what?"

"Everybody who's been in love thinks that you can't be happy unless you are too. But despite what you think, love is not the end-all and be-all. And if you think the love of a good woman will keep me from avenging Brodie's murder, you don't know me that well."

"Wanna bet?"

Chapter Four

♥

No. I don't want to bet," Nate said to Chase, more irritated than he should be. But he was tired of defending himself. Tired of people not getting why avenging Brodie's murder was important to him.

It didn't help that Chase had just provided him with evidence of how deep a hole he'd dug for himself by going along with Mrs. M's plan. The last thing Nate needed was his best friend partnering with the matchmakers of Highland Falls. "There's nothing between Ellie and me, and there never will be, so you might want to put out an alert to all your matchmaking buddies that we're no longer *fake*-dating now that her parents are gone."

"That's a bit harsh, don't you think?"

"How is it harsh? I'm not actually breaking up with her. We were never together."

Chase went to hold up his phone and then realized the incriminating photo was no longer there.

"We shared one little kiss, so what?" Nate said, addressing the photo anyway while also not acknowledging that what he and Ellie had shared was as far from a *little* kiss as you could get. "It didn't mean anything. The whole point was to protect Ellie from her family, and obviously that didn't work. Who knows, it probably made things worse. No one wants their daughter to bring home a guy like me."

"You might want to keep your voice down. Sound travels on water," Chase said with a pointed glance at Ellie, who was now sitting upright and paddling toward shore.

Nate couldn't tell if she'd heard him. Then again, what would it matter if she did? Everything he'd said was true. Mostly.

She lifted her gaze to his as she reached the shore. Her smile didn't quite reach her gorgeous violet eyes. She'd heard him, and for some reason, what he'd said must have bothered her. He wasn't sure why. Unless she'd picked up on his anger. He had to make her understand it had nothing to do with her.

He shot a look at Chase. "Thanks a lot, bro," he muttered as he headed for the shore.

"What? I didn't say anything."

Nate ignored Chase and focused on Ellie. "You okay?" he asked, holding out a hand to help her from the canoe. "Sadie told Chase that your mother wasn't happy when they left the inn."

"Unhappy I could have handled. Enraged and threatening were a little harder to deal with." She placed her hand in his, stepping out of the canoe onto the rocky shore. "Thanks."

"So it looks like Mrs. M was wrong. Me pretending to be your boyfriend didn't do you any good."

"I wouldn't say that." She let go of his hand. "Your phone call gave me an excuse to get out of the office and regroup, and my mother might have pushed harder for Joe to make an appearance if not for you. But I'm pretty sure Granny's plan had more to do with match-making than protecting me from my mother. I should have known better. Actually, I did know better, but I guess I was desperate. I'm sorry if I've put you in an awkward position, Nate."

He'd been right. She'd overheard him talking to Chase. "You haven't. I know Mrs. M almost as well as you do and should have figured out what she was really up to. But honestly, it's not a big deal, so don't give it a second thought. Although from what Joe and the judge said, Agnes isn't the only matchmaker you've had to contend with." And why he'd brought that up he had no idea. The voice in his head called him a liar. He was curious about the men her grandfather and the judge had set her up with.

Ellie sighed. "You'd think Grandpa and Jonathan caught spring fever. They were worse than Granny. I swear they were giving out my photo and stats to every man they met under forty."

"From what I heard, you might want to search online dating sites for your profile." He laughed at her horrified expression.

"I can't even..." She shook her head. "I'll have to get Sadie to do it for me. I'm afraid to see what they put on my profile."

"I doubt you have anything to worry about. It's obvious how Joe and Jonathan feel about you."

"You didn't meet the men they set me up with," she said, then smiled. "But I know they love me. That's the problem. They were afraid I was moving back to New York. They seemed to think if I fell in love with someone from around here, I'd stay."

He glanced at Chase, who was on the phone. His best friend was taking a page out of the old guys' playbook. Chase figured Nate would stick around if he and Ellie got together. "You're not moving back to New York?"

"No. I mean, I was thinking about it. Grandpa was doing well, and I had people in place to help out at the inn. But then I realized I really didn't want to leave. I'm happy here, and I love my grandfather. Jonathan too. Even when they're driving me crazy." She glanced across the lake. "And I love the inn."

"Your mother's going to contest your power of attorney, isn't she?"

She nodded. "She accused me of coercing my grandfather into making the changes to his will. She says he's obviously not of sound mind if he chose me over her."

"Right, her daughter who dropped everything to come look after her grandfather."

"That's not how she sees it." She rubbed her face. "I knew this would happen, but I didn't see any other way to stop her."

Ellie looked like she needed a hug but instead he gave her shoulder a reassuring squeeze. "I get how difficult this must be for you. But you're just abiding by your grandfather's wishes, and from what I heard, and saw, you don't have to worry that Joe will be declared mentally incompetent."

"He's not the only one she'll try to have—" She broke off. "Sorry. I shouldn't be dumping this all on you."

"Hey, just because we're not actually a couple doesn't mean I'm not here for you if you need me, Ellie. I am."

She gave him a smile that had him rethinking his offer. Not because there was anything flirtatious about it or the slightest hint that she wanted something more from him than friendship. It was because Ellie was a beautiful woman, but when she smiled, she took his breath away. "Not *here* here, obviously. I'll be heading out tomorrow. But feel free to call me anytime you need to vent or you need a sounding board."

"Thanks, Nate. I just might take you up on your offer."

Chase walked over. "Hey, Ellie. Sadie says not to worry about anything. They'll handle the cleanup. Abby's just about to tell everyone the party's over."

"No way. They've done too much as it is. I'll take care of the cleanup when I get back. I just need to get Grandpa. He has to take his meds."

"Let them help, Ellie. They don't mind, and you've had a rough day."

"I'm fine. Honestly, I am," she added when Chase raised an eyebrow.

"Just for the record," Nate said, "I have five older sisters, so I know when a woman says she's *fine*, she's not. Let them help, Ellie. You'll have your hands full with Joe. No way you're getting him out of there until he wins back his money."

"Watch me," she said, heading for the cabin.

"This I've got to see. Your dominatrix voice didn't work on him last time, remember?" Nate winced. That wasn't something he should say to a woman like Ellie. She probably had no idea what it even meant.

She cast him an amused glance over her shoulder. "I left my black leather and whip at the inn."

Nate tripped over a tree root. He was never teasing Ellie MacLeod again.

Beside him, Chase laughed. "That's the first time I've ever seen you stunned speechless by a woman."

Nate ignored him and followed Ellie inside the now-smoke-filled cabin. He walked over and opened a window while Ellie plucked the cigar from between her grandfather's lips. "Grandpa, your doctor told you no more cigars."

"I didn't inhale." Joe grinned, leaning back in his chair to look up at his granddaughter. "Did it work? Is your mother going to leave us alone now?"

"Everything's fine, Grandpa. Nothing for you to worry about. But we have to get back to the inn. It's almost time for your pills, and you really should thank everyone before they leave."

The other men at the table glanced at Nate, no doubt looking for confirmation. Joe couldn't see him where he leaned against the wall, so he shook his head. Ellie wouldn't be able to keep the truth from Joe for long, and he'd need the support of his friends.

"Your mother's gone then?" Joe asked.

"Yes. Chase, do you mind driving Grandpa and Jonathan back to the inn?"

"Not at all."

"Hold up there, Ellie my love. Game's not over yet. Shouldn't be more than an hour."

"I thought you might say that." She took a seat, pulled a handful of quarters from her pocket, and plunked them on the table. "Deal me in."

"You can't just join midgame. Besides, you don't even know how to play," her grandfather said.

"I say let her play," Ed said, and the judge and Colin agreed.

"All right, but don't say I didn't warn you, Ellie my love."

Chase leaned in to Nate. "Do you think I should volunteer to take her place?" Chase was a card sharp, not because he played a lot of cards but because he could count them.

"Let's see how she does. You can always volunteer after a couple of hands."

Ten minutes later, the game was over. Ellie had cleaned them out.

Nate felt Chase looking at him and thought he should probably stop staring at Ellie before he gave himself away. She'd surprised him again, and he decided he didn't like surprises.

"I don't know, bro," Chase said under his breath. "Seems to me Ellie is exactly your type."

Nate was afraid he was right.

* * *

Ellie leaned against the receptionist's desk after saying goodbye to her friends. It had been exhausting keeping up a positive front. Sadie and Agnes had seen through her act, but they hadn't pushed for more details about the meeting with her mother. Ellie didn't expect the reprieve to last for long.

She glanced at the registration book. Her grandmother had checked Nate in. Ellie had assumed he'd be spending the night either at Agnes's apartment above I Believe in Unicorns, her store on Main Street, or at Sadie and Chase's cottage on Willow Creek. But the three of them had suddenly remembered that their guest bedrooms were unavailable. Her family were pathetically transparent matchmakers.

They didn't seem to care that Nate had made it abundantly clear to everyone while cleaning up the dining room that they were friends, not lovers. It would have been amusing how he'd gone out of his way to treat her like one of the guys if it hadn't been embarrassing. Even more embarrassing, she thought upon closer inspection of his reservation, was that her grandmother had charged him the regular room rate. After what they'd put him through, the poor guy should be staying for free.

She leaned over the desk and picked up the landline, punching in the number she knew by heart. "Hi, Zia Maria. It's Ellie at Mirror Lake Inn. Is it too late to order a pizza for delivery?"

"Massimo," Zia Maria yelled at her son. "It's Ellie.

You got time to make her a pizza?" A moment later
Zia Maria chuckled. "He said for you, he'll make time.
My boy, he likes you. I like you too. When he dumps
that woman, you'll date him, yes?" Zia Maria didn't
hide the fact she wasn't enamored with her son's
fiancée. They had this same conversation every time
Ellie called.

Ellie laughed. "They're getting married next month,
Zia Maria. But tell Massimo I appreciate him fitting
in my order. I'd like an extra large…meat lover's
pizza." It seemed like the type of pie a guy like Nate
would go for.

"Eh? Meat lover's? But you like the vegetarian
best, no?"

"It's not for me. It's for Nate."

"Our Nate, he's in town?" The older women in Highland Falls loved Nate. In their eyes he was a hero.

"Yes. He helped out at the inn today so I thought
I'd treat him. I have food for breakfast and lunch but
nothing for—"

"He's staying with you?"

"Yes. I mean, no," she quickly amended. The last
thing she needed, or Nate wanted, was a rumor about
them going around town. Zia Maria was as bad as
her grandmother. "He's staying at the inn. Just for
tonight."

"You be careful. He's too handsome for his own
good, and he likes the ladies. *All* the ladies. He's
a heartbreaker, and your heart, it has already been
broken."

Ellie sighed. She should have said the pizza was for

a guest, a nameless guest. "You don't have to worry about me, Zia Maria. I'm immune to charming men and heartbreakers." Actually, she was drawn to them.

"That's good. You leave the order to me. I know what Nate likes. You tell him to come visit Zia Maria before he leaves."

"I'll do that." After saying goodbye and hanging up the phone, Ellie glanced in the direction of her grandfather's suite of rooms. He'd been his cheerful old self when they'd gotten back from the cabin, chatting with his friends and helping with the cleanup. But as the last of their guests had left, he'd grown subdued. Ellie didn't need to be psychic to know that he was anxious about the outcome of her meeting.

She walked past the office and caught a whiff of burning grass and cedar. Winter Johnson, the mayor, had used white sage to clear the negative energy from the room. Ellie inhaled deeply of the scent in hopes it would clear the confrontation with her mother from her mind. The only times she'd stopped thinking about it were when she lay back in the canoe with the sun warming the chill that had iced her insides at her mother's threats and when she'd placed her hand in Nate's and stood on the shore with him.

He had an oddly calming effect on her. She'd noticed it at the wedding and had wondered if she was imagining things, but today proved she hadn't been.

She could use some of that calm now, she thought as she raised her hand to knock on her grandfather's door. She had to confess that things hadn't gone as well as she'd suggested earlier. He had to be prepared for what would come next. She would have preferred to talk to him when Jonathan was there in hopes the judge could alleviate both their fears, but he'd gone to Sadie and Chase's for dinner.

There was one fear Ellie couldn't share with anyone though—the fear that she was the one her mother would try to prove incompetent. Nate's calming presence had almost lulled Ellie into confessing her fear to him. She could just imagine what he'd think of her if she told him she was psychic. Sharing her secret had never gone well for her in the past.

She knocked lightly, cracking the door open an inch. "Grandpa, it's Ellie."

"Everyone gone?" he asked, his voice gruff.

She walked into the room. "Yes. I wondered if you wanted me to heat you up some soup for dinner."

"I'm good. I had enough sandwiches and scones to last me until next week." He stood in front of the stone fireplace holding a framed photo of her grandmother. His hand trembled as he returned it to the mantel. "Mary would have enjoyed today. It was like it used to be." He glanced at Ellie. "You did a good job. She would have been proud of you."

"I had a lot of help." Ellie walked to his side, taking his work-worn hand in hers, giving it a gentle squeeze as she looked at the family photos lining the mantel. "She'd be proud of you too."

"I don't know about that, Ellie my love. I let you down today. I'm sorry."

"You didn't let me down. Come sit. There's something I need to talk to you about." She led him to the chairs by the window with a view of the lake, noting the way he dragged his left leg.

"Your mother hasn't given up, has she?" he said, lowering himself onto the chair.

"No, but I guess we shouldn't have expected her to. She's stubborn, just like you." At the moment that was the kindest thing she could think to say about her mother.

He looked at the lake, the sun setting behind the mountains in the distance. "Your mother never liked the inn, you know. She was after us to sell it for as long as I can remember. It didn't matter to her that it had been in the family for five generations or that your grandmother and I were happy here. We didn't care that we didn't make a lot of money, didn't mind the work either. Miranda blamed me, me and the inn, for her mother's heart attack. Probably thinks it's the reason I had my stroke."

Ellie wished she believed that. If concern that Joe was working himself into an early grave were her mother's only motivation, Ellie would be able to understand and forgive her. But that was the thing about being psychic. Ellie knew exactly what was motivating her mother. She just didn't understand why.

"Grandpa, I need to ask you something, and I don't want you to get upset. It's just a hypothetical question."

"Nothing you could ask would upset me, Ellie my love. I know you only have my best interests at heart."

"I don't know about that. You weren't happy when

I was thirteen and asked you about the birds and the bees."

He laughed, and she wished they could sit here and reminisce about the happy memories she had of visiting him and her grandma at the inn, but what she had to ask him was important. "Grandpa, if you didn't have to go into a home or leave Highland Falls, would you want to sell the inn? Don't answer me right away. I want you to think about it before you do. We'd get a place here. You'd live with me. Jonathan could live with us too if he wanted."

Her grandfather sat there, still and quiet, while memories of his life at the inn played out like a movie in his head. A small smile lifted the corner of his mouth as the images of him fishing with his grandfather, swimming in the lake with his friends, and building the dock with his father ran through his mind.

His face softened, and his eyes grew shiny when he thought about Mary, his wife. Images of them as newlyweds and all the hopes and dreams they'd shared. Their love for each other and Mirror Lake played out before Ellie. Their long walks, picnics under the shade tree, gardening together, working side by side at the inn. Her grandfather's memories included Ellie too. Their holidays together. Her grandma Mary calling out directions to Ellie and Joe as they put up the now-faded red floral wallpaper in the dining room.

Her grandfather cleared his throat. "I promised my father, just as he promised his father before me, that the inn would remain in our family, and it's a promise I mean to keep. But even if I hadn't, I'd fight until my dying day to hang on to this place. There's something about this land, this lake, that once it has you in its hold, it won't let go. It's home, Ellie. Mine and yours."

That was all she needed to hear. She stood up, leaning over to kiss his grizzled cheek. "All right, so we'll fight, and we'll keep fighting until we win, Grandpa."

Chapter Five

♥

Ellie's bravado faded ten minutes after she left her grandfather's room. She'd gotten carried away in the moment. Her grandfather's memories had fired her up, reigniting her determination to protect him and the inn. But now, as she stood in the dining room watching the evening sky reflected on Mirror Lake, her mother's threat as she'd left the inn threw cold water on that inner fire, and Ellie worried she wouldn't be able to protect either her grandfather or the inn.

She'd practically been shaking in her shoes at the promise of retribution in her mother's eyes and the contempt in Richard's. They didn't believe she had the spine to stand up to them. They certainly knew she didn't have the money to fund the legal battle they'd vowed to wage.

"You have the truth on your side," she told her watery image in the window. Surely that had to count for something. Except there were a few lies mixed in with the truth. Namely that the inn was a going concern.

The door to the inn opened, and she panicked,

thinking her mother had returned, this time with lawyers and the law as she had promised.

"Anyone here? I've got an order for Ellie MacLeod," a young male voice called out.

She berated herself for letting her imagination run wild and hurried to the reception area, forcing a smile. "Sorry. How much do I owe you?" She paid him, including a generous tip. Her winnings from the poker game came in handy.

"Wait a minute," she said when he went to leave. "I just ordered a pizza." There was a large takeaway bag sitting on top of the box.

"Nope, that's included in your order," he said, and left.

She peeked in the bag, the smells of dark chocolate, powdered sugar, and tart raspberries wafting up to greet her. It smelled so good she wanted to dive inside the bag but restrained herself, ignoring her grumbling stomach.

She picked up the box and bag and locked the front door before taking the red-carpeted staircase to Nate's room. Jonathan had a key, and if someone wanted a room for the night—unlikely, but she could always hope—the buzzer was connected to her phone.

Standing outside the door at the far end of the dimly lit hall, she contemplated leaving the box and bag outside Nate's room. But unlike her, he couldn't read minds. He wouldn't know that besides wanting to bring him a pizza, she craved a small dose of the feeling she got every time she stood close to him.

Being near him was like drinking a cool glass of water on a hot summer's day.

She lifted her hand and knocked. "Hi. I...," she began when the door opened, the rest of the words getting stuck in her throat at the sight of Nate standing shirtless with a towel draped around his neck. So much for her hope his mere presence would calm her worries and fears. Her pulse was racing like she'd run up and down the stairs ten times.

"Hey. Whatcha got there?"

Unable to look away from all that bronzed muscle and the swirls of dark ink on his arms, she shoved the box and bag at him. "Pizza."

"Nice. Do you want to join me?"

"Join you?" She managed to drag her eyes to his face.

"Yeah. I can't eat all this by myself." He moved away from the door, obviously expecting her to come inside.

Her gaze went to the rumpled bed, and she hesitated. Being in the close confines of the small guest room with a half-naked Nate, a man she was attracted to even if he wasn't attracted to her, was a bad idea. But the thought of being alone with her worries tonight held little appeal.

As though Nate had read her mind, he said, "It's warm enough that we can eat on the balcony if you want."

"I'd like that. Thanks." She closed the door and stepped into the room. "I wasn't sure what kind of pizza you like, but apparently Zia Maria knows. She sent you dessert too."

"If it's her chocolate pie, I can't promise there will be any left for you." He winked and dropped the towel on the sheets, then grabbed a gray sweatshirt from the black duffel bag lying open on the bed.

"Here. Let me take the food," she offered, moving to his side. She wanted him to put on his sweatshirt ASAP. The view of his back was as tempting as his front. "I promise. I won't eat your pie."

"You obviously haven't tasted Zia Maria's chocolate pie." He grinned, handing her the box and bag.

As Ellie walked to the sliding door, she couldn't resist one last peek at all that enticing muscle on display and glanced over her shoulder. His eyes met hers. She cleared her throat. "Do you want something to drink?"

"Whoever was in here last left an unopened bottle of red wine. I'm good with that if you are."

"I'm so sorry, Nate. I completely forgot someone was in here before you. I can clean the room while you eat."

"Don't sweat it. It's spotless."

She scanned the room.

"Seriously, Ellie. You should have seen the last place I stayed." He grabbed the bottle of wine from Three Wild Women Winery and two glasses from the bathroom counter.

"Okay, but at least let me change the sheets and get you fresh towels."

He reached around her to open the sliding glass door. "Yes to the towels, no to changing the sheets. No one slept in the bed, Ellie. Now let's eat before the pizza gets cold." He pulled out a chair for her on the balcony. "Sit."

She placed the pizza box and bag on the small round table and took a seat.

"So how's Joe doing?" Nate asked, taking a couple of napkins out of the bag before moving it aside.

"Still trying to figure out why my mother is doing this. I think we both are."

"In my experience, it comes down to jealousy, money, or revenge. Once you figure out what's motivating your mother, you'll stand a better chance of stopping her. You said all they were focused on was the money, so go from there," he said, twisting off the wine bottle's cap and pouring them each a glass.

"Thank you," she said, accepting the glass. "You're right. It has to be about the money. But what I can't figure out is why. It's not as if my parents need it. They have good jobs, good pensions."

"You'd be surprised how many families are torn apart over money. Whether they need it or not. Everybody seems to want more." He lifted the pizza box lid and cocked his head. "Did you say something to Zia Maria that I should know about?"

"No, why?"

He turned the box. On the inside of the lid someone had written, *You mess with Ellie, no more pizza for you.*

"That sounds like Massimo, not Zia Maria. He must have heard her when she was warning me away from you." She grimaced, realizing how that sounded. "Not that I said we were a thing. I didn't. I wouldn't because obviously we're not. I actually made it clear you were just staying at the inn and not with me. Zia Maria is as bad as Granny, so I made that really, really clear."

"You're cute when you babble," he said, handing her a piece of pizza. "So what did Zia Maria say? I thought she loved me."

"She does. She just doesn't love you for me. She told me to tell you to stop by on your way out of town tomorrow." Ellie took a bite of the pizza, savoring the tastes of prosciutto, garlic sauce, and mozzarella cheese.

Nate had inhaled his slice of pizza while she was talking and reached for another piece. "You didn't mention that I was going back undercover, did you?"

"No. I didn't know that you were."

"Good. I thought Chase might have said something to Sadie and that she'd told you." His phone pinged. He glanced at the screen and sighed. "Obviously he mentioned it to Mrs. M. He's turned into a regular mother hen since he married Sadie." His phone pinged again, and he groaned. "I'm going to kill him. My sister," he said at her questioning gaze. "He's brought in the big guns now."

"Chase doesn't want you to go undercover?"

"No. He wants me to drop the case." He wiped his hand on his napkin before responding to the texts with quick, irritated jabs of his finger.

"Is this about your friend Brodie?"

"Yeah. Chase wants me to move on, but I can't. Not yet. Not until it's done." He turned off his phone, reached for the glass of wine, and then leaned back in the chair.

"I'm sorry about your friend, Nate. It must be difficult for you to be on the case given your personal involvement."

"Thanks. It is, but I have to see it through to the end."

"I thought the people involved were in jail."

He nodded, then explained that he wasn't going after the people immediately responsible for Brodie's murder. Nate wanted to bring down the organization that had supplied the drugs.

"I don't know much about this kind of thing, but isn't that a job for the DEA?" she asked.

"It is. We're running a joint task force with them and ATF."

"At least you have backup."

He responded with a noncommittal grunt, straightening to grab another piece of pizza without meeting her gaze.

"You don't have backup, do you?" She took a fortifying sip of wine. The risks he was willing to take bothered her. And she had no doubt the risks were massive if Chase was worried about him.

Nate's eyes narrowed. "What? Are you psychic or something?"

She nearly choked on her wine, covering her reaction with a laugh. "No. I'm just good at reading facial expressions...and noncommittal grunts."

"Good. For a minute there, I thought you were like Mrs. M. She thinks she can tell people's futures, you know."

"You don't think she can?"

"You're joking, right? She pulled it on me once. Took my hand and zoned out, then started spouting a bunch of crap about soul mates and finding mine. I don't know what scared me more, her telling me that once I found my one and only, my life as I knew it would be over or that creepy voice she used."

Feeling defensive on her grandmother's behalf and her own, Ellie said, "You might not believe Granny can see the future, but there are people who do. Just ask Sadie and Abby."

"To each their own, I guess. As long as it doesn't hurt anybody. But I've seen the other side of it. You wouldn't believe how many crackpots come out of the woodwork when a kid goes missing. You ask me, they're a bunch of frauds who prey on people's tragedies." He winced. "Sorry. I don't mean Agnes."

Whatever he'd picked up on in her expression had nothing to do with her grandmother. It was that he'd hit too close to home. The summer she'd moved to New York, a little boy had gone missing from Central Park. She'd become obsessed with the case, wanting to help. Every time the father had been interviewed on TV, she'd gotten the feeling he was lying. That he knew where his son was. She kept seeing a dark car parked in an alley.

For years Ellie had hidden her gift, afraid that people would mock her, tell her she was crazy like her mother had. But a little boy's life had been on the line, so she'd pushed through her fears and gone to the police. Two of the investigating officers had brushed her off as just another crazy, but the woman on their team hadn't. Sadly, Ellie had been wrong.

It hadn't been the father; it had been his son from his first marriage. The teenager had left his sleeping brother in a parked car while visiting his girlfriend on a sweltering day. The little boy had died and his brother had hidden his body.

In the end Ellie's gift had proved a curse to that grieving family. Because of her, the father had been hounded by police. The press and his wife had turned against him. But no one had turned on Ellie. The female officer had protected her identity. No one ever knew of her involvement.

"Ellie, you know I'd never say anything like that to Mrs. M, right? I don't care that she's into the woo-woo."

"You think my grandmother's crazy?"

"No. Of course I don't." He shook his head. "I'm messing this up. Blame it on lack of sleep. All I'm saying is Mrs. M is like a grandmother to me. I wouldn't do anything to hurt her or let anyone else hurt her, for that matter."

"I know. She feels the same way about you. Sorry for getting defensive. I'm tired too."

He lifted his glass of wine. "Friends again?"

She touched her glass to his. "Friends," she said, her smile a little forced at the thought that all he wanted from her was friendship. Then again, given his opinion of her grandmother's gift and his feelings about psychics, that was probably for the best.

Chapter Six

♥

"Ellie, we have a problem," the judge said, joining her in the kitchen where she was making breakfast.

Her head pounded. She was a lightweight when it came to drinking alcohol, and she and Nate had finished the bottle of wine last night. "A little problem or a big one?" She prayed it was a little one. She didn't have the bandwidth to deal with a big problem today.

A thunderstorm had moved in at three in the morning, ensuring she couldn't get back to sleep and that she spent the rest of the early-morning hours tossing and turning, trying to figure out her next move with her mother. There also might have been a small amount of fantasizing about Nate. In her dream state, she hadn't seemed to understand the difference between friend and lover.

"A rather big one, I'm afraid," the judge said. "There's a leak in my room."

"Big leak or little leak?" she asked, wondering where to fit it in on today's to-do list. She had eight guest rooms to clean.

"The puddle is growing to the size of a pond as we speak."

"Wonderful." She smelled something burning and looked down. The chicken sausages were no longer a lovely golden brown. They were burned to a crisp. It was going to be one of those days, she thought as she moved the skillet off the burner. "Fruit-and-yogurt breakfast parfaits are in the fridge, and pancakes are in the warmer. I'll make orange juice as soon as I take care of your room." The judge and her grandfather were fussy about their orange juice. They liked it freshly squeezed.

"I'll look after the water in my room. All I need is a mop and a bucket. But that's only a temporary fix. From what I saw from my balcony, there are shingles missing on the roof. I remember your reaction the last time Joe and I tried to fix them, so I won't bother offering to do so again. Perhaps Mr. Black could be of service."

"Nate's leaving this morning. For all I know, he's already gone." She'd be disappointed if he was, but they'd more or less said goodbye last night. "But I wouldn't ask him anyway. I'll take care of the tiles once the rain lets up." Thank goodness for YouTube instructional videos. She'd become adept at dealing with minor repairs. She just hoped that replacing a few missing shingles would take care of the leak.

"He hasn't left yet. I passed him in the hall. He was going for a run."

That shouldn't cheer her up, but it did.

"Mr. Black also mentioned that your meeting with

your mother didn't go as well as you'd indicated to Joe. You should have told me, Ellie. I wouldn't have gone to Sadie and Chase's for dinner."

"I know. I didn't want to upset Grandpa. The tremor in his hand is back, and he was dragging his foot. Did you notice?"

He nodded. "It started soon after your mother's call."

"I wish you would have told me."

He patted her shoulder. "You had enough on your mind. I didn't think you needed the added stress." The judge looked out for her as much as her grandfather did.

"I ended up telling Grandpa the truth last night. Not how bad I think it will get, but that it wasn't over. I don't think he was surprised."

"I don't imagine he was. He'd said as much to me when I drew up the papers."

"What are you two jawing about?" her grandfather asked, walking into the kitchen. He sniffed the air. "I hope you burned those tasteless chicken sausages and not breakfast links." He went to the fridge, pulled out the freezer door, and heaved a put-upon sigh. "Not a pork sausage in sight. You're killing me, Ellie my love."

"No, your diet will do that if I let you eat whatever you want. But I did make you pancakes." She lifted the lid on the warming tray. "You and Jonathan sit and enjoy your breakfast while I get started on my day."

"Aren't you going to eat with us?" her grandfather asked.

"I have something I need to take care of." She

gave a barely perceptible shake of her head for the judge's benefit. She didn't want her grandfather stressing about the leak or offering to help. She walked a fine line between protecting him and not making him feel useless.

"Now, you don't need to do it all on your own. The judge and I don't mind giving you a hand, do we?"

"Not at all," Jonathan agreed, taking the juicer from the upper cabinet.

"Great. You can clean the bathrooms in the guest rooms Abby, Mallory, and the kids were in."

"You're an evil woman." Her grandfather's grin faded as he glanced at Jonathan. "We'll take care of the bathrooms for you, but before we do, we have an important matter to discuss. Our plan didn't deter Miranda, Judge. We need to come up with a new one."

"Grandpa, you don't have to worry about Mom. I told you I'd figure it out."

"Not on your own you won't. You said we'd fight, and we will. Together."

"Joe's right, Ellie," the judge said before she could argue. "He needs to be involved. He needs to know exactly what he's up against. The first thing your mother will ask for is a legal competency hearing, which Joe will have no problem passing. So both of you get that worry out of your heads."

"You're right. Of course you're right. Thanks, Judge." She kissed his cheek and then kissed her grandfather's. "I'm sorry I was keeping things from you, Grandpa. I was just trying to protect you."

He patted her cheek. "I know you were. So does that mean the judge and I get off bathroom duty?"

"Nope." She smiled at the two older men grumbling behind her, both her headache and her mood lifting thanks to Jonathan's optimistic outlook. Even the thought of the leak in his room couldn't dampen her spirits. She left the dining room, her steps light as she took the stairs two at a time.

She opened the storage closet directly across from the stairs and grabbed a mop and bucket. Tucking the mop under her arm, she looped the handle of the bucket over her wrist and pulled four fluffy white towels off the top shelf. She left the towels outside Nate's door and retrieved her phone from the pocket of her jeans. She sent him a text, letting him know that breakfast was waiting for him in the kitchen when he got back from his run.

Her mood deflated a little when she saw the state of Jonathan's room. He hadn't been exaggerating. She put down the mop and bucket, took off her sneakers, and rolled up the bottoms of her jeans to midcalf. Retrieving her wireless earbuds from the right pocket of her jeans, she pulled up a playlist on her iPhone. Listening to music was one of her favorite ways to deal with stress. It also made cleaning more fun. She stuck in her earbuds and turned up the volume as she sloshed through the cold water with the mop and bucket in hand.

Jonathan had an oversize corner room with a gorgeous view of the lake on one side and one of the woods on the other. The rain had slowed to a drizzle, the sun's weak rays peeking from behind the dark clouds that rolled across the sky. The early-morning fog that had blanketed the lake had dissipated into wispy fingers of mist.

She leaned the mop against the bucket beside Jonathan's brown leather chair. Books and paperwork were piled on the ottoman and side table. Thankfully the judge was a tidy man. It didn't look like any of his possessions had been damaged. She pulled up the round area rug and walked to the sliding glass door. When she opened it, a cool rain-and-pine-scented breeze rushed inside. She hung the rug over the balcony railing and then went back inside, closing the door behind her.

Time passed quickly and pleasantly as she sang and danced, mopping up the water in time to the music. She did a happy little shimmy while squeezing the last droplets of water into the bucket. She'd filled four of them.

"You traded me in for a mop," said a familiar deep voice from behind her.

She whirled around to see a grinning Nate leaning against the door frame. She didn't understand what he meant until she realized the song she'd been singing. The last song they'd danced to at her cousin's wedding. She hoped he hadn't been standing there long. If he had, he'd realize her entire playlist consisted of songs they'd danced to. How pathetic was that?

"Mr. Mop might seem like a stiff stick, but he has some pretty fancy moves."

Nate's grin widened. "I saw that." He wore boots,

jeans, and his black leather jacket, his helmet in his hand.

"Are you heading out?" She worked to keep the disappointment from her voice, telling herself it was because she was worried about him and not because she'd enjoyed having him around. Life had seemed a little brighter with Nate in it, a whole lot less boring too.

"I am." He looked up at the ceiling. "From the size of the leak, it looks like you might have a bigger problem than a few missing shingles, Ellie. You're not planning on tackling it on your own, are you?"

"No, of course not. I'll leave that to the professionals."

"You sure about that? The judge seems to think you'd give it a go."

He was such a tattletale. "I was, until I realized that it was beyond my level of expertise." Beyond hers but not her favorite YouTube fixer-upper channel's. "Good luck with Ryder. I hope you can get through to him." Nate had talked to her about Brodie's son last night while they devoured Zia Maria's chocolate pie.

"You and me both." He held up his phone. "Let me know how it goes with your mother."

"I will." She walked over and gave him a hug, feeling a little self-conscious as she did so. But there was a part of her that worried this would be the last time she saw him. "Be careful. You have a lot of people who care about you," she said, her voice muffled against his chest.

He hugged her back—a warm, friendly hug—then stepped away from her. "Careful is my middle name."

"That's not what I've heard." She'd heard he was a risk-taker, willing to do whatever it took to get his man, or woman, no matter the danger it put him in. "Thanks for everything, Nate. I wish you'd let me refund your room on your credit card though."

"It was nothing, and I had the best sleep I've had in months. Thanks for the pizza and pie. I enjoyed the conversation and company too."

"So did I." Their eyes met and held for several beats of her heart, the light rain pattering against the glass the only sound in the otherwise quiet inn.

He looked away first. "I'd better get going."

"There's leftover pizza and sandwiches in the fridge. I can pack them up for you, if you'd like."

"I'm good. Take care, Ellie," he said, then turned and walked away.

"You too, Nate," she said to his broad, leather-clad back. She leaned against the door frame, watching until he disappeared from view. He called goodbye to the judge and Joe and then the front door opened and closed. Moments later, his motorcycle started up. She stayed where she was, listening until the low rumble faded, whispering a prayer for his safety.

Her phone pinged. It was a text from her grand-mother.

Don't let Nate leave. Use your feminine wiles to keep him there. I'm on my way.

She snorted at the idea of flirting with Nate to get him to stay. She was running low on feminine wiles these days, she thought, looking down at her T-shirt and rolled-up jeans. Not that it would make any difference to Nate. He probably would have left sooner if she'd attempted to flirt with him.

You can save yourself a trip, Granny. He's already left. He's meeting with Brodie's wife and their son at Dot's Diner. She erased the part about his meeting at the diner before pressing Send. Ellie didn't put it past her grandmother to show up at Dot's.

As she waited for her grandmother's response, because Agnes MacLeod always had one, she heard a vehicle turn into the inn. "You weren't kidding, were you," she murmured, not sure she was up for a visit with her grandmother. She rolled down her pant legs, slipped on her sneakers, then went to collect the mop and place the bucket under the wet circle on the ceiling.

A dog barked from somewhere close by. Maybe it wasn't her grandmother after all. Maybe someone actually wanted to rent a room. Ellie closed the judge's door, hurrying down the hall to inspect the other rooms for one she could quickly make ready for a guest. But as she sprinted past the stairs, she caught a glimpse of the woman entering the inn. It was her sister.

Ellie backtracked. "Bri?" she said as she made her way down the stairs to the reception area, taking in the Irish setter sitting at her sister's feet. The dog looked as nervous as Bri. "What's going on?"

"Good morning to you too," her sister said, looking less than her perfect self. Her blond hair was disheveled, her face was makeup-free, and she looked like she'd slept in her clothes from yesterday.

"Sorry, but come on, Bri. You can't be shocked that I'm surprised to see you here after yesterday's meeting. I assumed you were heading back to Charlotte."

"No. We stayed with Mom and Dad just outside of Highland Falls. Richard's client has a vacation home that he let us use."

"Would that be the same client they're attempting to sell the inn to?"

"Ellie, please, I don't want to fight with you." Her sister sounded tired.

"What do you want?"

Bri searched her face. "When did you become so hard? This isn't like you."

"Dealing with family that would throw an old man out of his home and try to sell it out from under him will do that to a girl, I guess."

"It's not like that, Ellie. Mom's just trying to do what she thinks is best for Grandpa. I don't know why you can't see that."

"Grandpa can't either. Maybe you'd like to explain it to him. I'll call him right—"

"No, don't. I just ... I need a favor, Ellie."

She was about to tell her sister she had a strange way of going about asking for a favor when an image of Richard and Bri fighting came to her. She saw Richard grab Bri and the dog intervene. The dog—Toby, they called it Toby—lunged for Richard, pulling at his arm. Richard shoved him off, yelling as he kicked the dog.

Her sister went down on her knees, crying, cradling Toby in her arms.

Ellie gasped, the words tumbling out of her before she could stop them. "You have to leave him, Bri. Any man who could do that to a—"

Her sister backed away from her, looking as scared as Ellie was horrified. "Stop it. Stop saying things like that. Mom told me, Ellie. She warned me that this is what you'd do. That you'd pretend you can see things, pretend that you can read people's minds, but I didn't believe her. Do you know how crazy you sound?"

Ellie felt her pulse race, unable to contain the anger that had caused her barriers to drop and show her the images in her sister's mind in the first place. She held Bri's gaze and crouched in front of the dog. "Come here, Toby." She held out her hand. "Come here, boy."

Her sister shook her head. "That doesn't prove anything. I must have told you about him. You heard me call his name."

"I didn't even know you had a dog, Bri. You don't talk to me anymore." Not since Ellie had confronted her sister about her husband's controlling behavior. "So if you're not here to ask me to take Toby, why are you here?"

"I...I thought he'd be good for Grandpa. The client who left him to me had a stroke. Toby's a therapy dog. He can help with Grandpa's recovery."

"Grandpa doesn't need help, and I don't need some-one else to look after." It was true, but she couldn't stop the images of what had happened to Toby and her sister from playing in her mind.

"Okay, fine. If you're going to be like that—"

She reached for sister's arm to stop her from leaving. "Wait." When Ellie's fingers closed around Bri's bicep, her sister cried out. Toby growled, baring his teeth at Ellie. She backed away and held up her hands. "It's okay, boy. I'm not going to hurt her."

"It's not what you think," Bri murmured, facing the door. "Richard doesn't mean to hurt me. He doesn't know his own strength, that's all. He's been under a lot of stress lately."

"If a client said that to you, Bri, what would you tell them to do?" It was a question Ellie had asked herself many times over the past two years. She didn't understand how a brilliant woman who had everything going for her stayed with a man who was obviously abusive.

"You don't understand." She tugged on the dog's leash. "Come on, Toby."

"Stay, Bri. Stay with me and Grandpa."

"I can't. We're heading back to Charlotte in half an hour. I have clients this afternoon."

"Leave Toby with me." She couldn't in good conscience let him go. It was hard enough letting her sister leave.

Bri turned, her sky-blue eyes glistening with unshed tears. "Really? You'll take him?"

She nodded, retrieving the dog's leash from her sister's hand. "Don't you know I'd do anything for you? I love you. You're my baby sister."

Bri let out a small sob and threw her arms around Ellie. "I'm sorry I said the things that I did. I love you. I really do. And I'm sorry for what Mom and Richard said to you yesterday. I know you're just looking out for Grandpa."

Ellie gently rubbed her sister's back. "I don't want you worrying about that. I just need you to promise me that you'll take care of yourself." Ellie pulled back, holding her sister's gaze. "We're here if you need us. Call anytime, day or night. There's always a place for you here."

Her sister nodded and went down on her knees to hug Toby. "I love you, boy. I'm going to miss you."

"We'll take good care of him." She didn't need to read her sister's mind to know Bri was devastated at the thought of leaving Toby behind. "You can talk to him on FaceTime. I'll send pictures."

"Thank you. I have to go." She took one last look at Toby and then opened the door, practically running down the steps.

Toby whined, straining against the leash to go after her. Ellie closed the door, crouched in front of the dog, and took his face between her hands. "It's going to be okay, Toby."

"Ellie," her grandfather shouted, "come here. Me and the judge have a plan."

Toby started to shake, a liquid warmth seeping through Ellie's shoe. He'd peed on her sneaker. She bowed her head and sighed. "I'm here, Grandpa."

She straightened as Joe and Jonathan came down the hall from her grandfather's room. Upon seeing

Toby, the two men backed up against the wall. "Who's that?" Joe asked.

"Toby. Bri thought he'd be good for you. He's a therapy dog."

"We have a no-animal policy for a reason," her grandfather said. "I don't like them."

The judge held up his hands. "Don't look at me. I'm a cat person."

"He's not going anywhere, so you both better get used to him."

Chapter Seven

♥

Nate was still thinking about Ellie singing and dancing to Lewis Capaldi's "Someone You Loved" when he pulled into the diner's parking lot. Ellie couldn't sing worth a damn but the woman had some sweet moves. Except sweet wasn't how they made him feel—sweet or friendly.

No, his feelings for Ellie were clearly going in the wrong direction. A dangerous direction for a guy like him. Yesterday's kiss he could dismiss as a one-off—sort of—but his reactions to her beating the poker buddies at cards, his late-night dinner with her on the balcony, and her musical performance this morning weren't so easily explained away. It was a good thing he'd left today. She got to him, and that wasn't the kind of complication he needed in his life.

He shut down the engine, took off his helmet, and kicked the stand into place. Turning at the sound of rap music blasting from the black truck to his right, he narrowed his eyes at the long-haired kid with his feet up on the dash. Clouds of smoke puffed out of the open windows. Nate walked over to the driver's-side door and leaned in, turning off the music and snagging the keys.

Ryder's gaze shot to him. "What the hell?"

"Back atcha, kid. Your mother know you're out here smoking weed?"

His eyes were barely visible underneath all that hair, but Nate was pretty sure the question earned him an eye roll.

"Toss the joint, and let's get something to eat."

Ryder blew smoke in Nate's face and gave him the finger.

"Nice. Suit yourself." He forced himself to walk away. If he didn't, he'd be tempted to drag Ryder out of the truck and frog-march him into the diner. No wonder Gina had sounded desperate. The kid was obviously out of control.

He spotted Gina the moment he walked into the diner. She sat at the red vinyl booth with her chin propped in her hand, staring out the window.

"Hey." He leaned in to give her a hug. She wore a brown leather jacket over a white T-shirt paired with jeans and a truckload of vibrant jewelry around her neck and wrist. She looked exhausted. Beautiful, but exhausted.

"Hey, Nate." She returned his hug and then nodded at the window. "Did you have a nice chat with my delinquent son?"

"Saw that, did you?" He slid into the bench seat across from her. "So you know he's smoking a joint in your truck?"

"Oh yeah. He doesn't even bother hiding it anymore." She held up her phone. "I'm tempted to call the cops. Maybe that will scare him straight."

"How long has this been going on, Gina?" He glanced over his shoulder at the truck.

He'd spent time with Ryder after Brodie's funeral. The kid had been angry and grieving but nothing like the surly teenager Nate had just encountered.

The last time Nate had spoken to Brodie, he'd been bragging about how well Ryder was doing in school and on the basketball court. The kid had been a straight-A student and a natural athlete.

"He started acting out not long after the funeral."

"You should have told me."

She absently stirred the black coffee in her mug, turning her head to look out the window. "I was angry at you. I blamed you for Brodie dying. He wanted to be a teacher. He'd still be here if he'd followed his dream."

Nate leaned back in the booth, feeling like he'd been sucker punched. "I didn't talk him into joining the sheriff's department, Gina. You know that."

"You didn't talk him out of it either." She moved the spoon in slow circles. "He looked up to you, Nate. You were his hero. He would have done anything to make you proud."

And that's what got him killed. Gina didn't have to say it.

"I warned him he was in over his head." He had, only his warning had come too late.

"It doesn't matter. Nothing can bring him back."

She lifted her gaze to his. "Don't think I don't know I have my own blame to shoulder. I shouldn't have left him. Shouldn't have taken Ryder. He blames me too, you know. Ryder. I met someone six months ago. He went from surly to outright defiant and combative."

"You have nothing to feel guilty about, Gina. Brodie would want you to be happy."

"Try telling that to my kid."

"I will if you want me to."

"I want you to take him, Nate. That's what I really want. I'm scared he's going to get himself killed or hurt someone else. You're the only one I can turn to. The only one who stands a chance of getting through to him."

He stared at her, stunned. "I can't. I can't do it, Gina. I have a job. I—" He caught himself before he shared what he was doing. When he'd told her they'd put away the people directly responsible for Brodie's murder, she'd been relieved. He couldn't tell her it wasn't over. "Look, even if I could take a few days, there's no way Ryder would agree to stay with me."

"That's why he's here, Nate. I told him what I was going to ask you, and he came. Sure, he put up a fuss, yelled and ranted, but he still came. As much as you were Brodie's hero, you were Ryder's too."

"That's not fair." He waved off the waitress approaching with a pot of coffee.

Gina shrugged. "I don't care. I'll do whatever I have to to save my son. Even if it means guilting you into taking him. You're his godfather, Nate."

He swore under his breath. "I don't even have a damn place to stay. I didn't renew the lease on my place."

He'd thought it was a good idea at the time. In the past year, he'd spent a grand total of three weeks at his apartment in Asheville. The town was an hour and forty minutes from Highland Falls. He'd grown up there. His family still lived there. So did Gina. "What about school?" he asked, desperate for an out.

"He got expelled last week." She smiled.

He was trapped, and she knew it. "All right. I'll take him. For a week at most, Gina."

"Two weeks. That's how long his suspension is, and I have to work. I can't leave him on his own."

It sounded like a lifetime. "What about your mom or Brodie's?"

"They've washed their hands of him. I wasn't kidding, Nate. You're my last hope, and his."

"Now would you look who's here," said a familiar voice behind Nate.

He bowed his head and groaned. How the hell had Mrs. M known where to find him? She slid into the booth beside him, and Colin took a seat beside Gina, casting Nate an apologetic glance. That answered the question of how she'd found him. Leave it to Mrs. M to hook up with a former CIA agent.

"I'm Agnes, but everyone calls me Granny Mac-Leod." Mrs. M offered her hand to Gina. Nate grabbed Agnes's hand and put it on the table, covering it with his own.

At Gina's raised eyebrow, he said, "Don't ask."

"I have the second sight. It makes Nate nervous."

Agnes shifted on the bench to look at him. "You never did tell me what I saw when I did your reading."

"Yeah, and I never will."

She sat there grinning while Colin introduced himself to Gina, who totally ignored Nate's subtle head shake and told the older couple who she was and why she was there.

"Aww, the poor wee mannie," Mrs. M said.

"Hold your sympathy until after you meet the *poor wee mannie*," Nate said.

Mrs. M ignored him. "You've made the right decision, dear. We'll all be there to help the lad and to support Nate. Your boy will love the inn."

"Ah, Mrs. M, we're not staying at the inn. Ellie's got enough on her plate. She doesn't need—"

"She does, but that's why this is the perfect arrangement. You can help her with the inn, and she can help you with Ryder."

"She's getting the short end of the straw if you ask me," Nate muttered.

"How do you figure that? Richard and Miranda haven't given up, you know. She'll need your help dealing with those two. Besides, you'll be renting the two-bedroom suite, and they can use the money. I'm sure Ellie will give you a good rate if you help her around the inn though." An alarm went off on her phone. "We have to skedaddle. There's a special meeting of the town council. It was nice meeting you, dear. And don't you worry about your son. He's in good hands with this one." She patted Nate's cheek and slid out of the booth.

Colin joined her. "Nice meeting you, Gina. We'll see you around, son," he said to Nate, a hint of laughter in his voice.

Of course Colin was laughing at him. Nate had done it again. He'd walked straight into Mrs. M's matchmaking trap. But this time, he couldn't blame it on sleep deprivation or craving some lighthearted fun. He needed somewhere to stay with the kid, and Mirror Lake Inn, basically stuck in the middle of nowhere, was as good a place as any to keep Ryder out of trouble.

Nate couldn't say the same about himself. In his head he might have put Ellie in the friend zone, but there were other parts of him that weren't on board with the plan. A fact that would no doubt have the matchmakers of Highland Falls cheering, including his best friend, he thought, when his phone vibrated on the table with an incoming call from Chase.

Nate declined the call and scrubbed his hands over his face, looking over the tips of his fingers at Gina. "Don't you dare say she's sweet. She's not sweet. She's a manipulative busybody."

"Who obviously loves you." Gina glanced out the window. "Wow, she got Ryder out of the truck, and he's actually smiling."

"How can you tell? You can't see past his hair to his face."

"So what exactly happens when Granny MacLeod shakes someone's hand?" Gina asked instead of answering his question.

Nate pressed his face to the glass and swore. Pulling

a few bills from his wallet, he tossed them on the table and said, "Nothing good. Come on."

By the time they reached the truck, Mrs. M and Colin were getting into a cherry-red convertible. Ryder was staring after them. "That was way freaky."

"What did she say?" Nate asked.

He shrugged. "Something about me being lost, but the old guy pulled her hand from mine before she finished. That was some weird shit, man. Her eyes were wonky, and she spoke in a creepy monotone voice."

"Language," Nate said.

Ryder snorted. "Yeah, like you haven't heard it before. You swear all the time."

Colin beeped the horn as he pulled out of the parking lot. Mrs. M, with a kerchief over her hair, waved.

The kid smiled and gave them a two-finger salute. *Better than one*, Nate thought.

"The old lady said I'm staying with you at some inn."

"She has a name, and it's not old lady."

Ryder rolled his eyes. "Whatevs. Am I staying at the inn or not?"

Nate was tempted to say not, but Gina intervened. "You are, and I expect you to behave yourself, buddy. Remember, this is your last chance. The judge will place you in foster care if this doesn't work out."

Apparently Gina hadn't told him everything. She wouldn't meet his gaze. Tough. Whether she liked it or not, she needed to be up-front with him. He needed to know exactly what he was dealing with.

"That's a pile of bullsh—crap. I'm almost sixteen. No one's going to want me."

"I do. I want you." Gina pulled him in for a hug. "And so does Nate."

"Yeah, sure he does." But he didn't miss the tentative glance the kid slid his way. Gina was right. Ryder wasn't balking at the idea of staying with him. If anything, it seemed like he wanted to.

"I'm here, aren't I? Say goodbye to your mother. We've got things to do before we head to the inn."

Ryder's eyes narrowed. "Like what?"

"Getting your hair cut for one. You can't stay at the inn looking like that."

"How come you can?"

Nate swore under his breath. "I'm getting mine cut too." He hugged Gina goodbye, saying so only she could hear, "You and I need to talk. I'll call you tonight, and you can tell me exactly what trouble Ryder has gotten himself into."

She nodded and said a tearful goodbye to her son.

Nate walked to his bike, giving them a moment alone.

"Cool bike. Can I like drive it? Just in the parking lot," Ryder said as he joined him, a backpack slung over his shoulder.

"Not a chance." Then, noting the light dim in the kid's eyes, he said, "We'll see how this week goes. Toe the line, and I'll think about it." The inn was off the beaten path. He wouldn't have to worry about Ryder running into a car. He handed the kid a helmet and then put on his own, swinging his leg over the seat. "Get on, and hang on."

An hour later, the two of them freshly shorn, Nate

pulled into the inn's parking lot. Except for a red truck, the lot was empty.

Ryder got off the bike, took off his helmet, and looked around. "There's nothing here."

"Don't worry. There will be plenty for you to do." He kicked the stand into place and swung his leg over the seat. "Come on. We'll get settled, and then I'll show you around."

"That'll take about five seconds. What am I supposed to do for the rest of the day?" Ryder muttered, following him up the stairs.

"Read a book." Nate laughed when the kid groaned. Joe and the judge were on their hands and knees, looking under the reception desk, when they walked into the inn. "Hey guys, everything okay here?"

"No. We lost the dog." The judge helped Joe to his feet.

"Ellie will have our hides if we don't find him," her grandfather said.

Nate looked around. "When did you get a dog?"

"Bri foisted it on us this morning. Thought it would be good for me, or so she says. It's probably part of my daughter's plan to drive us from the inn." Joe scratched his head. "I thought you left."

"I did, but I've had a change of plans. Any chance I can book a room for a couple of weeks? The two-room suite if it's available. Ryder's staying with me." He introduced him to the older men.

"Sorry for your loss, young man. From everything we've heard about your father, he was a good man."

Joe added his condolences to the judge's and then perked up. "Do you like dogs?"

"Yeah, I guess."

"Good. You can help us find him. Come along now." Joe waved Ryder to the stairs. "He doesn't like me and the judge. Hightailed it out of here as soon as Ellie left. We haven't seen hide nor hair of him since."

"Do you have any dog biscuits for him? He might come if you bribe him with a treat," Ryder suggested. He'd said more in the last few minutes than he'd said to Nate the entire time they were in the barbershop.

"That's a grand idea. Ellie, that's my granddaughter," Joe explained to Ryder, "she went to Penelope's Pet Emporium and came home loaded down with five bags. There must have been treats in one of them. Do you remember where she put everything, Judge?"

"She left the food in the kitchen and the toys and dog bed in her room."

"Righto. Off we go." Joe pulled Ryder along with him. The kid shot Nate a wide-eyed glance over his shoulder but went along with Joe without protesting.

This might not be a bad idea after all, Nate thought, watching them head for the kitchen together. The older men might be a good influence on the kid. At least they'd help keep him busy.

"Where's Ellie?" Nate asked the judge.

"Up on the roof." He looked at the ceiling. "I haven't heard her hammering for a while now."

Stubborn woman, Nate thought, ignoring the surge of admiration rising up inside him. It seemed there wasn't anything Ellie couldn't handle on her own.

"I'll go give her a hand." He left his helmet and duffel bag on the chair by the stairs and headed for the door.

"See that's all that you do, Mr. Black. I'll be keeping a close eye on you," the judge called after him.

Nate smiled. The judge might just be his favorite person in Highland Falls. "Trust me, I don't have romantic designs on Ellie. We're just friends. And it's Nate."

As he rounded the side of the inn, he spotted the ladder. He made sure it was well secured before climbing up. She weighed a lot less than he did. "Ellie?" She was lying on the roof with her eyes closed.

She turned her head, shielding her eyes with her hand. "Hi." She smiled. "Nice haircut."

He ran his hand over his military-short hair as he walked over, stretching out beside her. "You don't seem surprised to see me. Mrs. M let you know I was on my way?"

"She did, and the twenty other people who've called me in the last hour also shared the news. I hear you've got Ryder with you."

He nodded. "And I hear you've got yourself a dog." He didn't tell her the dog was missing. He figured Ryder would find him. She didn't need something else to worry about.

"Bri brought him this morning and asked if we could keep him." Ellie filled him in on her conversation with her sister and on her concerns that Richard had hurt the dog. She'd taken him to the vet before she went to the pet shop. "The vet said nothing was broken or cracked, just badly bruised." She shook her head. "And I let my sister go back to Richard. I should have forced her to stay."

"You did what you could. You let her know you were here for her. It sucks, but there's not much more you can do for her, Ellie. It's up to Bri."

"My brother said the same thing. He's an ER doctor and has treated a number of abused women. He's going to talk to someone who specializes in abuse. Hopefully they can give us some advice."

"Does your brother know what your mother's up to?"

She nodded. "He's been through a lot the last year and a half, and I didn't want to unload on him. But he knew I was keeping something from him and wouldn't let it go until I told him. He's going to talk to my mother. If anyone can get through to her, it's Jace. He's her favorite." She turned her head to look at him. "Okay. Your turn. What's going on with Ryder?"

He told her as much as Gina had told him. "So obviously it's worse than she led me to believe if foster care is on the table."

"The poor kid. It has to be tough losing a parent at his age, and the way he lost his father must make it so much worse." She touched his arm. "I'm sorry. I know it's hard for you to talk about Brodie. This has to be tough for you too."

"It is. Gina blindsided me. I'm supposed to be out there getting the guy who orchestrated Brodie's murder, and I'm stuck here babysitting his son." He held up his hand. "That was a crappy thing to say. I love the kid, but do I really look like a guy you leave your fifteen-year-old with?"

"You probably don't want to hear this, but I think you're exactly who Ryder needs right now, and Gina must have thought so too."

"Time will tell, I guess." He looked around. "So what are you doing up here?"

"I fixed the roof." She sat up, leaning forward to pick up a hammer several inches from her feet. It caught on a tile and pulled it up. "Sort of fixed the roof, and now I'm hiding."

He grinned. There was something about her that made him smile, which was an impressive feat considering how he'd been feeling. "Who are you hiding from?"

"Life. Sadie, Abby, Granny, and the Sisterhood."

"They're not all on the matchmaking bandwagon, are they?"

"No. Just Granny. But that's only because Happy Ever After Entertainment announced the three finalists for most romantic town in America, and Highland Falls is one of them."

"That's a good thing, isn't it?" he asked, sensing she wasn't happy about it.

"Yes. It's awesome. But it would be even more awesome if Abby, Sadie, and the Sisterhood hadn't come up with the brilliant idea that I redo the guest rooms. They want the redesign to reflect romantic literary couples, and I have nine days to get it done. That's when the executives from the production company arrive to make their decision."

"Do you want to reno the rooms? I'm sure they'd understand that with everything going on, it's a big ask."

"I know they'd understand if I bowed out. But it's a good idea. The inn could use a face-lift."

"Okay then, I'll make you a deal. You help me with Ryder, and I'll help you with the renos." He held out his hand.

"Deal. But on one condition. You don't pay for the room while you're here. That way I won't feel guilty when I crack the whip."

He swallowed as an image of Ellie in black leather and carrying a whip came to mind. So much for keeping her in the friend zone. At least in his mind.

Chapter Eight

♥

Ellie sealed their deal with a handshake. Nate had great hands, big and strong and a little rough. She looked from his hand to his face and smiled. As dangerously sexy as he'd been with his long hair and beard, she preferred this clean-cut version of him. This was the man she'd spent the night dancing and laughing with at the wedding. The man who'd made her heart beat faster and made butterflies dance in her stomach.

She hadn't thought about Spencer and his betrayal once that night. She'd finally been ready to move on from her ex-fiancé and to dip her toe in the dating pool. A dating pool of one, maybe, but still, it had been a big step for her to admit, if only to herself, that she wanted to explore her feelings for Nate. That getting to know him better, seeing where the attraction led, was worth the risk of having her heart broken again. And then he'd disappeared for months on end, only showing up in her dreams.

Nate dropped her hand like it was hot cement and then cleared his throat. "I'll take care of the leak for you." He looked around. "Do you have any roof cement?"

She blinked, wondering what had happened or what she'd done wrong.

"Ellie?"

"I have some, yes," she said, glancing at him. He smiled, and she thought maybe she'd been imagining things. He was acting perfectly normal now. "It rolled off the roof. I'll get it for you."

He shrugged off his leather jacket, revealing a white T-shirt that hugged his broad chest and showed off his bulging biceps. "That's okay. I'll get it."

"I don't mind helping." She dug her phone from her pocket. "I have my trusty YouTube fixer-up guy's video right here."

"I'm good. Two of my brothers-in-law flip houses for a living. I give them a hand when I can." He lifted his chin at the ladder. "You should get started on your plans for the room renos. Figure out the couples you'll be using."

Nate and Ellie immediately popped into her mind. She blamed the thought on her grandmother putting ideas into her head. It didn't help that Highland Falls was in the finals for most romantic small town in the country. All this talk of romance was getting to her.

"You're right. No time to waste," she said in that over-the-top cheerful voice she used whenever her nerves got the better of her.

Be quiet before you really embarrass yourself, she told herself. It wasn't like Nate knew she was fantasizing they were a couple. Although in her defense, she didn't think a fleeting thought counted as fantasizing. *No, that's what you did last night.*

She pushed to her feet, the toe of her sneaker catching on the edge of the lifted tile. She tripped, gasping as she fell forward. Nate wrapped an arm around her waist and yanked her against him. "Thanks. I need to invest in a pair of work boots or at the very least sneakers with better treads." She tipped her head back. "You can let me go now."

"I need a minute to recover."

So did she, and having her back pressed against his chest, his arm wrapped around her waist, wasn't helping her regain her equilibrium. If anything, she felt a little lightheaded.

"Damn it, Ellie, you nearly fell off the roof."

"But I didn't." She went to remove his arm, but he simply tightened his hold. "Are you planning on keeping me here all day? Because I have lunch to make and rooms to redesign." *And I'm at risk of melting into a puddle of lust at your feet if you don't let go of me*, she thought but didn't say out loud.

"What's going on up there?" The judge was standing on his balcony, leaning back to look up at them.

"Ellie tripped and nearly fell off the roof is what's going on. So don't get your shorts in a twist, Judge."

"Maybe you'll listen to us now, young lady. We told you to call a roofer."

"I don't need a roofer. I was doing perfectly fine on my own."

"Sure you were," Nate muttered. "And stop leaning to your left."

"I can't see the roofing cement on the ground. Did it fall on your balcony, Judge?"

He disappeared from view and then came back, holding up the cement gun. "Is this what you're looking for?"

"That's it. Can you toss it up?" She held out her hands.

Nate snorted. "Don't toss it up until I get Ellie safely on the ground."

"I'm perfectly capable of getting myself safely on the ground, Nate. How do you think I got up here?"

"Humor me," he said, walking her across the roof toward the ladder, his front still pressed to her back and his arm still holding her tight. "Okay, now turn around. Slowly."

She huffed an annoyed breath but did as he directed. "Happy now?"

His lips twitched. "No, but my heart is no longer pounding out of my chest." He nodded at the ladder. "Probably a good idea if you go down on your knees before stepping onto the ladder."

"Really? You'd think I'd never done this before. Who do you think shoveled the snow and ice off the roof?" She lowered herself onto her knees, searching for a rung with her foot.

"You're killing me right now," he said as he crouched in front of her, holding the ladder steady as she made her way down.

She smiled up at him, jumping from the second-to-last rung to make the point that she wasn't athletically challenged and was perfectly capable of taking care of herself. Only there was something sticky on the right side rail of the ladder, and she couldn't get her hand off as quickly as her feet, and she nearly brought the ladder down on top of her. Well, she would have if Nate weren't still hanging on to it.

"Damn it, Ellie. Did you hurt your hand?"

"No, it's fine." It was stinging like crazy. She thought she might have taken off a layer of skin. "And my name isn't Damn It Ellie," she said before walking away.

He was still laughing when he told the judge to toss up the cement gun. She glanced over her shoulder. Of course he caught it easily.

As she rounded the corner of the inn, she nearly ran into a tall, lanky, freckle-faced teenager walking Toby. "Hi." She smiled. "You must be Ryder. I'm Ellie." She went to offer her hand and noticed the droplets of blood.

"What happened?"

"Little mishap on the ladder, but don't tell Nate." Her eyes narrowed on the smoke coming through the fingers of the hand hanging at his side. "And I won't tell him you're smoking. But I will tell you that it's bad for your health, and there's no smoking inside the inn. Besides, you're only fifteen."

"Almost sixteen, and it's not weed."

"I should hope not." She angled her head. "You don't actually smoke weed, do you?"

"Not anymore, I guess." He dropped the cigarette, putting it out with the toe of his Doc Martens.

He wore baggy jeans and an equally baggy navy

sweatshirt with the Jackson County Sheriff's Department logo emblazoned on the chest. His dad had worked for the sheriff's department. She could only imagine how Nate felt when he saw the sweatshirt. The sheriff, two deputies, and a woman from Highland Falls had been directly involved in Brodie's murder. Then again, the sweatshirt had probably belonged to Brodie.

"I'm sorry about your dad, Ryder. I never met him, but I heard he was a wonderful man."

"Yeah." He looked away and lifted his chin at the road. "Is it okay if I take the dog for a walk?"

"His name's Toby. We just got him today." She crouched in front of the Irish setter, scratching him gently behind the ears. "Lucky boy. You've made a friend." She straightened. "He was abused, so he's a little skittish. He's a rescue." It wasn't exactly a lie. She'd told the vet the same thing.

"I don't think he likes Joe and the judge. He was hiding from them. I found him under the bed in your room. I wasn't snooping or anything. Your grandpa was with me."

"I didn't think you were." She patted the dog's silky head. "I don't think Toby likes men, but he probably also senses my grandpa and the judge aren't dog people." She smiled. "I'm glad you are."

"They're okay, I guess." He hitched his thumb at the road. "So is it okay if I take him for a walk?"

Ellie had been dealing with her psychic abilities for so many years now that her barriers automatically slid into place whenever she was talking to someone. It was only when she was dealing with strong emotions that she had a problem. But right now, for Ryder's safety, and because she didn't want to embarrass him by asking Nate if it was okay—he was almost sixteen, after all—she opened her mind to his thoughts.

"You're not planning on going far, are you?" she asked in an effort to discover what he was up to. That he didn't like being questioned came to her clearly.

To him it felt like an interrogation. Like no one trusted him anymore. He couldn't do anything without someone thinking he was up to no good. The one thing Ellie didn't sense was that he was planning on running away. At least he wasn't yet. "It's just that I'm planning on making lunch. Is there anything special you'd like to eat?"

"Do you have pizza?"

"Unless Joe and the judge ate it, I have some leftovers in the fridge. Just don't tell Nate. It's his favorite."

"Prosciutto, garlic sauce, and cheese?"

"You know him well."

He shrugged. "He brought it every time he visited me and my mom last year."

The poor kid had been through a lot. It was no wonder he was acting out. Ellie had gone through her own rebellious stage at his age. For an entirely different reason, of course. But at least Ryder had his mother's support, and Nate's.

Ellie hadn't had anyone she could turn to at home in Durham. Her father was lovely and kind but not really there. A brilliant man who spent most of the time in his head, oblivious to what was going on around him. Her brother and sister had been equally oblivious to the tension between Ellie and her mother. But it wasn't like she could have shared her secret with them anyway. She couldn't have risked tearing her family apart.

She'd escaped to Mirror Lake Inn as often as possible, spending holidays and summers there. All her worries and fears had faded away the moment the inn came into view. She'd found peace here, peace and happiness. She hoped Ryder found the same.

"I have a better idea. It's your first day here. I'll order whatever you want for lunch from Zia Maria's." She pulled up the menu on her phone and handed it to him.

"Is it okay if I get an Italian panini?" he asked, handing back her phone.

"Absolutely." She glanced at the image on her screen. "It does look good. I think I'll order one for myself. We won't tell my grandfather or the judge though. I'm trying to get them to eat healthier."

"Joe found the bag of potato chips you had in your room," Ryder said with a grin before heading off with Toby obediently trailing after him.

Ellie sighed. At least her grandfather hadn't found her stash of chocolate bars. She had to find a better way to deal with her stress than eating chocolate and chips. Her phone vibrated in her hand. Better yet, she thought when her mother's name appeared on the screen, she had to deal with the reason for her stress.

"Enjoy your walk, guys," she called after them,

bringing the phone to her ear. She'd barely gotten out a hello when her mother went off on her.

"Is it not enough that you had my father threaten to take me to court for elder abuse, you guilted your sister into giving Toby to your grandfather? She's absolutely devastated, Elliana. She loves that dog."

Ellie stared at the phone. She had no idea what her mother was talking about, at least when it came to her grandfather. Her sister was another story. Obviously Bri had thrown her under the bus, using her as an excuse for why she'd left Toby at the inn. God forbid she tell their mother the real reason she'd left the dog behind.

Ellie walked up the steps and took a seat on a rocking chair. This wasn't a conversation she wanted her grandfather to overhear. And that's when it hit her. Earlier, Joe and the judge had said they had a plan, but like her, they'd been distracted by Toby. She'd been so busy with the dog afterward that she hadn't thought to ask them about it. They didn't just have a plan; they were waging a full-out assault.

"Do you have nothing to say for yourself?"

"I had no idea Grandpa was talking to you or that he'd threatened to take you to court."

"He didn't speak to me. He refuses to take my calls. His lawyer sent an email directly to mine!"

As far as Ellie knew, her grandfather hadn't retained a lawyer. It was something she'd been planning to talk to him about today. Jonathan must have sent the email. "I'm sorry it's come to this. But you must have known Grandpa wouldn't take this lying down. As far as he's concerned, you're trying to sell his home out from under him. Put yourself in his shoes for a minute. How would you feel if we did this to you and Dad?"

"It's not the same. Your father and I are healthy and have all our faculties."

"So does Grandpa. He might have had a stroke, but otherwise he's healthy." And she planned to keep him that way for as long as she could. "I can send you a report from his doctor, if you'd like. And he's happy to take a legal competency test."

"If he's fully recovered, as you claim, why did you tell your sister that he needed a therapy dog to help with his recovery?

Ellie ground her back molars together, feeling like Bri had played her and she'd walked into a trap. But no, Ellie had seen what she had seen. Bri hadn't meant for this to happen. She was trapped by a lie of her own making. And Ellie had no choice but to cover for her. She wouldn't risk Richard confronting Bri if Ellie told her mother the truth. Not that her mother would believe her anyway. She frowned, wondering if that was part of the problem. Maybe if Bri had their mother's support, she'd leave Richard.

"Grandpa doesn't like to go for walks. I thought having a dog would encourage him to get out more. Not to mention that the inn is a better place for a dog than a condo in the middle of a busy city. Was Richard upset? I got the impression he didn't like Toby."

"No, he wasn't," her mother reluctantly admitted. "Toby's very protective and territorial of your sister. This morning, he bit Richard."

"You might want to ask yourself why that is, Mom. Dogs are a good judge of character."

"What are you inferring?"

"I think you know. But if you don't, for Bri's sake, open your eyes. She needs you."

"So what, now not only am I a horrible daughter, I'm also a horrible mother? I'll have you know that everything I've done is to protect your sister. And if you have any love for Brianna and your father, you will stop fighting me on this. My father obviously listens to you. Tell him to let this go. If he doesn't, I'm afraid things won't go well for you, Elliana. I didn't want it to come to this, but I'll have no choice than to submit evidence to a judge why you're incapable of acting as your grandfather's legal guardian and power of attorney."

The phone in her hand trembled like the leaves on the sugar maples across the dirt road. And while the physical abuse her sister suffered at Richard's hands was far worse than what Ellie had suffered at their mother's, the latter was a form of mental abuse nonetheless. If she expected her sister to stand up to Richard, Ellie could do no less than stand up to her mother.

"I'd wondered how long it would take before you threatened me with my so-called mental instability. But here's the thing, I'm no longer a teenager you can intimidate. Go ahead, Mom, do your worst. Just remember, I can prove that I'm psychic. I also know why that terrifies you. Why you tried for all those years to convince me I was crazy in an effort to silence me. I watched you do the same to my grandmother. I won't let you get away with it again."

"You have no idea what I've had to deal with," her mother said, sounding like she was close to tears. "You have no idea what my life was like, how hard I'm trying to make things right. Please, Elliana, for your sister's and your father's sakes, convince your grandfather to let this go. He'll have enough money from the sale that he can live wherever he likes, do whatever he wants. He doesn't have to go in a home. I'm sorry I suggested it. I should have known how that would make him feel."

Her mother's 180-degree change of course had Ellie scrambling to keep up. "I suggested that to Grandpa last night. I told him I'd find a place in Highland Falls for us."

"Thank you, Elliana. I—"

"He refused, Mom. He's adamant about keeping the inn. You can try talking to him, but I honestly don't think there's anything you can say that will change his mind."

"He won't listen to me. You have to try again, Elliana. Convince him that this is the best thing for everyone concerned." In the background, someone called her mother's name. "I have to go. I'll call you later this week."

"Mom, what's going—" Her mother had disconnected. Ellie stared at the phone, trying to make sense of the conversation. She'd thought she'd had her mother's motivation nailed down.

After spending last night tossing and turning, trying

to solve the puzzle, she'd begun to think her mother might have made a bad investment with Richard and lost their pension money. But given what her mother had just said about Joe having the money to live wherever he wanted, to do whatever he wanted after the sale, it didn't sound like she wanted the money for herself. Unless it was a ruse to lull Ellie into complacency.

Chapter Nine

♥

Nate glanced at the tray of homemade patties Ellie handed him. "There's no way Joe and the judge won't know they're eating veggie burgers and not beef burgers."

"They won't if you don't tell them."

"All they have to do is look at them," he said.

"They won't see them. I'll put their burgers on the buns and cover them with the caramelized onions, tomatoes, pickles, and lettuce before I hand them over. Don't forget, no cheese on their burgers." She took off her apron and smiled at him. "Thanks for offering to man the grill."

Her smile and the scooped neckline of her sundress distracted him, and it took him a second to respond. "No problem. Ryder and I would be out a place to stay if you burned down the inn."

"Very funny. Joe and the judge were exaggerating."

"So you didn't blow up the last barbecue?"

"It was really old, and it was the first time I'd used one. I think there must have been a gas leak."

According to Joe and the judge, she'd started the barbecue with the lid down. "Too bad your YouTube fixer-up guy didn't have a how-to-grill video."

"Ha ha. Make fun of him all you want. His videos have been very helpful."

Going by the issues Nate had encountered on the roof, either the guy was an idiot or Ellie had gotten creative with her repairs. But he figured he'd teased her enough. "How's the hand?" he asked as she peeled off her gloves and tossed them in the garbage can.

"Much better, thanks." She picked up the bags of burger buns. "Thanks for doing the grocery run, but I really wish you'd let me repay you."

"Only if you let me pay for the room." She didn't know it yet, but he planned on buying the groceries while they were there.

"Between buying supplies for the roof and spending the entire afternoon repairing it, plus all of this, you've more than covered the cost of your room. You also missed out on spending time with Ryder."

"Trust me, the kid was happier spending his day with the dog than with me. All I got out of him when we went into town were one-word responses. The longest *conversation* we had was when he asked if I'd buy him a pack of cigarettes, and I said no."

"It's his first day. I'm sure he'll settle in. If it's okay with you, I can have him help me around the inn. I'd pay him, not a lot, but just enough that he'd have some pocket money."

"That's not a bad idea. But only if you let me cover his pay."

"We'll talk about it later." She nodded at Ryder, who'd opened the sliding glass doors leading into the dining room. "Table and chairs all set up on the patio?" she asked when he joined them in the kitchen.

"Yeah. Joe and the judge want to know when dinner will be ready." He glanced at the tray, pointing at the veggie burgers. "What are those?"

"Told you," Nate said to Ellie. "Grab the buns, will you, kid? You can help me grill the burgers." Chase, Sadie, and the baby were joining them for dinner and were set to arrive anytime.

"I gotta take the dog for a walk."

Ellie had no trouble getting the kid to do whatever she asked, but all he got was pushback. "It's okay, I've got them," Ellie said. "Don't go too far though. We'll be eating as soon as my cousin and her husband get here."

"It's okay. I'm not hungry."

"Too bad. You're joining us for dinner. And no *smoking* on your walk." He'd checked Ryder's bag for weed. He hadn't found any, but that didn't mean the kid hadn't stashed it somewhere.

Ryder ignored him, looking at Ellie instead. "I'm still full from the panini and fries."

"They were pretty filling. Maybe you can join us for dessert? Zia Maria sent her chocolate pie especially for you. Just do me one favor before you go. Distract Grandpa and the judge while Nate puts the burgers on the grill. If they see them before they're on the bun, they might figure out they're getting veggie burgers and not beef burgers."

Ryder actually smiled at her. "I can do that."

When she thanked him with that big, wide smile of hers, Nate figured he couldn't blame the kid. If she smiled at him like that, he'd do anything she asked too. Ryder took the bags of buns from her and headed for the sliding glass doors. Nate waited until he was outside to turn to her.

She grimaced. "I'm sorry. I know I shouldn't have overridden you, especially in front of Ryder, but I feel so sorry for him, Nate. It can't be easy being away from his mom and his friends. He just needs some time to adjust. Besides that, the paninis really were filling."

"He's playing you, you know. He's figured out you're a soft touch."

"I can be tough. Just ask Joe and the judge, my mother and my sister too."

Her expression clouded, and he decided to let it go. The conversation with her mother earlier today had left her pensive and subdued. He had a feeling she was holding something back from him, and he wondered if that was why he'd gotten a call from Chase midafternoon telling him they were coming for dinner. Ellie was close to Sadie. They seemed more like sisters than cousins. If anyone could get Ellie to open up, it would be Sadie.

"Yeah, you're real tough," he said, reaching out to give her bicep a gentle squeeze, and wouldn't you know it, that's when Sadie and Chase walked in. He sighed at the speculative gleam in his best friend's eyes.

Chase hadn't made an effort to conceal his amusement that Nate had found himself back at the inn.

He'd declared it was kismet. The Fates had decided Ellie was the woman for Nate, and they were conspiring to keep him in Highland Falls. Nate thought that was a pile of bullcrap. For a brilliant guy, his friend had developed some weird ideas since moving to the small town. Then again, he'd married a woman whose grandmother not only believed that she had the second sight but also believed in unicorns.

"Look who's here!" Ellie beamed, hurrying from the kitchen with her arms outstretched. The copper-haired toddler on Sadie's hip beamed back at Ellie, making grabbing motions with her hands. Ellie scooped Michaela into her arms. "Auntie Ellie's missed you so much! Did you miss Auntie?" she asked, showering the toddler's face with kisses.

Michaela giggled, babbling nonsensical words at Ellie, who nodded along as if she understood what the baby was saying. "I know. It feels like forever since we saw each other. We need to have a sleepover. Do you want to have a sleepover with Auntie Ellie at the inn?"

"No, she doesn't," Nate said as he walked through the dining room to the sliding glass doors. Four sets of eyes stared at him. "What? We've got a dog and a surly teenager. We don't need to add a crying baby to the mix."

At Chase's grin, Nate realized how that sounded. He should have kept his mouth shut. "Don't listen to your uncle Nate," Ellie said to Michaela. "He loves you too. Don't you, Uncle Nate?"

Ellie danced her way to his side, making Michaela

giggle. Her giggle stopped the second she looked up at him, her lower lip starting to tremble. "Aw, Nate. You made her cry."

"Ellie, she's fifteen months old. She doesn't understand what you're saying. Besides that, she hates me. Don't you, squirt?"

"Of course she doesn't. You love your uncle Nate, don't you, Auntie's sweet girl?"

Michaela shook her head, then buried her face in Ellie's neck. Ellie made a face. "It's your voice. It's deep and growly. You need to pitch it higher. And you might try smiling at her. Your expression is a little fierce." She nuzzled Michaela's cheek. "That's what it is, isn't it, baby? But see, Uncle Nate's not scary at all." Ellie rubbed her palm over his chest. "He's a good guy."

Michaela ignored him, reaching up to pat Ellie's face. "Good girl."

Ellie's eyes went wide. "Sadie, did you hear that? Oh my gosh, you are such a smart baby." She took Michaela's hand and patted it against Nate's cheek. "Good boy."

He rolled his eyes. "I'm not a dog."

"Woof," Michaela said, and everyone broke up, including Nate.

"Thanks for the laugh, squirt," he said, opening the sliding glass door to step onto the patio. "Chase, come and give me a hand."

"Michaela might not like you, but Ellie does," Chase said when he joined him at the grill. "And you seem to really like her."

"Not with this again. We're friends." He handed Chase the tray and called Ryder over. He was sitting at a table at the far end of the patio with Joe and the judge. The kid sauntered toward them, hitching up his pants along the way. "Ryder, this is Chase. He's with the FBI and worked on your dad's investigation with me last summer. He's the reason we broke the case."

"Don't listen to him. Nate wouldn't rest until we got everyone involved." Chase clasped Ryder's shoulder. "I'm sorry for your loss. Your father helped a lot of people. We're going to make sure he's not forgotten."

Mrs. M had been the one to suggest a charity in Brodie's name. She'd contributed all the money raised from last summer's We Believe in Unicorns event. Nate had matched her donation, and so had Chase. But Abby had raised the most money for the charity when she'd featured Brodie's story on her YouTube channel.

The donations were still coming in. There was a lot of money in the account, more than Nate would have thought possible. Someday in the near future, they needed to figure out what to do with it.

Ryder nodded, looking down at his feet. "Thanks," he mumbled. Then he asked Nate, "Can I go now?"

"Sure. Don't forget to join us for dessert." Ellie was right. He needed to cut the kid some slack.

"Sorry about that. I probably shouldn't have said anything. I made him uncomfortable," Chase murmured as Ryder opened the sliding glass door.

"I brought it up for a reason. He doesn't talk about Brodie. I'm not a shrink, but I think he needs to."

"Maybe you should take your own advice. You don't talk about him either."

"I'm not fifteen, and he was my friend, not my father." Nate slid the burgers onto the grill, glancing over his shoulder at the sound of Ellie laughing. Through the glass, he saw her sitting on the floor. Her hair was down, her feet were bare, and she was clapping for Michaela, who staggered toward her like a drunken sailor. Ellie said something to Ryder, and he crouched a few feet away from her, holding out his arms to Michaela, laughing when she lurched in his direction.

"Ellie's amazing with kids. She'll be good for Ryder. She'd be good for you too, if you'd let her in."

But he wouldn't be good for her. He wasn't cut out for long-term relationships, white picket fences, and a couple of kids. He had too much baggage, and that baggage weighed heavily on his conscience. He wasn't a good guy. He'd crossed the line too many times to count. Ellie deserved someone good and decent. And that wasn't him.

He turned back to the grill. "You don't have to try and set me up with Ellie to keep me from going undercover. I'm stuck here for a couple of weeks."

"I talked to your boss. You can have your job back if you want it. He'll put you on mandatory leave with pay while you're here with Ryder. You'll have to serve out the rest of your suspension behind a desk, but you'll be able to work with the task force."

"Are you kidding me? You went behind my back and talked to my boss?"

"If I didn't do it, your brother-in-law was going to. Your sisters haven't let up on him since they heard that you quit."

"And who did they hear that from?"

"My boss. Your brother-in-law."

"Who heard it from you." Nate shook his head. "You crossed a line."

"Too bad. You'd do the same for me. You're a hothead. You let your temper and this case get to you. You weren't thinking straight. You don't just throw away your career because your boss is trying to protect you from getting yourself killed. You're one of his best agents, Nate. He said so himself. But part of what makes you exceptional at your job also makes you a liability. He's just trying to help you find some balance. And just so you know, I wasn't the first one to plead your case. Several members on the task force had already spoken to him."

Nate looked out over the water and nodded. "I'll call him tomorrow." At least he wouldn't be cut out completely. He could talk to the members of the task force, see if they had a break in the case. "Sorry for jumping down your throat. I know you were just looking out for me."

"What's wrong with that burger?" said a voice from behind Nate.

Obviously he'd been distracted if Joe was able to sneak up on him. "Nothing. They all look the same to me."

"Bro, if you think they all look the same, you need to have your eyes checked," Chase said.

"You eat that one then. I want one of those." Joe pointed at a beef burger, which was how Nate ended up with two veggie burgers on his plate.

"Wow, you guys sure loved your burgers," Ellie said to the judge and Joe, casting Nate an *I told you so* smile.

He didn't have the heart to correct her or to tell her the veggie burgers tasted like sawdust.

She looked at the burger sitting on his plate. "Aren't you hungry?"

"I shouldn't have eaten the leftover pizza for lunch." Before she could examine the burger further, he took an oversize bite.

Joe and the judge snickered. He'd had his suspicions, but now he was positive they'd known exactly what Ellie had tried to pull. When she turned her head to listen to Michaela babbling in the high chair, Nate shot the older men a look, making a *zip it* motion with his fingers.

Michaela, who must have been watching him, did the same thing.

"Sadie, did you see that? Michaela just made a *zip it* gesture with her fingers. Did you teach her that?"

"Nate did," Sadie said, struggling not to laugh.

"So, who wants pie?" Hands went up around the table. "It's okay, Ellie. I've got it." Nate collected the plates and headed for the kitchen before she found him out. He went to open the door only to discover she was right behind him.

She grabbed the half-eaten burger off his plate. "I knew it." She wagged her finger at him. "No pie for you, mister."

"Hey, I'm the reason Zia Maria sent the pie. And it's not my fault Joe figured it out. If Chase hadn't distracted me, I would have heard him coming up behind me and closed the lid."

Ellie opened the door. "Sure. Blame it on Chase."

"It's true." He told her about Chase's conversation with his boss as he followed her into the kitchen. Stopping short when he spotted Ryder. He was bent over, pouring dog food into a bowl on the floor. Ellie followed his gaze and winced, mouthing *I'm sorry.*

Ryder straightened, staring at him with a look of betrayal in his eyes. "You told me and my mom you got the people responsible for murdering my dad."

"I'll give you guys a minute on your own," Ellie said, and slipped out of the kitchen. "Come on, Toby." As if sensing his new friend was upset, the dog nudged Ryder's hand with his nose.

"It's okay, let him be," Nate said to Ellie, setting the dishes on the counter. "We did get them. They're going away for a long time. They won't get out, buddy." He'd be at every parole hearing to make sure that they stayed behind bars.

"Then why did you say you'd be working with the task force, getting updates on my dad's case? Why are you going back undercover when I go home?"

"Because while we got the people directly responsible for your dad's murder, I want the people who supplied the drugs to the gang he was investigating.

I want anyone with the slightest involvement to pay. And I can promise you, however long it takes, I will bring them to justice. Every last one of them."

"My mom lied, didn't she? You didn't want to take me. All you care about is the case. You don't care about me."

"No, that's not true. Ryder, wait," Nate said when the kid turned to walk away. He reached for him.

"Leave me alone!" Ryder yelled, shaking off his hand.

Toby turned on Nate, snarling, his teeth bared.

Nate put up his hands. "It's okay, boy. I'm not going to hurt him." But he had.

Chapter Ten

♥

Nate moved his flashlight over the forest floor, looking for any sign that Ryder had come this way. He and Chase had been searching the woods for more than an hour. As Nate moved the decomposing leaves around with the toe of his boot his chest tightened, making it difficult for him to breathe. This felt all too familiar, and no matter how hard he tried to lock it away, the memory of searching the woods with Chase fifteen months ago came back to him in a rush.

They'd been searching for Brodie. They hadn't known it then, but they'd been too late. No one but Nate knew that he had missed their scheduled meet two days before, not even Chase. Nate would carry the guilt with him for the rest of his life. It didn't matter that he'd been in the middle of an operation and couldn't get away—to do so would have put other lives at risk. He'd tried calling and texting Brodie to change the time, but Brodie hadn't responded.

The last conversation he'd had with Brodie had been when he'd called Nate to schedule the meet. It hadn't gone well. He'd told Brodie to back off, told him to let Nate and the NCSBI take the investigation from there. It was too big a case for one person to handle on their own—too dangerous.

Brodie had been angry and offended. He'd accused Nate of underestimating him, of thinking that he was better than Brodie. Brodie wouldn't let them take the case from him. All he'd wanted was for Nate to run some prints through the NCSBI's data bank. Brodie couldn't do it without raising suspicions at the sheriff's department.

Nate had agreed, hoping that once they had a face-to-face, he could convince Brodie to let others help. But Nate never got the chance.

"Nate?" Chase's voice broke through his grief and his guilt. "What's going on? I've called to you three times."

"Did you see something? Hear something?"

Chase searched his face and then shook his head. "No. Nothing."

"He must have taken the other trail." Nate pulled out his phone. "I'll let Hunter know."

He'd called Abby's husband, Hunter Mackenzie, as soon as he realized he had no way of tracking Ryder. The last known location of Ryder's phone was the inn. The kid was smart. He'd turned it off. And that's when Nate knew that Ryder hadn't simply taken a walk to cool off; he'd run away. Hunter and his dog Wolf were two of the best trackers in the entire county. He was going to need them.

* * *

"Don't worry, Ellie. They'll find Ryder," Sadie said. They were sitting on the front porch, wrapped in plaid blankets.

"It's getting dark, and he's been gone for two hours." Ellie hugged the blanket around her; the temperature dropped at night on the water. "He was only wearing a T-shirt when he left. He doesn't know the area."

Her gaze went to the dark woods across the road. In the distance she heard people calling Ryder's name. She felt sick to her stomach, responsible for Ryder overhearing Nate talk about the case.

"If something happens to Ryder, Nate won't be able to forgive himself." Ellie was as worried about him as she was about Ryder. "He hasn't said anything to me, but I think he blames himself for Brodie's death."

"You can't read him?"

"No." She'd attempted to read his mind during their last dance at Sadie and Chase's wedding. Her argument for breaking her privacy rule at the time had been that she'd save them both from embarrassment. If she'd sensed he'd been the least bit interested in her, she'd planned to ask him out. "Some people have stronger walls than others, and all I get is a whisper of feelings and thoughts, but with Nate, it's like running up against solid concrete." She glanced at Sadie. "It's actually a nice change. When I'm with him, it feels like I'm standing in this quiet circle of calm while all around us the world is caught up in a violent windstorm." She shrugged, embarrassed she'd voiced the thought.

Sadie gave her a knowing smile. "You like him, don't you? No, don't bother denying it. I know you as well as you know me."

"I do, but it doesn't matter. Nothing can come of it. Nate has made it abundantly clear that we'll never be anything more than friends."

"You might not realize it, but for Nate, that's a big deal. He doesn't have women friends."

Ellie smiled at her cousin's attempt to make more of this than there was. She was just like their grandmother, looking for signs that Nate felt something other than friendship for Ellie. "So what are you, then? You and half the women in this town."

"I'm not talking about married women and women old enough to be his mother or his grandmother. I'm talking about the gorgeous, available women who flock to the man like bees to honey. I've yet to meet one of the women he's dated, and I use that word loosely. Nate is the poster boy for heartbreakers. Although, in his defense, I've never heard him pretend that he's open to anything more."

"No, he makes it pretty clear he won't let anything come between him and his job. But I get it, given what he does for a living. It has to be all-consuming when you're dealing with matters of life and death."

"You know who you're talking to, right? Chase was just like Nate. The job was all he thought about. Nothing and no one mattered to him more than his career. Until he met me and Michaela." Her cousin smiled.

Sadie and Chase were head over heels in love, and Ellie couldn't be happier for her cousin. But Nate wasn't Chase. "Nate seems more, I don't know, almost obsessed. Like he lives and breathes his job. Or maybe it's just this case."

"I've only known Nate since he was investigating Brodie's murder, so I can't really say. All I know is that Chase is worried about him. There's a darkness in Nate, which sounds crazy to say because he's always kidding around, and he's the life of the party."

That was it. That was what Ellie sensed in him, a darkness. In many ways, he was Chase's polar opposite.

Sadie continued. "Chase says he's never met another law enforcement agent who can get in a criminal's head as easily as Nate does. He thinks it's because after Nate got out of the military, he rode with an MC—motorcycle club."

"I didn't know that. I didn't know he was in the military either." There was a lot she didn't know about him.

"He was a sniper with Special Operations. One of the best, according to Chase."

"Let's hope he doesn't need to use that talent tonight," Ellie said, her eyes going back to the woods. "He had a gun. I saw it under his jacket."

Sadie tugged the blanket closer around her. "More out of habit than anything else, I imagine."

"Or maybe he's worried that trouble has followed him here. The man he arrested was supposedly high up in the organization that supplied the drugs to the Whiteside Mountain Gang."

"Don't even go there. You're just worried about

Ryder and letting your imagination run wild. Come on." Sadie shrugged off the blanket and stood up. "I should check on Michaela."

They'd put Michaela down in the judge's room. Ellie took one last glance at the woods before following Sadie inside. The judge put a finger to his lips when they opened the door to his room. "She just went to sleep," he whispered from the chair where he'd been reading. The soft glow of the lamp on the side table provided the only light in the room.

Asleep in the playpen beside the bed, Michaela noisily sucked her thumb.

"Where's Grandpa?" Ellie whispered. Joe and the judge had been playing with Michaela when she and Sadie had gone to sit outside. Ellie had used the baby to distract them. Her grandfather and the judge had wanted to join in the search for Ryder.

"His lawyer phoned him back. He took the call in his room. If you're staying up here, I'll go check on him." The judge laid his book on the table.

"What's going on?" Sadie asked when Jonathan left the room, closing the door behind him.

Ellie joined her cousin on the end of the bed. Keeping her voice low so as not to wake Michaela, she filled Sadie in on what Joe and the judge had been up to. "I asked Grandpa to hold off on the lawsuit, so I'm guessing that's what the phone call is about."

"Why didn't you want him to go ahead with it?"

"First of all, I think it would be hard to prove elder abuse. The judge disagrees with me. He says what my mother is doing is the very definition of elder abuse.

But my biggest concern is it will make everything worse. There's no way their relationship will recover from something like this. As much as I hate what my mother is putting Grandpa through, I know she loves him. And he loves her."

"She has a funny way of showing it."

"There's more to this than we know, Sadie. I talked to my mother earlier today. It's not about the money like I thought. It's not about Grandpa either. I think . . . I think it has something to do with my dad and Bri." She'd been mulling it over all day, and the more she thought about their conversation, the clearer it became that her mother was trying to protect her father and Bri. And there was only one thing she could be protecting them from.

Sadie frowned. "What does she have to protect them from? And what does the inn have to do with it?"

"You can't tell anyone what I'm about to tell you, Sadie. Not even Chase or Granny. You have to promise me."

"Of course. Nothing you say to me will leave this room."

"Do you remember when Bri had strep throat and ended up with rheumatic fever? She was around ten. I was fifteen."

"Vaguely," Sadie said. "They were worried about her kidneys, weren't they?"

Ellie nodded. "The doctor thought she might lose one of her kidneys and there was talk about a transplant. They didn't say anything to me, but because my *gift* had come online around that time, I knew they were looking at me as a potential donor."

"That must have been scary for you."

"It was, but not for the reason you might think. I'd walked into my mother's bedroom to find her crying and tried to comfort her, telling her I was okay with donating my kidney and Bri would be okay too. But that wasn't what she was worried about." She glanced at her cousin. "My mom had an affair, Sadie. Bri isn't my father's, and my mom was afraid he'd find out if she needed a transplant."

"She told you that?"

"No, I read her mind. I didn't mean to, but it was all new to me, and I hadn't learned to shield myself. And she was emotional, so she was broadcasting like a television with the volume on high."

"So how... You asked her?"

Ellie nodded. "She lost it and went on the attack. Telling me I was crazy just like Granny, and that if I ever said anything to anyone, she'd have me put away."

"Oh, Ellie, that's awful. I wish you would have told me." Sadie hugged her. "I'm so sorry." She leaned back, searching Ellie's face. "You know you're not crazy, don't you?"

"I do now. But those next few years when I was still living at home, I wondered if my mother was right. Looking back, I see that she was gaslighting me. Protecting herself and her secret by keeping me off balance. It got better when I left for college."

"That's why you spent all your holidays here, isn't it?"

She nodded. "I was lucky Grandpa and Grandma

let me. My mother didn't want me out from under her thumb. She was terrified I would tell them what she had done and made sure they wouldn't believe me. She told them I was mentally unstable and a pathological liar."

"You're the one who should sue her for abuse. How do you do that to your own child? Joe and Mary didn't believe her, did they?"

"They did that first summer. I can't say I blame them. I was acting out, trying to come to terms with reading other people's thoughts and feelings. Each holiday got better though."

"You should have talked to Granny about it, Ellie. Or me. You could have talked to me."

"She did the same to Granny as she did to me, Sadie, and I think I know why. Granny saw what I did. She must have told my mother her future, and whatever she told her had to do with Bri not being my father's daughter."

"But Granny goes into a trance. She doesn't remember what she tells people."

"We know that, but I don't think my mother does. But it makes sense that's why she worked so hard to discredit Granny and keep her at arm's length. The timing works too."

"I can't believe this. I can't believe how far your mother would go to protect her secret."

"The question is, What does any of this have to do with the inn? So far, the only thing I've come up with is that Richard knows, and he's blackmailing her. It's the only thing that makes sense to me."

"You can't read her?"

"Sometimes I can. She's good at shielding her thoughts from me. Most of the time she just lets me see what she wants me to. It's different when she's upset; I can pick up on things then. Honestly though, she's the last person I want to read. If I wasn't trying to figure out what's behind her deal with the developer, I'd stay out of her head."

"And Bri and your father have no idea about any of this?"

"No. They'd be devastated. And I'll do whatever I have to to make sure they never find out."

"What a mess."

"You have no idea." She was about to share her suspicions about Richard and Bri's relationship when the door opened. It was the judge.

"They found the boy."

Ellie jumped from the bed. "Thank God. Is he all right? Is Toby okay?"

"It would appear so. They've just arrived."

She squeezed past the judge, running to the stairs. She met Ryder on the landing. Toby was with him but Nate wasn't. "We were so worried about you." She hugged him. He was cold and shivering.

"I'm sorry," he said, his teeth chattering.

"It's okay. Everything will be okay, Ryder. What you need right now is a hot shower. I'll make you some soup and something hot to drink. Sound good?"

"I don't think I'm staying. Nate's angry. He's talking to my mom. I think he's going to take me home."

"Sometimes when we're scared, we say things we don't mean. Nate wants you here, Ryder, and so do I.

Now go have that shower. I'll be up in a few minutes with your soup."

"Thanks, Ellie." Head bowed and shoulders slumped, he walked to his room, the dog following on his heels.

"Sadie and Michaela up here?" Chase asked, coming up the stairs.

"They're in the judge's room. Where's Nate?"

"He needed a minute." He glanced at the door closing behind Ryder. "How's he doing?"

"Cold, sad, and worried that Nate is going to send him home. Is he?"

"I'm not sure." Chase rubbed the back of his neck. "It brought him back, Ellie. He tried to hide it, but I know he was remembering searching the woods for Brodie. He could use a friend."

"I'm going to heat up some soup for Ryder and get him settled in, and then I'll talk to Nate." She hugged Chase. "I'm glad you were with him. You should take Sadie and Michaela home."

"See if you can get Nate to open up to you. I'm worried about him, Ellie."

Once she'd said goodbye to Sadie, Chase, and a half-asleep Michaela, and had Ryder settled in his bed with chicken soup and hot chocolate, she went in search of Nate. She found him standing on the dock, looking out over the lake.

He glanced over his shoulder. "You shouldn't be out here, Ellie. It's cold."

"Then come inside with me," she said as she walked to his side.

"I will. I just need a few minutes." He didn't add *alone*, but it was obvious he didn't want company. He hadn't taken his eyes off the water.

She moved in front of him, slipping her arms around his waist. "I'll just wait right here until you're ready to come inside."

He sighed, his chest expanding under her cheek, and then his arms came around her. "I'm okay."

"I know you are. You're also right. It's cold out here, and you're warm. I figure if I'm waiting for you, I might as well share your body heat." She tipped her head back to look up at him.

His gaze drifted to her mouth. "This isn't a good idea, Ellie," he murmured, slowly lowering his head.

"Probably not," she said, going up on her toes to meet him halfway. But nothing felt so amazing as being kissed by Nate on a moonlit night in May.

Chapter Eleven

♥

Nate walked into the kitchen, determined to put the woman singing about love while tossing fruit into a blender back in the friend zone. He cleared his throat. "Ellie, about last night."

She turned with a smile that lit up her face and sucker punched his rehearsed speech out of his head. None of the well-intentioned arguments he'd come up with in the shower withstood the beauty of that smile. Maybe because this was new to him.

He couldn't remember the last time a woman had gotten so deeply under his skin in a matter of days. Possibly because he never stuck around long enough to give them a chance. Then again, Ellie was special, so he shouldn't be surprised he'd spent more than an hour coming up with reasons why being anything more than friends was a bad idea. She wasn't the type of woman you loved and left. She wanted more, deserved more, more than he was willing or able to give.

"Don't give it another thought, Nate. The judge's

reaction was over the top. I honestly don't know what's gotten into him."

He, for one, was grateful the judge had interrupted their kiss on the dock. There was no doubt in Nate's mind where that kiss had been headed—to Ellie in his bed. And the last thing he wanted was to have been having this conversation the morning after.

She made a face at the blender. "Maybe it's this new eating regimen I've got them on. Diets make me cranky."

Don't laugh or smile, he told himself. This was a conversation they needed to have. It was serious. His lips twitched. Love, he reminded himself, she'd been singing about love. "He's just being protective, Ellie. He knows I'm not the guy for you."

"I'm a thirty-three-year-old woman who knows her own mind. I don't need protection." She grimaced. "I mean, of course I need protection. No woman should have sex without it. But I certainly don't need a man telling me who I should or shouldn't date."

What was he supposed to say to that? He could barely think straight. The blood had left his head and headed south. Now all he could think about was Ellie and sex. He needed a do-over. He'd grab a coffee, take a shower, a cold one this time, then come back down and try again.

Except she wasn't finished. "Not that I think we're dating," she said, scooping protein powder into the blender. "So you can stop worrying that I'm expecting a declaration of love and a proposal of marriage, Nate. It was just a kiss."

"It wasn't just a kiss, Ellie. It was..." What the hell was it? It had felt like a whole lot more than just a kiss to him. But like she'd said, she knew her own mind. Who was he to argue? For all he knew, he was projecting his feelings onto her. "Whatever it was, we shouldn't do it again."

"It was a kiss between friends. One of those friends had had a rough night, and the other friend was trying to make him feel better. That's all. Nothing more, nothing less."

"So you're saying it was a pity kiss? You didn't feel like the world had tipped on its axis and the stars had exploded in the sky?" He stepped closer to her. "You didn't feel like you needed that kiss like you needed your next breath?"

She shook her head, her cheeks flushed. "No. No I didn't," she said, and turned on the blender.

He bent his head and whispered in her ear, "Liar."

She stabbed the Off button with her finger and whirled around to face him. "What do you want me to say? You've made it clear that you don't want anything more from me than friendship. Do you want me to bare my soul to you, embarrass myself and say, *Yes, Nate, that's exactly how I felt*? The world turned upside down, and the stars exploded, and I felt like I needed that kiss like I needed my next breath. There, are you happy now?"

"No. I'm not." He cupped her shoulders with his hands. "I was talking about me, Ellie. That's how your kiss made me feel."

"I don't understand. If you feel the same way that

I do, why did you say it can't happen again? Why wouldn't you want to see where this goes?"

"Because I know exactly where it goes. I'm not like Chase or Gabe or Hunter. I don't stick around. I don't do promises, and that's not going to change. I'm not going to change. I like my life the way that it is."

She stood there looking dejected, the light extinguished from her beautiful violet eyes. He hated that he'd done that to her, but she needed to know the truth. He let his hands fall to his sides before he did something stupid like pull her in for a hug. With Ellie, a hug wasn't just a hug.

She looked away from him, wrapping her arms around her waist.

"Do you want me to leave?"

She nodded. "Yes. Yes I do."

He felt like he'd been sucker punched again. Only this time, the blow hit him in the heart instead of the head. He didn't blame her though. He'd hurt her just like he'd known he would. "Okay. We'll go as soon as Ryder wakes up. If that's okay with you."

"What are you talking about?"

"You said you wanted me to leave."

"The kitchen. I wanted you to leave the kitchen." She shook her head. "I can't believe you'd think I'd ask you leave the inn. If that's the type of woman you usually date... What am I saying? You don't date. Ryder needs you, Nate, and you need a place to stay." She narrowed her eyes at him. "Unless you've decided your two-week commitment to him and Gina is too much for you."

After what had happened with Ryder last night, he'd been more than ready to throw in the towel. Except Gina had cried when he told her it wasn't going to work out, and he'd caved. Besides that, he owed Brodie.

"No. I'm not bailing on the kid, and I appreciate you letting us stay. He seems to like it here."

"Good. And I've just decided you should stay here, and I'll go." She took off her apron and handed it to him. "I have a meeting in town this morning. You can make breakfast."

"Okay. But you're not going to town right now, are you?"

"Yes. Yes I am. I'm walking out of this kitchen, getting into the truck, and heading for town. I plan to stop at the bakery before my meeting. Is that all right with you?"

"Uh, yeah," he said, fighting a smile. "But you might want to change out of your pajamas."

"You might want to change out of your pajamas," Ellie muttered under her breath as she stood in line at Bites of Bliss. Nate had ruined her dramatic exit.

She would have figured out she was wearing her purple T-shirt and matching unicorn sleep pants before heading into town. Then again, maybe she wouldn't have. She didn't remember the last time she'd had a fit of temper. Clearly, Nate brought out the worst in her.

"Hey, Ellie. I'm so glad you stopped by. I was going to call you about the menu for this weekend's tea," said Bliss, the bakery's pretty blond owner.

With everything going on, Ellie had completely forgotten she'd agreed to hold afternoon teas this coming weekend. And not only had she agreed, half the women attending last Saturday's tea had made reservations before they'd left the inn. This time they were actually paying, so it wasn't like she could afford to cancel. She'd need the extra money to put into the guest rooms' redesign. She swallowed a groan and forced a smile. "I'm sure whatever you've come up with will be fabulous, Bliss."

"I found the cutest flower cookie cutters online, and I thought you might like to use them for the sandwiches."

Right, the sandwiches, Ellie thought, her stress levels going through the roof. "That's a great idea. If you email me the link, I'll order them." If she was lucky, they wouldn't come in on time.

"It's okay. I've got extra you can use. I'll just run back and get them now."

"Perfect. Um, before you do, would you mind giving me a slice of that chocolate cake?" She pointed at the decadent-looking confection in the glass showcase.

"Sure. I'll pack it up to go."

"I'll just eat it here, thanks. My meeting at the bookstore isn't for another thirty minutes."

"That's right. I heard you're redoing the guest rooms at the inn. I love the idea of using romantic literary couples for the theme," Bliss said as she removed the chocolate cake from the showcase.

"We have to do our part to keep up the image of America's most romantic small town, don't we?" Romance, shomance. She was so over the idea of romantic love it wasn't even funny.

Bliss frowned. "Are you okay, Ellie?"

"Great, thanks." She looked at the slice of cake Bliss was cutting. "Maybe a little bigger." Bliss moved the knife over a smidgen and glanced at her. "You know what? Just give me the whole cake."

"You want the whole cake?"

"Yep, the whole thing. And a chocolate hazelnut coffee, thanks."

Bliss nodded slowly. "Ah, sure. Whatever you want. Why don't you sit down and I'll bring it over to you?"

Ellie had just settled down at a table when her cell phone pinged. It was a text from Nate, who wanted to know if it was okay to give her grandfather and Joe something other than fruit smoothies for breakfast. She was about to respond with some healthy options when Bliss placed the cake and coffee on the table. "Thanks, Bliss."

"Are you sure you're okay, Ellie?"

Thanks to Nate, Ellie's barriers had slipped, and she sensed Bliss was worried about her.

"Never been better." Ellie smiled, stabbing out a response to Nate as Bliss walked away, glancing at her over her shoulder.

Feed them pork sausages for all I care. I. Am. Off. Duty.

But she didn't want her grandpa to have another stroke or Jonathan to have a heart attack. She followed up with Chicken sausages and eggs. Scrambled, not fried. As an afterthought, she added Thanks. Just because she was mad at Nate didn't mean she shouldn't be polite. But that didn't mean she wanted to continue texting with him.

She turned off her phone, picked up the fork, and dug into the cake. It was incredible. She felt the weight of someone's gaze and glanced at Bliss, who was watching her while talking on her cell phone. Ellie pointed at the cake with her fork and mouthed *So good.*

It wasn't long before she realized whom Bliss had been talking to. Sadie rushed into the bakery with two bags from Three Wise Women Bookstore, followed closely by Abby, who carried two other bags. Bliss pointed at Ellie.

Sadie and Abby hurried over. "What happened?" her cousin asked, setting down her bags and pulling out a chair at the table.

"Why would you think something happened?" she asked, blocking the waves of worry coming off both women.

"You're stuffing your face with chocolate cake at nine in the morning," Abby said as she put her bags on the floor and pulled out a chair. "What did Nate do?"

"Why do you think Nate has anything to do with it? I love chocolate cake, and this one is to die for. Here. Have a bite." She picked up the spoon beside her coffee cup and handed it to Abby.

Bliss arrived with dessert plates and napkins. "Can I get you guys something to drink?"

"It's okay, Bliss," Ellie answered for them. "We have to leave in ten minutes for the meeting."

"We decided to bring the meeting to you," Sadie said, hefting a bag onto her lap. "I'll take a coffee, Bliss. Thanks."

"Me too," Abby said, helping herself to a spoonful of cake. "Oh my gosh, you're right. This is amazing."

Ellie frowned. "Why are you bringing the meeting to me?"

Abby leaned over to pick up a bag. "We didn't think you wanted to discuss your love life in front of the Sisterhood."

"When would I have time for a love life? Not that I want one, because I don't." She wagged her fork at them. "You guys are getting as bad as Granny. It's all Happy Ever After Entertainment's fault for holding the contest. The town's become obsessed with love and romance. You can't go anywhere without being smacked in the face with it." She lifted her chin at the wedding cakes lining the top of the bakery's showcase.

"Ellie, it's wedding season, and this is a bakery," Sadie pointed out.

"I'm talking about the *Love Is in Bloom in Highland Falls* poster on the wall. They're all over town."

"There's a billboard going up tomorrow," Sadie said, fighting back a grin when Ellie shoved a forkful of cake into her mouth.

Abby pressed her palms together. "Please don't tell me you're thinking of bowing out of the guest rooms' redesign. My contact at the production company loved the idea, and she thought her bosses would too. Everyone in town is just as excited as she was. The bookstore is running a contest for most romantic couple in Highland Falls. The couple with the most votes will have a room at the inn named after them. So far Sadie and Chase are in the lead."

"You and Hunter and Mallory and Gabe are like two votes behind us. Granny and Colin are three." Sadie grinned. "You and Nate aren't that far behind."

"Who put us on the list? We're not a couple." Ellie sighed. "Granny did, didn't she?"

"I don't know. It's secret ballots. But Granny isn't the only one hoping you guys get together; so is Chase. Hunter volunteered to make the name plaques, by the way."

That was one job off her growing list of things to do. "Tell him I appreciate it. I'll have the names of the literary couples to him this week. When will the winner of Highland Falls' Most Romantic Couple be announced?" Ellie asked, praying that Nate didn't get wind that they were on the list. Not that there was a chance of them winning. Unless her grandmother rigged the contest, she thought on a sigh.

"We thought it would be fun if Happy Ever After Entertainment made the announcement the same day that they announce the winner for Most Romantic Small Town in America, which will be Highland Falls, of course."

"But what if we don't win?" Ellie asked.

"Not a chance. I've been scoping out the competition," Abby said. "Christmas, Colorado, is a beautiful town, but, as its name suggests, they're all about the holidays. If the production company was shooting a Christmas movie, we probably wouldn't stand a chance. But they're not. I know for a fact it's a summer romance. So our main competition is Harmony Harbor in Massachusetts. It's gorgeous too, but the town has a coastal, seafaring vibe, and I have it on good authority from my source inside the production company that they're looking for a romantic mountain setting."

Abby moved Ellie's coffee and cake out of the way. "Let the romantifying of Mirror Lake Inn begin," she said, glancing up from piling the books on the table. "No pressure, but you and the inn are the key to us winning this thing, Ellie. There's an inn featured in the story line, and with the guest rooms reflecting romantic couples, there's not a chance we can lose."

Sadie followed suit, making a stack beside Abby's.

No pressure indeed. But no matter how much Ellie wished she could cancel the guest rooms' redesign, she knew how badly the business owners in town were counting on winning the competition. The local economy would benefit big-time if Happy Ever After Entertainment filmed its movie here. And not just in the short term. Abby would promote the heck out of the town's connection to the movie before, during, and after, ensuring that Highland Falls benefited from added tourist dollars for years to come. Which the inn would also benefit from.

"I know it's a lot of work," her cousin said as she continued stacking her books beside Abby's. "But you'll see. In the end it'll be worth it."

"A lot of money too. It will eat into our operating budget for the next few months." Who was she kidding? She'd have to dip into her savings. But now that she'd decided to stay, that didn't worry her as much as it would have if she'd been moving back to New York.

"I bet the local antique store would be willing to barter with you or even lend you things on consignment," Sadie suggested.

"That's a good idea. I've been meaning to stop in anyway. One of my clients at Custom Concierge has been looking for a few pieces for his library." A client whom she hadn't gotten back to since late last week. She needed to schedule a couple of hours a day to work on her own business.

"Exactly how long do you think the redesign will take?" Abby asked.

"I'll probably be finishing it up an hour before the executives from the production company arrive." She caught the glance Abby shared with Sadie. "They haven't moved up their date, have they?"

"No. They're arriving next Tuesday. But I might have mentioned that you'd be doing tours after this coming Sunday's tea." Abby winced, no doubt in response to Ellie's jaw dropping. "Sorry. I thought it would be a good way to boost reservations. I bet people would be willing to move their reservations from Saturday to Sunday. That way you could just focus on the room redesign. You could do two or three seatings."

"Don't worry. We'll all pitch in," Sadie said. "And I'm sure Nate won't mind helping out."

Ellie snorted. "I don't see that happening. The last thing Nate wants is to be stuck in a room with me discussing how to turn it into a tribute to romantic love. He'd probably run in the other direction if I suggested it."

Sadie nodded at the cake. "So this does have to do with Nate. What happened?"

Ellie sighed, then shared this morning's conversation with Nate. "So helping me out with guest rooms isn't exactly something he'd be on board with."

Abby pressed her hands to her chest. "That's so romantic."

Ellie stared at her. "Were you not listening to me?"

"I can see why it might not have felt romantic to you, Ellie. But if you look at it from our perspective, as women who've known Nate longer than you have, you'd see what we see."

"And what's that exactly?"

"You rocked his world with a kiss. He said so himself. For him to admit that to you is huge, Ellie. He has feelings for you, and for a commitment-phobe like Nate, that must be pretty terrifying. Yet he didn't pack up Ryder and find somewhere else for them to stay. That to me speaks volumes," Sadie said. "As afraid as he is of falling for you, he can't make himself leave."

"It doesn't have anything to do with me. Ryder likes it at the inn. He and Toby have bonded. He's vulnerable right now. Nate wouldn't want to move him."

Sadie rolled her eyes. "He has five sisters, who have dogs and kids of their own. They adore Nate. They'd welcome him and Ryder with open arms."

"Face it, Ellie," Abby said. "Nate has a thing for you, and whether he wants to admit or not—obviously not—him sticking around is a big deal. If you're interested in him, you should totally take this as an opportunity to show him how great you are together. You are interested in him, aren't you?"

"Yes, but I was engaged to a man who was afraid of commitment." Until this morning, she hadn't realized that was Nate's problem. She'd thought it had more to do with his job. "So afraid that Spencer had an affair with his costar days before our wedding, and he dumped her a month later. He's now a serial dater. Sound like anyone you know?" Ellie wrinkled her nose at Abby's and Sadie's shocked expressions. "I guess I forgot to mention that."

"You said Spencer left you at the altar," Sadie said.

"Not exactly. Granny said that, and I didn't correct her. It was better than people learning the truth. It's not like Spencer or his costar were publicizing their affair."

The movie's publicist had hounded Ellie for days after she'd ended the engagement, begging her not to say anything to the press that would tarnish Spencer's reputation. Ellie had finally agreed to issue a joint statement with Spencer—that they wanted different things from life and wished each other the very best—to get the publicist to leave her alone.

"Never in a million years would Nate do something like that. He might have some commitment issues, but he's a good guy. A really good guy. And you're the last person he'd hurt."

"Sadie's right," Abby said. "Nate wouldn't mess around on you. You're his best friend's wife's cousin, and he'd never do anything to upset your grandmother."

Abby made a good point, and Ellie couldn't help but wonder if the family connections were another reason Nate wanted to keep her at arm's length. It would be nice if he gave her a say. That's what really bothered her. He framed his rejection as though he was protecting her. Like she'd told him, she was more than capable of protecting herself.

She glanced at the stacks of books on the table. "We should probably pick the couples. If I'm going to have the rooms ready for Sunday, I have to get started right away."

"I have a better idea," Abby said. "We'll help you eat your cake and come up with a plan for you to seduce Nate. And then you two can go through the books together and pick the most romantic couples."

"That's actually a great idea," Sadie said. "You can make a comparison between the couples in the books and yours and Nate's relationship."

Ellie pulled a copy of Shakespeare's *Romeo and Juliet* from the top of Sadie's pile and a copy of Emily Brontë's *Wuthering Heights* from the top of Abby's. She held them up. "Right, because their love affairs ended so well."

Chapter Twelve

♥

Nate walked into his room. The door to the adjoining bedroom was closed. Obviously Ryder was still in bed. Nate hesitated, debating how he should handle things after last night. Ellie would probably tell him to go easy on the kid. Or she would if she were talking to him. She hadn't responded to any of his texts after the first one. He'd messed up with her. He didn't want to mess up with Ryder too. But when he smelled cigarette smoke coming from the kid's room, he decided that what the situation called for was tough love.

He opened the door. Ryder was lying on the bed, his head hanging over the edge of the mattress, his feet up on the wall. "You were told there was no smoking inside the inn. Put it out."

Ryder ignored him, blowing a couple of smoke rings.

Nate gritted his teeth as he walked over and took the cigarette from between Ryder's fingers.

Toby growled and bared his teeth at Nate.

Since the dog didn't move from where he lay curled up on the end of the bed, Nate ignored him and tossed the cigarette in the cup of water on the nightstand. "Get up. Now."

"Hey! That was my last one," Ryder said, jerking into an upright position.

"Good. You won't be tempted to break the rules again."

Ryder shrugged, then reached over to pat the still-growling dog. "It's not like I'll be here anyway."

Last night, the relief of finding Ryder alive had quickly dissipated in the face of the kid acting like it was no big deal they'd been looking for him for hours. That was when Nate told him he was taking him home. It wasn't his finest moment. He'd been shaken up, still dealing with the memory of searching for Brodie.

"You're not going anywhere." Nate was about to tack on a couple of conditions when the belligerent expression on Ryder's face was replaced with one of relief. "And neither am I."

"Whatevs," the kid said, pulling Toby half onto his lap and burying his face in the setter's fur.

"Come on. The dog needs to go out. We'll take him for a run."

Ryder lifted his head. "So what, you're like my jailer now? I can't go anywhere without you?"

Nate was tempted to say yes but fought the urge. "No. I just thought you'd like to come for a run with me." He shrugged and turned to walk away. "I left breakfast for you in the warming tray."

"I guess we can go with you. Toby could use a run."

* * *

Ellie pulled out of the Forever Treasures parking lot feeling like she might actually be able to pull off the redesign in time for the tours on Sunday. Her meeting with Sadie and Abby had been productive, if she didn't count the time they'd wasted plotting Ellie's seduction of Nate. The only seduction going on at the inn would be between the literary couples featured in the books they'd chosen. At least until they reopened for overnight guests.

Abby had suggested that Ellie close for two weeks and that they promote the reopening at the same time they announced that Mirror Lake Inn would be featured in an upcoming movie. The woman was nothing if not confident. But the idea worked for Ellie and went a long way toward relieving her stress.

Well, it had until Abby decided she'd film the stages of the reno for her followers and have them vote on the design elements of each room. In the end she'd gotten Ellie on board with her plan. When it came to promotion, no one did it better than Abby.

Ellie's stomach grumbled as she sat at a traffic light on Main Street, and she glanced at the time on the dashboard. It was almost two. She hadn't realized she'd been in the antique store that long. Then again, she'd accomplished quite a bit. She'd found several pieces for her client's library in New York. He'd responded within minutes of her sending him the photos, thrilled with her and her finds.

She'd pretty much found everything she needed to decorate Jamie and Claire's room, Westley and Buttercup's room, Beauty and the Beast's room, and

Elizabeth Bennet and Mr. Darcy's room. Four down and four to go. Although she wouldn't be able to decorate Highland Falls' Most Romantic Couple's room until the winner had been announced.

Hopefully, Abby's followers would give Ellie's choices a thumbs-up. But even if she had to make a few changes, it would be worth it. The owner of the antique store was thrilled with the added publicity and had worked out a payment schedule that was more than generous. She'd also offered Ellie a volume discount.

The light turned green, and Ellie went to put her foot on the gas, but none of the cars in front of her moved. She rolled down her window and stuck her head out to see what the holdup was. It didn't appear as if there was a fender bender. She glanced at the drivers in front of her, following their gazes to where Nate and Hunter were loading Sheetrock into the back of a truck in the hardware store's parking lot.

Seriously? Since when did the sight of two men in T-shirts and cargo shorts cause a traffic jam? Okay, so they were exceptionally handsome men, and their muscles and show of strength were equally impressive, but they weren't exactly an uncommon sight in Highland Falls. Several of the drivers honked their horns. Nate glanced over his shoulder, spotted Ellie, and waved her over.

She looked from him to the load of building supplies in the back of the truck. The Sheetrock and two-by-fours couldn't be for the roof. But they could be for the damaged ceiling in the judge's room. If the damage was really, really bad. She put on her turn signal, easing out of traffic to turn into the parking lot. Several cars did the same, their drivers no doubt hopeful that Nate had been waving them over. She would have laughed at the dumbfounded expression on his face if she weren't adding up the cost of the supplies. Plus, she was still mad at him.

By the time she pulled up beside the truck, Hunter was walking into the hardware store, and Nate must have informed the other drivers that he'd been waving Ellie over, because she was on the receiving end of tight-lipped looks as the women drove away.

"What's going on?" she asked when Nate came to stand beside the driver's-side door.

"I wanted to check if you were okay with me ordering lasagna from Zia Maria's for dinner. The kitchen is kind of a mess, so I thought it would be easier to order in."

She took a deep breath. He'd made everyone breakfast and probably had made lunch for them as well, seeing as it was midafternoon. She couldn't really get mad at him for not cleaning up. "Don't worry about the mess in the kitchen. I'll deal with it. I'm on my way home now."

"I want to put in a few more hours on the demo, so you might as well just leave it until I'm done taking down the other wall."

"Why are you taking down a wall? Was there another leak?"

"Joe didn't talk to you? He said you'd okayed the demo."

"No. I had my phone off. I just turned it on twenty minutes ago." She thought about what he'd said about the kitchen. "Nate, what wall did you take down?"

"The wall off the kitchen."

Her eyes went wide. "My bedroom wall? You took down my bedroom wall?"

He grimaced, then nodded. "Yeah. I'm sorry, Ellie. I assumed Joe had talked to you. I thought it was just my calls you weren't taking."

She waved off his apology. She was the one who'd gone radio silent. For five measly hours! "Why does Joe want...Oh no, please don't tell me he asked you to build an entertainment room." Her grandfather had been talking about getting a big-screen TV since she'd arrived in August. When she vetoed him putting one in the dining room, he'd suggested the inn could use an entertainment room. He'd gone so far as to pick the furniture.

Nate rubbed his jaw. "I probably shouldn't have told him I needed something to do."

"Cutting the grass or painting the Adirondack chairs is something to do, Nate. Adding an entertainment room is on a whole other level. I never should have introduced him to HGTV."

Nate laughed. "I'm sure my brothers-in-law wish my sisters hadn't discovered the channel either. But me taking this on isn't a big deal. I like to keep busy and work with my hands. Then again, I'm not the one who lost their room."

"Losing my room isn't the problem. Cost is, and so is time." She told him about Sunday's tour.

"Shouldn't be a problem having it done by Saturday night. Hunter offered to give me a hand, and I'll put Ryder to work. He needs to stay busy. He's already cut the grass, and he was painting the Adirondack chairs when I left. Joe and the judge were supervising."

And she'd offered to put Ryder on the payroll. Between that and the costs of the renovations and redesign, she'd blow through her savings in a couple of weeks. "How much did all that cost?" She nodded at the supplies in the bed of the truck.

"A lot less than it would to rent a two-room suite at the inn, so don't worry about it."

"At the rate you're going, you'll have a room at the inn with your name on it." *Just what a commitment-phobe wants to hear*, she told herself, but at that moment she was too overwhelmed to think of something else to say.

A car door slammed. Nate glanced in the direction of a black BMW and grimaced before refocusing on Ellie. "You should get back to the inn and check on Joe and Ryder's progress. I won't be long." He moved away from the truck, turning toward a leggy blonde striding in his direction. She wore a tight-fitting red T-shirt with short shorts and four-inch platform sandals. It was a look Ellie couldn't hope to pull off, but this woman rocked it.

"Hey, Tiff," Nate said, sounding uncomfortable.

"'Hey, Tiff'? That's all you've got?" The blonde drilled a cherry-red fingernail into Nate's chest. "You told me you didn't do relationships, and I actually appreciated your honesty."

Nate glanced at Ellie over his shoulder, raising an eyebrow. She started the engine, but instead of pulling away, she sat in the idling truck, too intrigued to leave. She was pretty sure Nate sighed before saying to Tiff, "I didn't lie to you. I don't do relationships."

"Really, so what's this?" She held up her phone. "You're obviously in a relationship with this woman. You're in seventh place for the Most Romantic Couple in Highland Falls."

"Oh, crap," Ellie murmured, putting the truck into Drive. It was time to get out of Dodge. No way was she explaining to the ticked-off blonde that she was the other half of that couple, even if they were on the list under false pretenses. She had a feeling Tiff wouldn't believe her. Besides that, Ellie didn't feel like sticking around to see how Nate reacted to them being on the list. She'd rather do that without an audience.

She'd left Forever Treasures feeling like she had things under control, but all it had taken was a five-minute conversation with Nate to prove she was kidding herself. And not just about the room redesign. Her crush on Nate was alive and well. She didn't stop thinking about him and Tiff the entire drive back to the inn. She wondered if he'd take Tiff out to make it up to her. Nate might not do relationships, but as she knew from personal experience, he also didn't like to intentionally hurt people.

A tiny spark of jealousy flared to life inside her at the thought of Tiff and Nate on a date in Highland Falls. Every business in town had jumped on

the love-and-romance bandwagon. Tiff looked like a
woman who'd use that to her advantage.

"Get a grip, Ellie," she muttered as she parked the
truck at the inn. She had more important things to do
than obsess about Nate's love life. She had to confront
her grandfather, for one.

The first place she checked was his room. He wasn't
there. He wasn't in the dining room either. But the
gaping hole to the right of the dust-covered kitchen
was. She went to stand in the wide-open empty space
that had been her bedroom for the past eight months.
It used to be part of her grandparents' suite. She'd
reconfigured the room the day she'd arrived. She'd
wanted to be close to her grandfather in case he needed
her in the night.

But as she stood there surveying the space, she
had to admit converting it to an entertainment area for
guests was a good idea. It was the timing of the reno
that she wasn't on board with. She glanced out the window and spotted Ryder sitting on the dock painting an
Adirondack chair. Toby was the only one with him.

"You can't hide from me forever, Grandpa," she
called out, and headed for the sliding glass door. She
heard a bang—like something had dropped, and it
wasn't a body—as she stepped onto the patio. She'd
deal with her grandfather later. Right now she wanted
to check on Ryder. She hadn't spoken to him since
she'd tucked him into bed last night.

"Great job," she said as she walked across the lawn
to the dock.

"You don't mind that I painted the chair different

colors?" he asked, looking nervous. "There were a bunch of half-empty paint cans, so I thought I'd use up what was there."

He'd painted the chair a pale turquoise, the three middle back slats mint green. "I don't mind at all. It looks amazing. You're very creative. Do you like to paint?" She crouched beside Toby, waiting until he nudged her hand with his nose to pat him.

Ryder shrugged, but a small, pleased smile turned up the corner of his mouth. "Other than finger painting and that kind of stuff in grade school, I've never painted before. It's okay, I guess."

He liked it better than he was letting on. "I love to paint. I find it relaxing, rewarding too." She used to get lost in her painting. It was the best form of stress relief. But she hadn't painted in years.

"Were those your paintings in the closet? I wasn't snooping," he quickly added. "It's just that we cleaned out your room this morning."

"To make room for my grandfather's man cave. Yeah, I heard."

He grinned. "I bet the guests will like it. Especially if they have kids. Joe's plans for it are pretty sweet."

"I bet they are. He should be watching *Low-Budget Designs* instead of *Bargain Mansions* on HGTV."

"That's what Nate told him." He laughed, then glanced at her. "So the paintings, are they yours?"

She nodded. "I painted them years ago. I got my bachelor's degree in Fine Arts from Columbia."

"They're really good. Why don't you paint anymore?"

Because every time she did, she heard her mother's withering critiques. It hadn't been long before Ellie's internal critic had parroted her mother. Self-doubt, Ellie had discovered, was crippling when it came to artistic expression.

"Thanks. I'm glad you like them. But I discovered pretty quickly that I wasn't going to make a living as an artist. My degree wasn't a complete waste though. I make my living finding special pieces and artwork for my clients." She told him about Custom Concierge.

"That's cool."

"It is." She smiled and glanced at the chairs lining the beach. "If you're up for it, you can paint the rest of the chairs. They look boring compared to this one."

"Yeah, I can do that. I have to help Nate with the entertainment room, but I can paint the other chairs when he doesn't need me."

"Great. Maybe I'll paint one too." She could use the stress relief.

"Cool." He glanced at his phone. "I'd better clean up. Joe and the judge are taking me to dinner."

Which meant she and Nate would be alone, at least for a couple of hours. Unless he went straight out on his date with Tiff. In the end, maybe it would be for the best if he did. The less time Ellie spent alone with him the better.

Ryder stood up with the paint tray in one hand and the paint can in the other. He glanced at Toby, who'd been about to follow him. "Sorry boy, you can't come."

"Don't look so glum, Toby. You're staying with me. We'll have fun." She picked up a tennis ball from the dock and tossed it. "Go on, get your ball."

Toby looked from the ball to her and hung his head.

Ryder transferred the paint can to his other hand and dug in the pocket of his jeans. "Look, I've got a treat for you. Be a good boy for Ellie, and I'll give you another one when I come home."

Toby took the treat but stayed glued to Ryder's leg.

"It's amazing how fast he bonded with you." Ellie wondered if Toby sensed Ryder had suffered a loss too, which reminded her of her promise to her sister. "Would you mind posing with Toby, Ryder? I told my sister I'd send her pictures every day. She'll be happy he's made a friend."

"Sure." He put down the paint tray and can to kneel beside Toby, wrapping his arms around the dog's neck. Ellie took a couple of shots, smiling when she viewed them on her screen. Both the dog and the teenager looked happy. "Do you want to send one to your mom?"

"Nah, it's okay. Come on, Toby." Ryder retrieved the paint tray and can. "You can stay in my room while I clean up," he told the dog. Then he glanced at Ellie. "Is that okay?"

"Absolutely. If you want, I'll move his bed and his toys into your room. I'm pretty sure he'll be happier staying with you than with me."

Ryder's face lit up with a smile. "That'd be awesome. Thanks, Ellie."

"No, thank you. You've been a big help with Toby, and I really appreciate you cutting the grass and painting the chair."

"It's not a big deal," he said, sounding like Nate.

As Ryder and Toby walked across the lawn together, she snapped another picture. She took a photo of the chair as an afterthought. She'd send them to Nate, and he could forward them to Gina.

But first she'd send them to her sister. Ellie typed Toby has a new friend. She attached the photos and pressed Send.

Taking a seat on a chair near the edge of the lake, she waited for her sister's response. Dots appeared on her screen and then disappeared. She added Everything okay with you? in hopes her sister would respond. Her phone buzzed in her hand. She'd gotten her wish. Hopefully, she'd also get some answers from her sister.

"Hey, Bri."

"Hi. Thanks for the pictures. I've been wondering how he was doing."

"Sorry. It's been a bit crazy around here. But you know, you could have called."

"It hasn't been much better around here." Her sister sighed. "Ellie, did you say something about Richard to mom?"

"Do you mean after she accused me of being selfish for insisting you give Toby to Grandpa for his therapy?"

"I'm sorry. I didn't know what else to say. You didn't tell her the real reason I did, did you?"

"How could I? It's not like you told me the truth. I had to figure that out for myself."

"Please, don't. I can't deal with that now." Her sister paused, and Ellie heard what sounded like a door closing. "Have you talked to Mom today?"

"I haven't heard from her since yesterday morning." This was the opportunity Ellie had been hoping for. She'd just have to be careful not to reveal her suspicions that the deal with the developer had something to do with their mother's affair. "But there's something going on, Bri. Mom's backed down on insisting Grandpa have a legal competency test and putting him in a home. It doesn't sound like she wants to sell the inn for the money either, so I can't figure out why she's pushing for this deal. Can you? Does Richard have any idea what this is really about?"

"I'm in the dark too. When Mom first told me what she planned to do, she was clear that she was only concerned for Grandpa's well-being. But this morning, she called to talk to Richard. She hardly said two words to me. She was upset, Ellie. Panicked even."

"What did Richard say?"

"He told me I needed to do whatever I have to to convince Grandpa to sell. He wanted me to leave for the inn today. When I told him I couldn't afford to take time off work right now, he... he was upset."

"How upset was he?" Her sister didn't respond. Ellie knew what would happen if she pushed too hard, so instead she said, "For Grandpa's sake and for Mom's, we need to figure this out, Bri. Why don't you come Friday and spend the weekend? I could use your help." She told her about the guest rooms' redesign and Sunday's tour.

"Is Mom coming?"

Ellie bowed her head. The last thing she wanted was her mother underfoot. She'd criticize Ellie's every decision. But if that was what it took to get her sister away from Richard for the weekend, she'd suck it up. "I haven't asked her yet. But I will if you want me to. Do you want me to?" She closed her eyes and crossed her fingers.

"I know she's hard on you, Ellie. But if we want to find out what's really going on, it would be better if she comes. Maybe between the two of us we can convince her to let this go."

"If I don't murder her first," Ellie muttered after disconnecting from her sister.

Chapter Thirteen

♥

I'm going to pretend I didn't just hear you contemplating murder. I'd hate to have to arrest you." Ellie whipped her head around, her eyes wide. "I'm kidding," Nate said as he took a seat on the chair beside hers. "Who's on your hit list?"

"My mother." She filled him in on her conversation with her sister. "I was afraid if I didn't agree to invite her, Bri wouldn't come."

Nate frowned. "Back it up a sec. What do you mean you and Bri need to get to the bottom of it? I thought you'd decided it came down to the money."

"I did. Until I spoke to my mother yesterday." She caught her bottom lip between her teeth, then glanced at him. "The only person I've told this to is Sadie. If I tell you, Nate, you have to promise not to say anything to anyone."

"I'm a vault, Ellie. You can trust me with your secrets." Unless they put someone in danger.

"My mother had an affair. My dad isn't Bri's

biological father." After dropping her bombshell, Ellie repeated what her mother had told her yesterday.

"I see what you mean, and I get why you don't want to tell your sister. But that's a pretty big secret for you to carry, Ellie."

"I've been carrying it for the past eighteen years. Most of the time I've been able to shut it away. Now I can't."

"So your mother's aware that you know?"

She nodded. "I found out by accident. Knowing what I do now, I wouldn't have confronted her. She basically made my life hell from that day forward." She smiled. "You look like you want to beat her up for me. I was just being dramatic, Nate. It wasn't that bad. We didn't have a typical mother-daughter relationship, that's all."

He'd met a few drama queens in his time, and Ellie wasn't one of them. If anything, she had a tendency to underplay things. He had a feeling she was doing that now. "I don't think so. Don't forget, I met your mother. I also know she put Agnes through hell."

"She did, and that's something I can't forgive her for. But I have to figure out what's going on, and if that means putting up with my mother, I will. If nothing else, Bri will be out from under Richard's thumb for a few days."

"The one thing I don't get is, if Richard's using your sister's paternity to blackmail your mother into going along with the sale, he's getting something out of it. My guess would be a substantial sum of money for brokering the deal. So why would he risk your sister coming here to uncover the reason your mother is hot and heavy to sell the inn? If Bri found out the truth, Richard would lose his leverage."

"He doesn't know that's why she's coming. The only reason he wants her to come is to convince Grandpa to sell."

"You better make sure she doesn't tell him the truth, Ellie. It could put her in danger."

She pressed a hand to her chest. "Don't tell me that."

"Look, maybe I'm overreacting." He didn't think he was, but he didn't want to scare Ellie. Richard was a man who had no compunction about hurting his wife and a dog and blackmailing his mother-in-law. When you added a substantial financial windfall to the equation, it equaled a volatile situation in Nate's book. "It's a hazard of the job."

"No, you're right. I shouldn't have said anything to Bri. If something happens to her—"

"Nothing's going to happen to your sister." It wasn't a promise he could or should make. He knew that better than anyone. "But Ellie, this isn't on you. It's on Richard and your mother. If your mother wants to protect Bri, she should tell her the truth."

"She won't."

"Will you?"

"I can't. I can't do that to Bri or to my Dad. They wouldn't believe me anyway. My mother would make sure of that."

He'd been in law enforcement long enough to know she was holding out on him. He decided to let it go. At least for now, because according to Abby, Ellie was stressed about the room redesign and Sunday's tour. He'd actually been trying to alleviate her stress, not add to it, which he'd unwittingly done by agreeing to build an entertainment room for Joe. "If you want, I can look into Richard. I might find something that'll give your mother leverage against him."

"If you wouldn't mind, I'd really appreciate it." She closed her eyes and shook her head. "I'm sorry for dumping all this on you. And don't say it isn't a big deal, because it is." She glanced over her shoulder. "Hey, wait a minute. Where's Hunter?"

"Abby called just as we were about to leave. She said you were stressed about redesigning the guest rooms and suggested I should help you work on that instead of Joe's reno. Actually, she demanded that's what I do. Hunter'll drive the load over first thing in the morning."

"I wasn't that stressed about it."

"You ate an entire chocolate cake at nine in the morning." And that was on him, him and his unwillingness to see where their obvious attraction took them.

"I did not. Sadie and Abby ate at least half the cake." She wrinkled her nose. "Okay, more like a quarter of it. But it was closer to eleven by the time we finished the cake and our meeting. And if anyone is to blame for me being stressed, it's Abby. Thanks to her, the rooms have to be ready for Sunday." She sighed and got up from the chair. "Which, in the end, turned out to be a really good idea. Abby's ideas always are, so I guess I shouldn't be surprised. But you don't have to help me, Nate. Go on your date with Tiff."

"I have a date with Tiff?" he asked as he came to his feet.

"Right, you don't date. Well, whatever you do with a woman. You can go do it with her. I'm good. Thanks for the offer though." Her smile looked forced.

He put out his hand to stop her from walking away. "Wait a sec. I'm confused. Who said I was taking Tiff out?"

"I just assumed you would. She was upset that you're on the Most Romantic Couple in Highland Falls list with me, and you don't like to hurt women who are pining to be in a relationship with you. So I thought you'd want to explain that we're not a couple, have never been a couple, and never will be a couple and that you didn't break your no-relationship rule with me somewhere other than a parking lot on Main Street."

"Tiff isn't pining for me. She was just—"

Ellie rolled her eyes. "Of course she is. If she wasn't, she wouldn't have reacted the way that she did."

"Her ego was hurt, not her heart, Ellie. She wanted to know why I was willing to break my no-relationship rule with you and not her."

Ellie snorted. "I hope you cleared that up for her. And just so you know, I had nothing to do with us being on the list."

"I have a feeling, after today, we won't be on the list for much longer."

"Wishful thinking. I already tried to get us taken off and was told that the only people who can remove their vote is the voter."

"I know one voter who's removing hers, and the

way gossip spreads in Highland Falls, I wouldn't be surprised if the rest remove theirs by the end of the day."

"How did you manage that? Put a sign on the back of your motorcycle saying *Ellie and Nate are friends, not lovers* and drive around town?"

His laugh came out a little hoarse as the image of them as lovers flashed through his mind. He cleared his throat. "No. One of your grandmother's customers saw me with Tiff and saw you drive off and assumed I was cheating on you. She hit me with her I Believe in Unicorns bag. Don't laugh," he said, rubbing his head. "She either had a ceramic unicorn in her bag or paperweights."

"Hopefully not the ceramic unicorn. Granny won't give her a refund if she broke it on your head."

"Hey, my head's not that hard."

"Pretty hard," she said, raising her hand to gently prod the back of his skull. "No bump or cut. You'll live. But I think you've suffered enough on account of me today. You should go for dinner with Grandpa, Jonathan, and Ryder."

At the feel of her fingers running through his hair, heat gathered low in his belly. He should definitely go out for dinner. Staying at the inn, alone with Ellie, was a bad idea. Except she was stressed, and he'd promised Abby he'd help her with the guest rooms.

"I forgot. I wanted to send you these," she said, holding up her phone. "I thought Gina might like them."

His phone pinged in his pocket. He took it out, smiling at the pictures she'd taken of Ryder and

Toby. "These are great, Ellie. Thanks. Gina will love them."

The thoughtful gesture had him rethinking his plan to stay and help out with the guest rooms. Ellie wasn't only beautiful; she was also sweet and kind, and for a minute there, he wished he were a better man. A decent man who was worthy of her love.

She leaned in to him, pointing at the freshly painted Adirondack chair. "Didn't he do a great job? I think he really enjoyed painting. He's very creative."

The sun glinted off her long, black hair, her light floral scent filling his nostrils and making it difficult for him to think straight. "Yeah, really great," he said, his voice little more than a rough rasp.

Ellie stepped back. "Please tell me you're not laughing because he's creative."

It was so far from a laugh that it wasn't funny. "No, of course not. I think it's great that he likes to paint."

"Okay, good. Because I think we should encourage him to paint more. It's a great therapeutic tool for kids dealing with trauma. In Ryder's case, loss."

She glanced at him. "Maybe it's something you could do together."

"I'll stick to painting walls, thanks. I'm not creative. You are though," he said, needing a distraction before she started talking about the loss he shared with Ryder. "I saw your paintings when we moved your stuff upstairs. They're incredible, Ellie." They were. She was a talented artist. "Do you still paint?"

"No. But I probably should. It's a great way to relieve stress."

"Probably a better way to deal with it than eating chocolate." He grinned. "We found your chocolate bar stash in your room. We weren't snooping. The nightstand drawer fell out when were moving it."

"I'll have to find a new hiding place. My grandfather will—" She broke off, her eyes narrowed on Joe, who was rounding the side of the inn. He took one look at Ellie and started to backtrack. "Oh no, you don't. You and I have to have a chat, mister."

"Now, Ellie my love, what would you have me do? Nate wanted a project to keep him busy."

"Don't throw me under the bus, Joe. This one's on you."

"You said it was a good idea when I brought it up to you." Joe cocked his head. From the direction of the parking lot, the judge called his name. "We'll talk about it later. We can't be late for our reservation. You know how Zia Maria gets."

"Nate's going with you, so—"

"No, I'm not," he said, despite knowing he should. "I ordered a lasagna, Joe. It'll be ready to bring home when you leave. It's paid for."

"You told him it was a good idea?" Ellie asked when Joe disappeared from view.

"After he told me you okayed it, I did." He reached around her to open the patio door. "I know the timing isn't ideal, but look at how it opens up the dining room."

"You're right. It is brighter, and we could use a lounge area for guests."

"Don't forget the big-screen TV and the bar."

She pressed a hand to her face and looked at him through her fingers. "Please tell me Grandpa didn't eat my chocolate bars."

Nate laughed. "No, but you'll ruin your appetite for lasagna if you do."

"Trust me, I won't. By the time Sunday rolls around, I'll probably have gained ten pounds."

Keep your eyes on hers, he told himself, resisting the urge to do a visual tour of her body while contemplating where those ten extra pounds would go. Ellie wasn't tall and lean; she was tall and curvy. And while Tiff dressed to flaunt her assets, Ellie didn't, which Nate found more appealing. It was also distracting.

"I have a better way to get rid of your stress," he said, and one of his favorite ways to deal with stress immediately popped into his head. He stifled a groan, thinking he should run after Joe and the judge and jump into the back of the truck. "Let's map out which literary couple goes in which room, and we can brainstorm ideas for the decor that won't cost much or take much time to do."

"Really? Mr. I Don't Do Romance wants to brainstorm romantic literary couples for the guest rooms? Nate, have you ever read a romantic novel or watched a romantic movie?"

"I bet I've watched more rom-coms than you." He held up ten fingers at her raised eyebrow. "Five sisters and five nieces. That's all they watch, and whenever I visit, they make me watch with them."

"Okay, so have you read or watched *Pride and Prejudice*?" she asked as she walked through the dining room to the reception desk, leaning over to grab a pad of paper and two pens.

"Too easy. The version with Colin Firth as Mr. Darcy was my sisters' favorite. What else have you got?"

"How about *The Princess Bride*?" She picked up a bag of books from the chair.

"Seriously?" he said, taking the bag from her. "Who hasn't watched the romantic adventures of Princess Buttercup and Westley?"

She laughed. "Me. It was Abby's pick."

"See, you need my help after all. What else?"

She glanced over her shoulder as she headed up the stairs. "*Bridget Jones's Diary*."

"I actually didn't mind that one. I stayed awake for the entire movie. What was your favorite part?"

"When Bridget went to the non–costume party dressed as a Playboy Bunny."

He laughed. "Same."

"How about *The Count of Monte Cristo*?"

"Someone has good taste. I loved that movie."

"Thank you. I loved the book and the movie. What about *Outlander*? Have you read any of the series?"

"No, but my sisters are addicted to it. I caught an episode with them and then refused to watch any more. There are just some things a guy can't watch with his sisters, sex being one of them. But Abby being Abby, I've heard more about the show than I needed to. So I should be able to brainstorm ideas for Jamie and Claire's room with you."

"I'm impressed, but I doubt you'll have watched this one: *Beauty and the Beast*."

"You're kidding, right? I've seen the movie so many times, I've got most of the songs memorized. I've even read that one. Bedtime stories," he clarified in case she thought he'd read it for his own enjoyment.

"That's all six guest rooms covered, then. I can't decorate the seventh until Highland Falls' Most Romantic Couple is announced, and I'll be staying in the eighth guest room now." She opened the door to the room a few down from his. "I'm thinking this one for Belle and the Beast. It's bigger than the others." She pointed to the wall behind the bed. "I thought I'd frame the bed with a wall of navy bookshelves."

"That'd work." Nate dumped the books on the bed. Taking the pad of paper and a pen from Ellie, he sketched out her vision for the bookshelves. "Something like this?"

"Exactly like that. How long do you think it would take me to build the shelves?"

"Would you be using your fixer-upper guy's You-Tube videos?"

"Ha ha. I'm being serious."

"So am I. Hunter and I can do it for you in a day. You can do the painting though."

"Thanks for your vote of confidence." She walked to the window and held out the drapes. "I'll have to change these and the bedding. I want to go white, romantic, and flowy." She tapped a finger to her lips. "I'll put a rose under a glass dome on the middle shelf above the bed. And I'd love to find a cute teacup and teapot. You know, like Mrs. Potts and Chip. They'd look amazing on the gold breakfast tray I saw at the antique store."

"I might be able to help you out there. I bought two of my nieces Mrs. Potts teapots and Chip teacups for Christmas a couple years ago. The oldest might be willing to part with hers. I'll give my sister a call." He cocked his head. "Why are you looking at me like that?"

"For a guy who doesn't do relationships, you obviously have a wonderful relationship with your family. You sound like you're a pretty great uncle too."

"My brothers-in-law hate me." He smiled, disconnecting when the call went to voice mail. "I'll give her a minute." Sure enough, his phone rang a second later. Only it was a FaceTime call. He hit Accept, and his thirteen-year-old niece's face filled the screen. "Hey, princess. You're just the girl I wanted to talk to."

"Mama is not happy with you, Uncle." She frowned. "Who's that?"

He swore under his breath. Ellie had moved to check out the wall and into his niece's line of sight. "Ah, my friend."

"Mama, Uncle has a girlfriend!"

"No, Uncle does not have a girlfriend. He has a friend." He bowed his head when Ellie moved in beside him and waved at his niece.

"You have no idea what you've just done," he said out of the side of his mouth.

"Hi, I'm Annalise." His niece waved, grinning from ear to ear. There was nothing that his nieces and sisters wanted more than to marry him off.

"What a beautiful name. I'm Elliana, but everyone calls me Ellie."

"I'm named after my nana. She died when I was eight. She wanted to join my pop pop in heaven. She loved him very much, didn't she, Uncle?"

"She did." His parents had died six months apart. They'd been married for fifty-five years. His sister joined his niece on the screen. "Hey, Val. I was—" he began, about to get out the reason for the call so he could get off it ASAP.

"Hi, Ellie. I'm Val," his sister said, totally ignoring him. "So how long have you known my baby brother?"

"Seven months. We met at my cousin's wedding. Not that we really got to know each other that well. We just danced and talked. But now that he's living here with Ryder, we've gotten to know each other better."

Nate shot Ellie a *stop talking* look. He got that Val's penetrating stare was unnerving, but the more Ellie said, the more his sister would make of it. "Listen, Val—"

"My baby brother's living with you?"

His niece disappeared from the screen. In the background he heard her whispering to someone that he had a girlfriend and that she was beautiful and really, really nice and that they were talking to her now.

He glared at his sister, who was pretending to ignore him, but he caught her smirk.

"No. Well, I mean yes," Ellie said, "but not in the way it sounds. I run my grandfather's inn. The Mirror Lake Inn in Highland Falls."

"Is that my brother's room you're in?"

"No. Nate's and Ryder's rooms are down the hall. I'm planning to redecorate this one in a Beauty and the Beast theme." She filled his sister in on her plans and Sunday's deadline, taking her on a tour of the room while telling her the changes she was thinking of making.

"I love your ideas, Ellie. What are you doing with the other rooms?"

"This is the first one Nate and I discussed. You know, for a guy who doesn't do romance, your brother has been surprisingly helpful." She walked past him and out the door, telling Val the themes for the other rooms.

Nate sat on the end of the bed and bowed his head as the two of them laughed and chatted like old friends.

"Oh, hi. Wow, there are a lot of you." Ellie laughed as his sisters and nieces introduced themselves.

Nate shot off the bed and down the hall to grab the phone from Ellie's hand. "Okay. Listen up. Ellie and I aren't—"

"Uncle has a girlfriend. Uncle has a girlfriend," his younger nieces sang.

"Give the phone back to Ellie," his second-oldest sister said over his still-singing nieces. She was even bossier than Val.

"No. We're helping Ellie. I called—"

"Nate, I want to hear your sisters' and nieces' ideas for the rooms. Val already gave me a good idea for Jamie and Claire's." Ellie took the phone from him. "Okay. Where were we?"

"You were about to tell my sisters how you met Nate," he heard Val say as Ellie walked into the other room.

Chapter Fourteen

♥

Anxious to get an early start on Beauty and the Beast's room, Ellie opened the guest room door. Sunlight streamed through the window and danced on a beautiful white comforter. She stopped in the middle of stepping into the room, staring at the Mrs. Potts teapot and two Chip teacups sitting in the middle of the bed, a glass dome with a red rose suspended inside on the nightstand.

Pressing a hand to her mouth, she turned at the sound of heavy footfalls. Nate frowned, coming to stand behind her. "What's wrong?"

She stared up at him. "I thought you left because you were mad at me."

Ryder, Joe, and the judge had arrived while she was on the phone with Nate's family. He'd barely spoken two words to her while they ate the lasagna from Zia Maria's, and then he'd taken off on his motorcycle. He hadn't returned by the time she'd finally given up and gone to bed. A part of her worried that his family's insistence they were a couple had sent him running to

Tiff. If only to prove to himself and to Ellie that he had no intention of being tied down.

"But you went to your sister's and got everything I wanted for the room." She hugged him. "Thank you. You have no idea how much this means to me, Nate."

His chest expanded under her cheek, and he put an arm around her, smoothing his other hand down her hair. "I wasn't mad at you, Ellie. My sisters drive me crazy, and I knew what I'd be walking into. They're seriously nuts."

Yet he'd still gone—for her. Maybe she was making more of it than she should, but his actions last night made her wonder if he'd had a change of heart and was now open to exploring their feelings for each other. *Get a grip*, she told herself. *He was just being a friend.*

She tipped her head back. "They're seriously nuts about you. They absolutely adore you, Nate. For good reason, from what I heard." If she hadn't already had a crush on him, she would have developed one after talking to his sisters and nieces.

He gave her hair a playful tug, then stepped away. "Don't listen to them. They've been obsessed with marrying me off since I turned thirty. They'd say anything to convince you I'm husband material."

It wouldn't take much convincing, she thought. "Don't worry, I have no delusions you're the marrying kind." Nate was right. She'd gotten caught up in his sisters' fantasy.

They'd convinced her that she was the one woman who could get him to break his no-relationship rule. In their minds she had something going for her that no other woman had had—time. Time enough for her to get past Nate's defenses and capture his heart. After all, she was the only woman Nate had ever introduced to his family. Except he hadn't introduced her. She'd introduced herself, and it had been obvious he'd wanted to get her off the phone as quickly as possible.

"You should tell that to my brothers-in-law. They've been texting me since six this morning. Two of them wanted to know when we're getting married so they could mark it on their calendars. One wanted to know if he was my best man. Brother-in-law number four wanted to know if I'd been in an accident and had amnesia. I like him best. My least-favorite brother-in-law, Val's husband and Chase's boss at the FBI field office, he wanted your number. I didn't give it to him, but don't be surprised if you receive a text from an anonymous number listing all the reasons you shouldn't hook up with me."

"If he does, he better hope your sister doesn't find out. And not just Val. They all think you can do no wrong. It must be nice to have such a close, supportive family."

"Your definition of *supportive* must be different than mine. But yeah, when they're not trying to run my life, I lucked out."

"You did, and so did I." Ellie walked into the room and smoothed a hand over the comforter. "Where did you get this? It's beautiful and exactly what I pictured for the bedding but had no idea where I'd find anything like it by Sunday."

"Val. My mom bought it for her hope chest.

According to my sister, my mom started filling it when Val was thirteen." He ran a finger over the comforter and smiled. "I guess they inherited their wedding-obsessed gene from her."

"Nate, I can't keep this. Val should save it for Annalise."

"I said the same thing, but I was outvoted. They'll be offended if you don't accept it, Ellie. Besides, my nieces liked the idea their stuff would be part of the Beauty and the Beast room. They think my mom would too."

"Your mom sounds like she was a wonderful woman. You all must miss her very much, her and your father."

"Yeah, we do. They were great parents. That first year without them was tough, but Val stepped into my mom's shoes. If we missed a Sunday family dinner, family birthday, or holiday at her place, there was hell to pay. She's relentless. You're just lucky she doesn't have your cell phone number. She—" He dropped his chin to his chest. "You gave it to her, didn't you?"

She nodded. "Yesterday when we were on the phone."

"You mean, all my sisters and nieces have your number now?"

"What did you expect me to do? Say no?"

"If you valued your sanity, you would have."

"You're exaggerating. Besides, I really liked them. I think they're great. They seem like a lot of fun."

"Yeah, they liked you too," he muttered.

He was obviously not pleased, and she knew why. But she shrugged, pretending she didn't. "I'm a likable person."

"Hey, Ellie," Ryder called up the stairs. "Joe wants to know what's for breakfast."

"Tell Joe and the judge it's about time they start making their own breakfast. Ellie's busy."

"Nate! I'll be right down, Ryder."

"You have to stop catering to them, Ellie." Nate followed her from the room. "You can't do everything by yourself."

"If you saw what they were making themselves for breakfast, you would have taken over too. But you're right. At least for the rest of this week, they can look after themselves. I'm making an exception this morning because I have to break the news to Grandpa that my mother's coming for the weekend. I called her last night."

"You talk to Joe, and Ryder and I will make breakfast."

"You don't have to do that. You're already doing enough for us." The phone rang at the reception desk, and Ellie hurried the rest of the way down the stairs to answer. "Mirror Lake Inn, Ellie speaking." She pressed her lips together when the woman's voice came over the line, turning her back on Nate. "Hi, Val. Thanks so much for the comforter. It's perfect, and so are the teacups, teapot, and rose. Please let the girls know how much I appreciate them." She felt Nate behind her and shooed him away.

He stepped in front of her, crossed his incredible arms, and looked at her with a *see what I mean* eyebrow raised.

"Twenty-two? Wow, there really are a lot of you.

No, no, I'm sure it'll be fine." She turned to open the reservation book, flipping to Sunday's afternoon tea. "I should be able to fit you in at the one o'clock seating. Does that work for—" She broke off, talking to her empty hand. "Nate!"

He had the phone to his ear, clearly unhappy Val was booking his entire family for Sunday's tea. She might have appreciated how sexy his gruff and growly voice was if she weren't annoyed with him. She made a grab for the phone, and he put out his other hand to keep her at arm's length. The man had a very long arm. "Nathan Black, you give me the phone right now."

He snorted, turned his back on her, and continued arguing with his sister. Ellie moved in front of him, warding off his outstretched hand with her own while attempting to take the phone from him. She had to jump a little because he was at least six five and she was five nine. When Nate once again blocked her, she dipped her hand under the neck of her long-sleeved T-shirt and pulled her cell phone from her bra.

Nate's argument with Val abruptly ended. Ellie looked up, thinking his sister had hung up on him, only to find he was staring at her.

She shrugged. "I don't have pockets in my leggings." Then she gave him a smug smile and called his sister. Her call went to voice mail, and she left a message. "You have a reservation for twenty-two at one on Sunday, Val. I can't wait to meet everybody. If anyone has allergies, just let me know." As she disconnected, she was thinking of ways to show her appreciation to Nate's family.

Her musings were cut off when Nate slammed the phone in the cradle. Without saying a word to her, he strode into the dining room.

She followed him to the kitchen, where he was taking a carton of eggs out of the fridge. Ryder winced when Nate plunked the eggs on the counter. "I'll help Nate make breakfast, Ryder. Why don't you take Toby for a quick walk before we eat?"

"Sure," he said, and left the kitchen while casting an apprehensive glance over his shoulder at Nate. "Joe and the judge said to call them when breakfast is ready. They're in Joe's room drawing up plans for the reno."

"Thanks," she said, turning to Nate when Ryder had disappeared from view. "Stop taking your anger at me out on the eggs."

He ignored her, reaching for the frying pan in the oven drawer.

"You have a lot of nerve being mad at me for accepting your family's reservation when, thanks to you, the inn is under construction."

He dropped the pan on the burner, turned, and walked to her, backing her up against the counter. He slapped his hands on the counter on either side of her hips, caging her in. "I told you my sisters have been trying to marry me off for five years. I told you they like you. I told you about my brothers-in-law's texts. So you tell me, why are they coming? Or better yet, tell me why you want them to."

"Because they wanted to visit the inn and take the tour, and they're your family!"

He raised an eyebrow. "And…"

"Oh come on, you can't be serious. Are you really suggesting I have an ulterior motive for wanting them here? Like what, Nate?" Her jaw dropped when it hit her. "Oh my gosh, you actually think I've joined forces with your sisters and nieces to trap you into marriage." She shook her head. "And how exactly would that happen? I don't want to get married, and neither do you. It's not like I'm planning to seduce you and then spring a secret baby on you. I think you've been watching too many romantic movies with your sisters."

"I never said anything about you seducing me." His voice was huskier than usual, his eyes on her mouth.

"Oh, so you're okay with me seducing you? You want us to be friends with benefits?" She bit her lip to keep from laughing.

He lifted his gaze to hers, his eyes almost black, his sun-bronzed skin flushed. "You're making fun of me."

Yes, but apparently the joke was on her, she thought when the muscles low in her stomach tightened with desire. "I was just making a point." About what? What point was she trying to make? She couldn't think straight with his body so close to hers, his fingers brushing against her hips.

"And what point is that, Ellie?"

Had he moved closer? Was that a hint of amusement in his voice? "Um. I, um. *Get a grip*, she told herself. She was going to make a fool of herself, and she'd already done that yesterday morning. Obviously the kitchen was a dangerous place. "My point is, it doesn't matter what your family or my grandmother or the voters for Highland Falls' most romantic couple say or do, they can't influence our feelings for each other. They can't make us fall in love. They can't make us—"

He placed a finger on her lips. "I get the picture," he said. Then, lowering his hand, he stepped away from her. "But what they can do is drive us insane. And just remember who will be here when my sisters start hinting that there's something more going on between us. Your grandmother and half the matchmakers in Highland Falls. Don't forget your mother will be here too. How do you think—"

"Miranda is coming here?" her grandfather said, standing where the wall had once been.

She glared at Nate, who grimaced and mouthed *Sorry*.

Forcing a smile for her grandfather, she said in her cheeriest voice, "Yes. Mom and Bri are coming for the weekend. It'll be a good opportunity for you two to talk and clear the air, Grandpa. Maybe we can straighten everything out this weekend, and you won't have to worry about it anymore."

"I'm not worried. It's your mother who should be worried. If she sets foot on my property, I'll have her arrested." He turned and walked to his suite, then slammed the door shut behind him.

Ellie winced and grabbed a mixing bowl off the shelf. "That went well."

Nate took the bowl from her. "Go talk to Joe. I'll handle breakfast."

"It's okay. I said I would help, and it's probably

best if I give him a few minutes to cool off." She
opened the fridge, bending over to get the cheese, and
her backside brushed against Nate.

"Seriously, Ellie. Please get out of the kitchen." He
rubbed his face. "I mean, go deal with Joe."

* * *

"Wow, it's really coming along," Sadie said from
behind her.

Ellie turned on the step stool, where she was hanging the plaid curtains in Jamie and Claire's room. It
was nice to see a friendly face. Nate was avoiding her,
and her grandfather wasn't speaking to her.

"Thanks," Ellie said to her cousin, and she stepped
off the stool. "Granny brought over some bedding she
had, and it works perfectly with the plaid accents.
The antique store dropped off my order this afternoon.
Don't you love this washbasin and pitcher?"

Sadie walked over, running a finger along the earth-
enware bowl. "I do, and I love the stand too. I peeked
my head in the Beauty and the Beast room. Hunter and
Nate are doing a great job on the bookshelves. They
said they'll be finished with them in another hour or
so. You're painting them navy?"

Ellie nodded. "Hopefully I'll get to them tonight."
She frowned at Sadie. "Why do you look nervous?
Nate and Hunter didn't damage the wardrobe when
they brought it up, did they?"

"No. Can't you read my mind?"

"I don't read minds without people's permission,

remember?" Except she had read the judge's mind when he'd first arrived in Highland Falls, and Ryder's. "Unless I have a very good reason to invade someone's privacy."

"Please invade mine. Then I don't have to tell you."

Ellie lowered herself onto the edge of the bed. "What's wrong?"

Sadie joined her and took her hand. "It's probably nothing, but—"

"Why are you thinking about Spencer?"

"Go ahead, read the rest of it."

"It doesn't work like that. Now tell me what's going on."

"Okay. Well, after you told us about Spencer, Abby was curious, and she stalked him on social media. And ah." She made a pained face. "Ellie, he was posting about the contest for most romantic small town in America. Abby's positive he's somehow involved with Happy Ever After Entertainment."

"Maybe she stalked the wrong Spencer," Ellie said, grasping at straws. This couldn't be happening.

"It's the right Spencer. But for all we know, he's got the lead role in the movie, so let's not panic just yet. Abby's contact at Happy Ever After is away until Friday. She'll call her then."

"Okay, I know why I'm panicking. But why are you?"

"Because given your history with Spencer, if he is one of the judges, there's no way Highland Falls will win."

Chapter Fifteen

♥

It's a three-chocolate-bar day," Ryder said as he met Nate at the top of the stairs. Three days ago, they'd begun gauging Ellie's stress levels by how many chocolate bars she ate. It was the only way to tell how she was really feeling. She was one of the most relentlessly cheerful and easygoing women Nate had ever met.

Ryder glanced over his shoulder at the open guest room door down the hall. "She doesn't even know Joe's big-screen TV arrived. Maybe we should hide it."

The kid had fallen for Ellie, which didn't surprise Nate. As he knew from personal experience, she was easy to fall for. It was not giving in to his feelings for her that was hard. Almost as hard as acknowledging he had them.

"I doubt we'll be able to keep the news from her for long, buddy. The delivery guy was setting the TV up for Joe when I left him."

Nate and Hunter had finished the entertainment room a couple of hours ago. They'd worked through the night. Ellie had done the same. But it wasn't Joe's TV that was stressing Ellie out. It was her mother's impending arrival today.

"Yeah? Is it okay if I go have a look?"

It wasn't the TV Ryder wanted to check out. It was the gaming console Joe had ordered to go with it.

"Did you finish painting the Bridget Jones room for Ellie?"

"Yeah. It looks pretty cool. Ellie said I did a great job. She's putting the last coat on the iron bed frame and then that room is done. Except for the door. She said it won't take her as long to paint as the other ones did though."

Ellie had used the book covers for inspiration. He'd known she was talented, but what she'd done with the doors had blown him away.

"Okay, sounds like you deserve a break." Nate gave the kid's shoulder a squeeze. "You've been a big help, Ryder. I'm proud of you. So is your mom."

Gina had been thrilled with the changes she'd noticed in her nightly phone calls with Ryder. He was no longer the angry teenager she'd foisted on Nate. According to Gina, Ryder was beginning to sound like the happy-go-lucky son he'd been before he'd lost his father.

Ryder shrugged. "It's not a big deal. I like helping out with the rooms. Come on, Toby." He patted his leg, and the Irish setter obediently left his place outside the Bridget Jones door. Ryder was the dog's favorite human, but Ellie was a close second. Nate wasn't even in the running. "Maybe just tell Ellie I'm working on ideas for our room," Ryder added.

"Wait a minute. I thought Ellie was only doing the six rooms for the tour." She had enough on her plate without taking on any more.

"When Ellie's grandmother and the Sisterhood stopped by yesterday, they sort of vetoed the *Count of Monte Cristo* room."

"Are you kidding me? That was my favorite room."

Ryder grinned. "Ellie's too. But they said nobody voted for it in their poll. So they suggested, more like ordered, really, that she change it to the top pick— Simon Basset and Daphne Bridgerton's room. The series is playing on Netflix, and everyone in Highland Falls is hooked on it."

"So our suite is *The Count of Monte Cristo*?"

"Nope. Ellie let me choose, and I picked Katniss and Peeta from *The Hunger Games*. She said I can help design the rooms. But we won't start until Monday."

"When you're designing the rooms, buddy, just remember which one of us goes in which. I get the Peeta room."

"Ellie says you're more like Gale. But Katniss picked Peeta, so you can't be Gale." Ryder grinned. "If it makes you feel better, Ellie says she would have picked Gale over Peeta."

Nate groaned. Just what he needed, Ryder joining the matchmakers of Highland Falls. "Go and check out the gaming console, kid," Nate said, and walked to the Bridget Jones room.

Ellie was sitting cross-legged on the floor in front of the freshly painted turquoise bed frame, eating a chocolate bar, and not a small one.

"Room looks great," he said, leaning against the door frame. Three of the walls were painted pale yellow, and the one behind the bed was a blue gray.

"Don't bother," he added when she tried to hide the mostly eaten chocolate bar under her leg. "The chocolate at the corner of your mouth and on your fingers would have given you away."

She licked the tips of her fingers clean, then dabbed at her lips. "That was my last one. I need to go to the store and buy a family pack. Maybe two packs. I won't survive the weekend without them."

"I have a better idea. Come on." He walked over and held out his hand.

"Where are we going?"

"For a run. It's the best way to deal with stress. Better than giving yourself a sugar rush. Besides, you need some fresh air. We both do."

"You might be able to run with very little sleep, but I can't. Actually, I don't particularly like to run on a good day." She wiped her fingers on her leggings before placing her hand in his. "But some fresh air sounds good. How about a walk instead of a run?"

"Let's compromise. We'll jog instead of running."

"I have a feeling what you think of as jogging is what I think of as running." She glanced up at him. "Are you stressed too?"

She had no idea. Living under the same roof with Ellie while keeping her at arm's length was about as stressful as not eating when you were starving. "Not like you, no. Just frustrated with the case. The task force hasn't made any headway." He checked in three times a day. "And I'm still waiting to hear back about your brother-in-law. Hopefully I'll have something by the time your mother and sister arrive."

"If Bri even comes at all. I called her this morning, and she says something came up but that she'd try, with an emphasis on *try*, to come tomorrow afternoon. I managed to push my mother off until then, except I made the mistake of using the renovations as an excuse. She threw a fit. In her mind, the inn is being torn down so all I've done is waste a lot of time, energy, and money for nothing."

Instead of taking her in his arms like he wanted to, he said, "Go put your sneakers on. We'll talk while we jog."

"I'll be lucky if I can breathe, let alone talk." She looked down at her long-sleeved purple T-shirt. "I'm seriously out of shape, Nate."

Not from what he could see. The woman had a body that would tempt a saint, and he was no saint. The only thing that had saved him from doing something stupid, like act on that temptation, was working almost day and night on the renos. "You might be surprised. Ryder didn't think he was in shape either." He'd been taking the kid with him on his early-morning runs.

"He's fifteen!" She unwrapped the last of her chocolate bar and glanced at him. "Don't judge. I need a sugar boost if I'm going to survive our jog. I'll meet you outside."

Twenty minutes later, he'd almost given up on her when she joined him on the road. "Did you find another chocolate bar in your room?" he teased.

"Ha. I wish. I heard shouting and cheering coming from the entertainment room and discovered Grandpa, Ryder, and the judge sitting on the floor playing a video game. They were so into shooting each other on the screen, they didn't even realize I was there." She narrowed her eyes at him. "You knew, didn't you?"

"I might have had an inkling." He touched her arm. "Come on, we'll jog off your stress. And focus on the positive. Video games are supposed to be good for seniors."

"Not from what I saw. Grandpa was yelling at the screen and at Jonathan. His blood pressure is probably through the roof. Which is where mine went when he told me that he'd ordered a leather sectional off Facebook Marketplace."

"If it makes you feel better, I checked it out. The owner is legit, and the sectional is in good shape. Joe got a great deal."

"Maybe we should jog *without* talking," she said, and set off down the road.

He slowed his pace to hers. Her jog was more of a walk for him. "I'm not supposed to tell you this, but the judge pitched in on both the TV and sectional, Ellie."

He figured she'd eventually find out, but more than that, she'd let it slip the other day that she was burning through her savings to pay for the guest rooms' redesign. And it wasn't as if the inn was bringing in much revenue while it was temporarily closed.

She stopped in the middle of the road. "I can't believe Grandpa let the judge do that."

"Jonathan was pretty insistent. He's loaded, Ellie. It's not like it's going to break him."

"I know, but that's not the point. He's a paying guest. He shouldn't feel obligated to furnish the entertainment room."

"A guest who you treat like a member of your family. He feels the same way about you and Joe, in case you hadn't noticed." He nudged her. "Come on. Let everything go for now. You can worry about it later. There's nothing better for clearing your head than a good run. Jog," he corrected with a smile at her sidelong glance. "Besides, it's a beautiful day."

"You're right. It is."

They'd jogged for twenty minutes in silence when he noticed her lagging behind. "You okay back there?"

"Very funny. I'm just taking in the scenery."

He slowed to a walk, waiting for her to catch up. "I've run in a lot of places, but this is by far the most beautiful." So was his current jogging partner.

"The scenery here is one of the reasons I couldn't go back to New York." She inhaled deeply. "Thanks for suggesting this. I didn't realize how much I needed to get outside. The last couple of days have been brutal. For you too. The room looks great, by the way."

"A lot better than if I had done it on my own. Hunter does amazing work. Using the reclaimed wood"—a glint of light from across the lake caught his eye—"on the walls was inspired."

"What are you looking at?"

"Nothing." He drew his gaze from the stand of trees. He'd noticed lights last Saturday when he and

Ellie were eating on the balcony, but he'd figured it was a couple of teenagers looking for a place to make out undisturbed. "There's a trail around the lake if you're up for it." He'd have a clearer view of the spot to the left of the cabins where he'd seen the flash of light. If he was right, someone was scoping out the inn with a long-range lens. Then again, these days he was more hypervigilant than usual. So it might be nothing at all.

"Sure. I used to take the path to the cabins when I was younger. It's not exactly conducive to running or jogging though, especially now. We're liable to slip and fall into the lake."

"Now I know why you agreed so quickly." He winked, placing a hand lightly on the small of her back to guide her off the road and into the woods.

"You just wait. Once I get in shape, I'll challenge you to a race."

"You're on." He lowered his hand when they reached the trail. "You go ahead of me. The path's too narrow for the both of us along here." They could manage, but he wanted to scope out the area without Ellie being aware of what he was doing.

"Sure it is. You just want me to act as your early wildlife warning system. Don't you?"

He laughed. "You're mistaking me for Chase. The guy is a wuss. At least when it comes to snakes. Wait a sec, you're not afraid of them, are you?"

"No, and thanks to Sadie, I know which ones to stay far away from. We have a lot of wildlife other than snakes around here, you know."

"I saw a fox the other morning and a couple of deer. No bears though," he said, retrieving his phone from the pocket of his shorts. He brought up his camera, enlarging the screen. He'd been right after all. A green truck was parked among the trees, and a guy was aiming a long-range lens at the inn. There was a sign on the truck's side panel, but the vehicle was angled in such a way that Nate couldn't make it out. He couldn't see the license plate either. He took a couple photos anyway. If he had to guess, whoever Ellie's mother had signed the sale agreement with had someone surveying the inn.

Ellie was talking away to him, oblivious to the fact that he'd fallen behind. He lengthened his stride, tuning back into the conversation. "Skunks, racoon, deer, and rabbits are a common sight at the inn. Last fall, we had a visit from a black bear and an elk, which was pretty exciting."

"Does Joe own all this land too? Or just the inn and the cabins across the lake?"

"All of it. Years ago, he sold off a few parcels of land at the far end of Mirror Lake. The only reason he did was because he knew the families and they planned to live there year-round. Hunter and his brother each bought a parcel. Hunter sold his, but his brother built a beautiful home there a few years back."

Nate bet whoever was interested in buying the property would develop the entire area. He thought that was a real shame, and one more reason to ensure the sale was stopped.

"Whoa, what was that?" Ellie stopped to look down

at her top. She laughed. "I forgot I brought my phone. It's on vibrate."

He really didn't need to know that. *Keep your eyes on the trees*, he told himself when she dipped her hand into her T-shirt and pulled out her phone.

"Hi, Abby." She nodded while listening to the other woman. Seconds later, her shoulders drooped. "Are you sure?" She blew out a breath and then shook her head. "No. No way. I can't do that. I know. I know how important it is. Okay, I'll think about it. Thanks. Yeah, I'll see you tomorrow."

"What's up?" he asked when she disconnected. She looked about ten times more stressed than when they'd started out.

"That was Abby. She called to give me the awesome news that my ex-fiancé owns majority shares in Happy Ever After Entertainment. He's part of the contingent arriving on Tuesday to decide whether Highland Falls is the most romantic small town in America."

"So I'm guessing by your reaction that you guys didn't part on the best of terms." He shouldn't be relieved by that, but he was.

"That's an understatement. He cheated on me with his costar a few days before our wedding. I didn't take it well. I covered for him in the press, but I shared how I really felt with Spencer. I haven't talked to him since. He reached out a few months ago, and I blocked him."

"He's lucky you covered for him. The guy's an idiot." Nate called him a lot worse in his head. He couldn't believe a man who'd been fortunate enough to be loved by Ellie would throw it all away for a roll in the hay. "But I don't think you have to worry about him not casting a vote in Highland Falls' favor because of your past. He's the guilty party. I'd think it's more likely that he'll vote for Highland Falls rather than against it. You could always remind him that he owes you."

"Your idea is almost as bad as Abby's. She thinks I should seduce him." Ellie pressed a hand to her stomach. "I feel like I'm going to throw up."

At the thought of her seducing anyone but him, Nate didn't feel so hot either.

Chapter Sixteen

♥

Ellie texted her sister. Where are you? You promised you'd be here. You're the reason I invited Mom in the first place! And it was going as badly as she had expected it would.

"Mom, keep your voice down! Everyone will hear you," Ellie whisper-shouted as she pocketed her phone.

Sadie, Abby, and Mallory had arrived with their families at noon to help Ellie finish the *Bridgerton* room. The men and the kids were outside playing tag football. Thankfully, they were louder than her mother. They were also outside, while Ellie was stuck in the newly renovated entertainment room with her mother and grandfather.

"If your grandfather would take off his headphones for five minutes, I wouldn't have to yell!"

Ellie glanced at Joe, who was sitting on the recently arrived leather sectional playing video games with said headphones on. His lips curved in a smirk as he worked the controller with an expertise that surprised her and cheered. Ellie was positive he was picturing her mother in place of the zombie he'd just blown up.

"Maybe if you hadn't criticized every change we've made from the moment you arrived, he'd be willing to listen to you."

Ellie would have thought she'd be immune to Miranda's criticism by now. But her mother belittling the guest rooms had hurt. Ellie had been proud of what they'd accomplished, especially proud of how the doors had turned out. Praise from Nate, Ryder, the judge, and her grandfather had made her think she might have a modicum of talent after all. Now she wondered if they'd just been humoring her all along.

Her mother threw up her arms. "What do you expect? You promised you'd talk him into selling the inn. Instead, you've spent money you don't have on these ridiculous renovations."

Joe cast Ellie a betrayed glance. Obviously, he could hear more than he was letting on. "I didn't promise I'd talk Grandpa into selling," she said, as much for her grandfather's benefit as for her mother's. "I said I'd talk to him about it." And the only reason she had was that her mother had brought Ellie's father and sister into it. "But I also told you how much the inn means to Grandpa."

"Don't waste your breath, Ellie my love," Joe said, removing the headphones. "She won't listen to you. It's always been her way or the highway." He tossed the controller and headphones onto the sectional. Then he looked at his daughter. "But you'll not get your way in this, Miranda. Listen to me, and listen to me good, for this is the last time I'll say it. The inn is not for sale. Not now, not ever. I'll draw my last breath here, and when I do, everything goes to Ellie."

A look of shock came over her mother's face. "What have you done? What have you said to your grandfather to turn him against your sister and brother? Against me, his own daughter. His only child!"

As they tended to do when strong emotions were involved, Ellie's barriers slipped, and so did her mother's. Miranda was afraid she'd shared her secret. But she was even more afraid that she'd misjudged her father and there was nothing she could do to convince him to sell. Her fear had turned to anger that she directed entirely at Ellie.

The bitter emotions coming from her mother were so strong that they choked off Ellie's defense of herself before she got the words out of her mouth.

"Ellie hasn't said a word against Jace and Brianna. Nor you for that matter. And there's plenty she could have said given how you treat her. But I changed my will for one reason and one reason only. Ellie loves the inn as much as me. Her connection to this place runs almost as deep as mine. Not a surprise, I suppose, since you shipped her off to spend her holidays and summers here with me and your mother."

Ellie flinched. She knew her grandfather loved her, but for just a second, she wondered if she'd been a burden on them.

Joe must have noticed her reaction because he reached for her hand, took it in his, and gave it a comforting squeeze. "Some of my best memories are of those times, Ellie my love. You were a blessing to me and your grandmother. Just as you've been one to me all these months."

"I'm sorry I haven't been able to be here with you like Elliana. I actually have a job." Her mother left *I have a life* unsaid, but Ellie heard it as clearly as if she'd said the words out loud.

"And what would be your excuse for trying to sell the inn out from under me, then?"

"You wouldn't understand." Her mother turned away to look out the window.

"Probably not," her grandfather agreed. "But be that as it may, you'll tear up that agreement with the developer today."

Her mother whirled around. "I can't. I can't do that."

Ellie tried to read her mother's panicked thoughts, but they were so tangled up with her fear that her secret would be revealed that Ellie had a hard time seeing the answer she needed. It was like trying to find a clear image beneath a screen of static.

Anger, Ellie thought, her mother's thoughts were easier to read when she was angry rather than scared. "You don't have a choice, Mom. Grandpa has made his decision. You have to abide by it."

"And if I don't…what are you going to do about it, Elliana?"

Ellie pushed past her mother's anger and silent threats to an image that was still coated with Miranda's fear. Two men stood over a map of Mirror Lake. One of the men was Richard, and the other man, she assumed from her mother's reaction, was the developer. Ellie frowned. If Richard was blackmailing her mother, why wasn't her fear directed at him?

"You're asking the wrong person, Miranda. And I've told you exactly what I'll do if you continue with this. I'll bring charges against you for parental abuse."

"That's a lie! I have never abused you in any shape or form," her mother cried.

"Maybe not physically. But what would you call it when a daughter sneaks behind her father's back and signs a paper that she has no legal authority to sign, in an effort to deprive him of his home and his livelihood? I have it on good authority a judge would agree with me."

"I had legal authority until Elliana coerced you into signing power of attorney over to her! If anyone will be charged with elder abuse, it will be her. And don't think I'd hesitate to bring charges against her."

She wouldn't, not if it meant saving her marriage and Brianna.

"So you may want to think twice before you threaten me, Daddy."

Joe slumped on the couch, and Elliana's throat clogged with emotion. He wouldn't press charges against her mother, not if it meant Miranda would go after her. But it was more than just the thought of her mother leveling charges of elder abuse against Ellie that worried him, she realized. He was worried his daughter would do to Ellie what she'd done to Agnes. Her grandfather had known all along that Ellie was psychic. He was afraid of the censure and ridicule she'd face if her secret came out.

"You tried that threat on me the other day, Mom. It didn't work then, and it won't work now. You might want to think back to our conversation." Ellie reached for her grandfather's hand and gave it a reassuring squeeze. "You and I had a conversation too, Grandpa. We agreed to fight and not give up until we win."

"But Ellie, what if she—"

Ellie looked her grandfather in the eye. "I don't care. She can do her worst. All that matters is that we keep the inn in the family." She lifted her gaze to her mother. "If family is so precious to you, I'd suggest you give this up now."

"Don't you dare threaten me with that! The law is on my side." She took her phone out of her purse and brandished it at Ellie. Her mother didn't believe she had the spine to stand up to her. She also knew Ellie was bluffing. She'd never do anything to hurt Bri or her father. "Would you like me to prove that to you? I'll call the police right now and test your theory." Her mother gave her a smile that wasn't a smile at all. "It would be too bad if you were unable to attend tomorrow's big event because you were behind bars, wouldn't it?"

Nate walked into the room. From the vitriol-filled glance he sent her mother, he'd heard what she'd just said.

He moved to Ellie's side, sliding his hand beneath her hair to give her neck a gentle squeeze. "Hey, babe. You okay? It sounded like the conversation was getting a little heated in here."

Her grandfather looked as relieved to see Nate as she was.

Before she could respond to him, her mother snapped, "Who are you?"

Nate placed his left palm on his chest. "I'm wounded you don't remember me, Mrs. MacLeod. We met last weekend. Nate Black. The love of Ellie's life." He winked at Ellie, and Joe chuckled. She could kiss Nate for making him laugh when he'd been close to tears less than a few minutes ago.

"I didn't recognize you without all the hair." Her mother waved her hand as if that was neither here nor there. "As you can see, we're in the middle of a family meeting. A private meeting." She turned her head and nodded at the door, silently ordering him to leave.

"You really know how to hurt a guy, ma'am." He dipped his head to look into Ellie's eyes. She couldn't read his mind, but she didn't need to. His eyes held a promise that everything would be all right. "I count as family, don't I, babe?" he said, then quirked an eyebrow at her grandfather. "Joe?"

"Sure do," her grandfather said while all Ellie could do was nod. She was afraid that if she tried to speak, all that would come out was a half-hysterical laugh.

"Looks like you're outvoted, Mrs. MacLeod. But to be honest with you, no way in hell was I leaving after hearing you threaten Ellie." His lighthearted tone had been replaced by one that sent a chill down Ellie's spine. But he'd misjudged her mother if he thought she'd be cowed.

"Then perhaps you should suggest to Elliana that

she not threaten me, Mr. Black. Or I will have no choice but to call the police."

"Take a look out the window, ma'am."

Her mother drew an annoyed breath through her nose before complying with Nate's request. "And what exactly am I supposed to be looking at, Mr. Black?"

"You see the guy carrying the football? The one all the kids are chasing? That's Gabe Buchanan, Highland Falls chief of police. But I'll save you the embarrassment of calling him in here to level your charge against Ellie. It won't stick, ma'am. If anything, you'll be charged with making a nuisance call. Possibly a charge of harassment if Ellie and Joe are inclined to press charges. Which I'd advise them to do."

"You'd advise them?" Her mother laughed. "Please, you know nothing about this."

Nate slid his warm hand from the back of Ellie's neck and reached into the pocket of his cargo shorts. "That's where you're wrong." He flipped open his wallet to reveal his badge. "I'm an agent with the North Carolina State Bureau of Investigation."

Her mother's gaze jerked from the badge to Nate. "No. You can't be. You're a physiotherapist."

"I might have exaggerated my qualifications to Ellie. In my defense, I was looking for an in with your daughter, and helping out Joe with his therapy was mine."

Clearly, Nate was an accomplished liar. He hadn't missed a beat.

"Now, if you'd like to check out my credentials, feel free to call my boss at the NCSBI." He reeled off a number. "Word of advice, don't share with him that you plan to bring charges against Ellie. He'd be about as unhappy with you threatening her as I am. And seeing as I'm handing out free legal advice today, here's another piece for you. Drop this now, tear up the sale agreement that you made illegally with the developer. Because if you don't, if you harass Ellie and Joe again, I'll open an investigation into you, your son-in-law, and the developer, and I won't stop until I find enough to tie the three of you up in court for a very long time."

The color drained from her mother's face. She fumbled her phone, nearly dropping it before shoving it into her purse. With her head bent, she spent an inordinate amount of time rearranging the contents of her purse. An attempt, Ellie suspected, to regain her composure. Then, with a decisive snap of the clasp, her mother lifted her chin and turned to leave the room. Before she left, she glanced over her shoulder at Ellie. "Whatever happens next is up to you."

Chapter Seventeen

♥

Moments after her mother's dramatic exit, the front door of the inn slammed so hard that the big-screen TV above the mantel shuddered. Ellie blew out the breath she'd been holding and sagged against Nate. "It's over. It's really over. And it's thanks to you." She hugged him. "You were amazing."

He smiled and gave her hair a gentle tug. "Let's hold off on celebrating for now. I don't think you'll have to worry about your mother harassing or threatening you and Joe, but I got the information on Richard's finances that'd I'd been waiting for. He's in financial trouble, Ellie. He made a couple of investments, two that stayed just this side of legal, and he got burned. If this deal is as big as I think it is, he'll have a hard time letting it go."

"Never did like the man. All show, if you know what I mean," Joe said. Then he beamed at Nate. "But I do like you. Consider yourself an honorary member of this family, son." Her grandfather got off the couch and slapped Nate on the back. "I'll go tell Jonathan the good news. I have a feeling this will change his mind about you, and he'll be all in with you dating my granddaughter."

Ellie had been all in with dating Nate for a while now, but this totally sealed the deal. At least for her. Nate looked decidedly uncomfortable at the idea of having another matchmaker to contend with.

"Grandpa, I need to talk to you for a minute," Ellie said.

Her grandfather nodded as if he guessed what she wanted to talk about. He sat down and picked up the video game controller.

Nate glanced from her to Joe. "I'll give you a minute. Let everyone know you guys are okay and there was no bloodshed. Sadie, Abby, and Mallory were worried about you."

Ellie glanced at the vent in the ceiling. The *Bridgerton* room was right above it. "They heard everything, didn't they?"

Nate nodded, the corner of his mouth twitching as if he was holding back a grin. "You're lucky you got me instead of Sadie, Abby, and Mallory. They were all set to pick up the swords they're decorating the walls with and come to your rescue. Those are three bloodthirsty women."

Ellie laughed. They weren't decorating the walls with swords. She'd vetoed the idea. But even if they'd come to her rescue brandishing swords, she didn't think they would have shut her mother down as completely and as effectively as Nate. "They're also very good friends," she said. "Tell them I'll be up to help them in a minute."

"They were finishing up the wallpaper when I left, and I've been given strict orders that you need to take it easy."

"That's sweet, but I have to get ready for tomorrow's brunch and tours. There are sandwiches to make, and—"

A disembodied voice that sounded a little like Abby's came through the vent. "Nate, get her out of here. She needs a break, and she won't take one if she stays."

Ellie rolled her eyes at the vent. "I don't need a break."

"Do too," her grandfather said without looking away from the TV screen, where he was happily blowing up more zombies.

"Sorry, Ellie. They're a lot scarier than you are," Nate said as he walked away. Then he glanced over his shoulder. "You might want to change before we go."

To avoid her mother criticizing her appearance, Ellie had put on a sundress. "I'm not going for another jog. I won't be able to get out of bed tomorrow." The muscles in her calves had protested when she'd gotten up this morning, which went to show how terribly out of shape she was.

"Yeah, I didn't think you'd be up for another *walk*. I saw you inching your way down the stairs this morning, remember?"

"How could I forget? You told me I was walking like I was a hundred."

"I was being kind."

"Goodbye, Nate."

She shook her head as he left the room laughing, then turned to her grandfather, who was grinning at her. "He's a keeper, Ellie my love."

"I agree with you, Grandpa. But Nate is a man who likes his freedom. He's not interested in a relationship."

"Never knew a man who thought he was. Not until the right woman came along. Trust me, I know what I'm talking about. I had no intention of settling down until I met your grandmother." He put down the controller. "It was your grandmother who figured out you'd inherited Agnes's gift, you know."

Ellie glanced at the vent. This was one conversation she didn't want anyone to overhear. "Maybe we should talk in your room."

Her grandfather followed her gaze and nodded, standing up to lead the way into his room. Ellie closed the door behind them, following him into his sitting area by the picture window. Outside, the kids were laughing, running after Finn, Sadie and Chase's golden retriever, who'd stolen the football.

Ellie spotted Ryder and smiled. This was the happiest she'd seen him since he'd arrived. Down by the dock, Chase was laughing at something Nate had said. From Nate's exasperated expression, it wasn't the response he'd expected or wanted. She drew her gaze from Nate's handsome face and took a seat in the chair beside her grandfather.

"How did Grandma Mary know?"

"She went to a church tea and heard the talk about Agnes. At the time, we had no idea what your mother had put Agnes through. We would have put a stop to it had we known. The mayor took your grandmother aside and filled her in at the tea, asking her to stand up with them against some of the church ladies who wanted Agnes cast out. They believed her abilities were the work of the devil."

Her mother had said the same thing to Ellie after one of the therapists Miranda had dragged Ellie to had concluded she was psychic, not crazy. "Grandma Mary didn't think that, did she?"

"No, she thought they were a bunch of closed-minded ninnies, which was what she told them. It made a difference coming from her, given that your mother was the one who'd started the rumors. Mary was as mad as a hornet when she got home from the tea. She called your mother straight away and gave her a tongue-lashing the likes I've never heard. Their relationship was never the same after that." He cast a sad glance at the photo of Ellie's grandmother and mother on the mantel. "After seeing the way Miranda treated you, neither of us wanted much to do with her. But we held our tongues. We were afraid she wouldn't let you come and stay with us or let us see your brother and sister."

So it wasn't just that Ellie had learned a secret her mother would guard with her life—Miranda blamed her for the loss of the love and respect of her parents. Her mother wouldn't think to look at her own actions. As Ellie had learned over the years, nothing was ever

Miranda's fault. She was always quick to cast blame elsewhere.

"How did Grandma Mary figure out I was psychic?"

"She used to sneak you kids over to see your Granny MacLeod whenever she got the chance. On one of those visits, your granny told Mary that you'd inherit her abilities. Agnes asked Mary to promise we'd protect you from your mother. Your grandmother gave her word, but truth be told, Mary didn't believe in the all that woo-woo nonsense. Neither did I."

"But Grandma Mary stood up for Granny MacLeod."

"She did, and she'd do it again. Didn't mean she believed Agnes could tell someone's future. But nor would she allow your granny to be persecuted for her beliefs."

"What changed Grandma Mary's mind?"

"It took a while. You were careful to hide your abilities. But your grandma was a smart one. She began noticing that you'd do things before we even asked, so she made a game of it. Got me in on the act."

"What do you mean?"

"We'd take turns thinking about the most outlandish things we'd want you to do. They had to be something out of the ordinary or it would be too easy to brush off as coincidence." He gave her a mischievous smile. "Remember the time you painted the tree by the lake blue? Or the time you made cupcakes frosted with ranch dressing and topped with bacon bits and cherry tomatoes?"

"Or the time I dug up Grandma Mary's wildflower garden in the front and filled it with rhododendrons?"

He laughed. "I forgot about that. Your grandmother wasn't happy with me about that one. I slept in a guest room for a week." The twinkle in his eyes faded. "It wasn't five minutes after we'd think the thought that you'd be rushing out to get it done. You were so anxious to please us, as though you were afraid we'd send you away if you didn't. It broke our hearts, Ellie my love. It truly did. We tried to get your mother to leave you with us full-time, but your father wouldn't hear of it. I blame myself for that. I should have told him. I should have told him everything."

"Don't blame yourself, Grandpa. If anyone should have told Dad, it should have been me." She'd come close a few times, but she'd been afraid her father would reject her like her mother had, and she couldn't risk him learning why her mother hated her. "But why didn't you ever say anything to me?"

"It was our way of protecting you. We didn't want you to suffer like your granny." He reached for her hand. "It didn't make a lick of difference to us. But as Agnes can attest, people aren't always kind to those who are different. They can be cruel."

She leaned over and hugged him. "I was lucky to have you and Grandma looking out for me. Thank you, and thank you for telling me."

"As I told your mother, you were a blessing to me and your grandmother. And don't you worry, your secret is safe with me. I'd never tell anyone." He patted her back. "Now off you go and enjoy yourself with Nate. You deserve to take a break."

"I really shouldn't. There's too much to do for tomorrow."

"You leave it to me and Jonathan. All we have to do is slap some of those fillings you made this morning onto the bread and cut them into triangles."

Now she was more nervous about leaving than she had been. But her grandfather countered every argument Ellie made to stick around. So in the end she reluctantly agreed.

She kissed his cheek and headed for her room. Once she'd changed into a yellow T-shirt and a pair of denim capris, she checked out the *Bridgerton* room.

The wainscoting Nate and Hunter had put up that morning worked beautifully with the blue wallpaper with its lacy white pattern that Abby, Sadie, and Mallory had hung on the upper two-thirds of the walls. The blue satin drapes with gold piping looked as wonderful as Ellie had hoped, as did the gold-and-blue floral satin bedspread against the powder-blue velvet headboard. All that was left for Ellie to do was hang the prints in their heavy gilded frames and dress the nightstands.

It wouldn't take her long to finish up, she thought, looking around for the hammer and finishing nails. She'd feel better if the room was complete before she left. She found what she was looking for on the dresser and picked up one of the framed prints.

"I told you she'd be here," she heard her cousin say behind her.

Ellie turned to see Sadie, Chase, and Nate watching her from the doorway.

Sadie walked over and took the hammer, nails,

and print from her and put them on the bed. "We've got this."

"I know you do. You guys did an amazing job on the room. It's just—"

Sadie put her hands on Ellie's shoulders, turning her toward the door. "Go."

"But—" Ellie went to object, only to be cut off by her cousin again.

"Chase and I will take care of this, and Abby, Mallory, and the kids have the sandwiches covered."

"Okay, okay. If Grandpa and Jonathan want to help, don't let them cut the sandwiches. The flower cookie cutters are on the counter on top of the bread box."

"Yes, and we found the pink-, yellow-, and blue-dyed sandwich bread," Sadie said, giving Ellie a light push toward Nate. "Go have fun, kids."

Chase handed Nate a black duffel bag and waggled his eyebrows. "Don't do anything we wouldn't do." He closed the door in their faces.

From behind the door, Sadie released a startled shriek. Ellie went to open the door to see what was wrong, but her cousin's shriek was immediately followed by laughter. Then the room went quiet.

"Don't you dare mess up the bed, you guys!" Ellie called through the door.

"I can pretty much guarantee they'll mess up the bed, but you'll never know it. Chase is a neat freak. He won't leave the room until everything is in order." Nate nodded at the stairs. "Let's get out of here."

"What about Ryder?" she asked, following him down the stairs.

"He won't even know we're gone. He's having a blast with Gabe and Mallory's boys."

"Okay, so where exactly are we going? And what's in the bag?" she asked as they left the inn.

"A picnic, according to Chase and Sadie." Nate walked toward his motorcycle. "And we're not going far. Just over to the cabins. Sadie says there's a great spot for a picnic."

"She's right. We used to go when we were kids. It was one of our favorite spots. We decorated the trees with solar fairy lights. Actually, now that I think about it, those were probably the lights you saw from the balcony last Saturday."

"Could be," he said, but there was a skeptical tone in his voice.

Before she had a chance to question him, he shut the compartment he'd put the duffel bag into and handed her a helmet. "Hop on."

She swung her leg over the seat and put on her helmet.

He laughed. "Good try." Placing his hands on her hips, he positioned her on the back of the bike instead of the front, where she'd been sitting.

"You're no fun," she said as he got on and put on his helmet.

He glanced at her over his shoulder. "That's the first time anyone has ever said that to me." He winked and put down his visor. Then he started the motorcycle. "Hang on."

She just bet all the women Nate *dated* thought he was a whole lot of fun. She put her arms around him, wishing she'd have the opportunity to experience what those other women had with him. Except in some ways, she had. Nate was fun to be with. He made her smile. He made her laugh. It's just that she wanted more from him, she thought, as his hard stomach muscles flexed beneath her fingers.

She pushed the thought from her head and enjoyed the ride. It was exhilarating with the wind rushing around them, freeing even. Being pressed snug against Nate only added to her enjoyment. She admired the power in his big frame, the ease with which he maneuvered the motorcycle off the dirt road and onto the rutted path through the woods. Her only disappointment was that the ride was over too soon. He brought the Harley to a stop on the outer edge of the clearing.

"I told you," she said as she got off the bike and removed her helmet. She lifted her chin at the lights draped among the upper limbs of the trees.

"How the hell did you get them up that high?" Nate asked, removing his helmet to look up at the trees.

"Sadie climbed the trees. I used a ladder. She's more daring than me." Ellie smiled at the memories and glanced around. "It hasn't changed that much. The cabins have, obviously. They're looking pretty run down."

"I had an idea about that that I wanted to run by you."

"Ah, so you had an ulterior motive for bringing me here."

"I did," he said, then sighed when he opened the duffel bag. "And apparently Sadie and Chase had an ulterior motive for sending us here." He tilted the bag to show her the contents. It contained a bottle of wine, candles, grapes, cheese, cold meats, and buns.

She pointed at the navy nylon fabric rolled up at the bottom of the bag. "Is that a sleeping bag?"

"Knowing Chase, it is." He shook his head. "How did he get all this crap in here?"

"I have no idea, but I really need him to teach me how to pack like that."

"You and me both," Nate said, walking through the clearing. "This spot look good to you?"

Above them the sky was clearly visible, and the trees didn't completely block out the view of the lake. "Perfect," she said, and Nate began unloading the bag. He piled the food in her arms and then took out the sleeping bag and laid it on the ground.

"Seriously. How does he do it? The guy's a magician," Nate said, staring down at the double sleeping bag.

And a matchmaker with no shame, Ellie thought, positive her cheeks were flushed. "It'll certainly make it more comfortable than sitting on the ground."

"I'm pretty sure he didn't intend for us to sit on it, Ellie," Nate said, sounding amused.

She rolled her eyes. "I know what he intended us to do with the sleeping bag, Nate. I'm not a twenty-year-old virgin. I'm a sexually experienced thirty-three-year-old woman."

He opened his mouth and then closed it, taking the bottle of wine and the candles from her arms.

"Don't worry, in a couple of days you won't have to put up with the matchmakers of Highland Falls. I can almost guarantee that, as soon as Spencer arrives and they find out we were once engaged, they'll turn their matchmaking sights on him and me." She sat on the sleeping bag, wanting nothing more than to lie back and close her eyes and not wake up until Spencer left town. Having everyone trying to set up her and Nate was one thing—she'd totally be on board with that plan. But having them set up her and Spencer was a whole other story.

"No way. They've already decided we're a perfect match, and nothing will change their minds." He joined her on the sleeping bag, opened the bottle of wine, and poured the merlot into the tiny plastic glasses. "Trust me, I know what I'm talking about," he said as he handed her a glass of wine.

"I wish you were right, Nate. But you're not. Just think about it," she said when he went to object. "Spencer is judging the contest, and there's nothing this town wants more than to win. They'll think I'm the ace up their sleeves. It won't matter to them that we're no longer together. I told you, Abby already suggested I seduce him," she said, laying out the food on the paper plates.

"She was joking. There's no way she'd expect you to do something like that."

"Maybe not, but that's because she's a friend. Some of the other business owners in town might not have any qualms asking me to take one for the team."

Nate choked on his wine. "Damn it, Ellie." He wiped off his black T-shirt with a napkin. "Anyone suggests you sleep with the guy, you tell me, and I'll make sure no one says that crap to you again."

She raised an eyebrow. "You do realize I'm perfectly capable of telling them myself, don't you?"

"Five older sisters, remember? And I'll tell you the same thing I'd tell them. No one talks smack about the people I lo...care about and gets away with it."

Ellie's glass of wine stalled halfway to her mouth when he nearly used the L-word in reference to her. *Get a grip*, she told herself. *He* cares *about you. He doesn't* love *you.* She took a sip of her wine to moisten her suddenly dry throat. "To be honest, I'm not as worried about the ones who are open about their expectations. I'm worried about the sneaky ones. The business owners who've pulled out all the stops. Everything they do and say leads back to love and romance. I guarantee that when I take Spencer on the tour of Main Street, they'll seat us at their most romantic spots and do everything they can to put us in the mood for love." Like having them sit on a sleeping bag drinking wine surrounded by the faint glow of fairy lights in the forest and a view of the sun setting on Mirror Lake.

"What do you mean you're taking your ex on a tour of Main Street?"

"It's not just the tour of Main Street." She removed her phone from the pocket of her capris and brought up the itinerary. She turned the screen toward Nate.

A muscle in his jaw pulsed as he scanned the list of events. "Why the hell is your name beside his at every one of the events?"

She sighed. "Why do you think, Nate?"

He tossed back his wine and then poured himself another glass before topping up hers. He stared at the lake and then glanced at her. "You know, you could avoid all of this if we just pretend we're together. Half the town thinks we are anyway, so they're not going to call us out on the lie. Same goes for the other half that wish it were true."

"That might work," Ellie said, fighting back a smile. Even if she could read Nate's mind, she didn't have to. He was clearly jealous of Spencer, and the poor man had no idea. If it wouldn't give her feelings for him away, she'd stand up and do a happy dance.

"Might? Be serious. It's the perfect plan."

"I don't know. It would be pretty embarrassing if Spencer figured out that we were fake-dating. He'd probably think it was because I'm still in love with him."

His eyes narrowed. "You're not, are you?"

"No, of course not. But he always had a bit of an ego. He's also good at reading body language, and I don't know if we're good enough actors to pull it off. It's hard to fake physical chemistry."

"We don't have to fake it, Ellie. We have it in spades," he muttered, not looking particularly pleased about it.

"You're right. We—"

"Thank you," he said, all gruff and growly.

"You didn't let me finish," she said, barely managing to keep the laughter from her voice. "I was going to say couples in love act differently than we do. Just look at Sadie and Chase, Mallory and Gabe, Abby and Hunter. When they're in a room together, they're either standing close or they're following each other with their eyes. They always know where the other one is, sharing secret glances and smiles. And they can't keep their hands off of each other. It's probably because they're intimate, and that's not something we can fake."

Nate choked on his wine again, but this time he didn't spill any on himself. "Damn it, Ellie. You can't keep saying stuff like that to me."

"Why not?"

"You know damn well why not." He put down his wineglass and placed his hands on her shoulders, turning her to face him. "You know I want you. You know I have a hard time keeping my hands off you, a hard time keeping from kissing you every time we're within five feet of each other."

She put down her glass and slipped her arms around his neck. "There's less than six inches between us now, and you don't seem to be having trouble not kissing—"

He swore softly as he pulled her against him, his eyes holding hers as he lowered his head, claiming her mouth in a kiss unlike any kiss he'd given her before. He cradled the back of her head in his big hand, lowering her onto the sleeping bag, his body hot and heavy covering hers. She wanted, no, needed to be closer and wrapped her legs around his hips, deepening the kiss as she did, her tongue tangling with his in a wild, passionate dance.

Nate's groan reverberated against her lips as he

broke the kiss and rested his forehead against hers. "I don't think this is a good idea."

"I think it's a really good idea," she said, kissing her way down his throat.

"You're killing me here, Ellie. I can't give you what you need."

She rocked her hips. "I'm pretty sure that you can."

He choked out a laugh. "I'm not talking about sex. I'm talking about what happens after. I'm not a guy who sticks around. I don't do love and romance. I don't do long-term relationships and marriage."

"I'm not asking more from you than you're willing to give. I just want this, us together, making love under the stars."

"Are you sure about that?"

Maybe he was right. Maybe this was a mistake, a mistake that she might not recover from because, while Nate had made it clear that he didn't want more than a physical relationship, she did. She wanted so much more. Afraid she'd get a little emotional if she said the words, if she told him she wasn't sure at all, she went to shake her head instead. But the rebellious side of her stopped that unhappy head shake with a thought. What if this was exactly what needed to happen for Nate to realize how good they could be together?

"I've never been more sure of anything in my life," she whispered, drawing his mouth back to hers.

Chapter Eighteen

♥

Nate opened one eye, squinting up at the bright blue sky and then down at the woman asleep in his arms. With her long silky hair spread over his chest, Ellie was pressed naked against his side with one leg flung over his. And instead of feeling trapped, a feeling that had him reaching for his boots the moment he woke up after spending the night with a woman, all he wanted to do was lie there with Ellie in his arms. He swore under his breath.

She lifted her head, kissed his chest, and offered him a sleepy smile. "H—" She broke off as she took in their surroundings. "Nate, it's morning!" She nearly emasculated him trying to get out of the sleeping bag.

"Damn it, Ellie, give me a minute."

"I don't have a minute!" she said, wriggling out of the open end of the sleeping bag. She searched the ground. "I can't find my phone. Where's yours? I need to know the time." With her hand, she motioned for him to hurry. But apparently he wasn't fast enough because, less than a second later, she was running from the clearing.

"Ellie, you're naked!" And so gorgeous, with the sun glistening off the midnight-black hair streaming behind her and on that incredible body he'd worshipped every inch of last night, he nearly swallowed his tongue.

She stopped, looked down at herself, then shrugged. "No one can see me here."

"You don't know that," he shouted after her, thinking about the guy who'd been taking photos the other day. Nate tossed the sleeping bag aside, found his jeans, and quickly pulled them on. As he did, he scanned the area for their phones and her clothes. He spotted her T-shirt a couple yards away and had a visceral memory of stripping it off her. It was a memory he wouldn't soon forget. He had a feeling he wouldn't get a single second of the night they'd spent together out of his head. Worse, he didn't want to.

"Idiot," he muttered at himself as he walked to retrieve her T-shirt. He'd messed up big-time. He never should have made love with Ellie. *Sex, you had sex,* he told himself. But even as he repeated the word in his head, he knew it wasn't true. It had been more. Everything with Ellie was more. He scooped up her T-shirt, spotted their phones nearby, and grabbed them.

"Ellie, it's six thirty. We've got plenty of time," he called out, jogging in the direction she'd gone. He found her half-hidden behind the cabin closest to the lake, peeking around the side of it.

"What are you doing?" he asked, then remembered he had her T-shirt in his hand. "Here." He tossed it to her from where he stood, afraid that if he got too close, he wouldn't be able to resist the temptation that was Ellie MacLeod.

She caught it, seemingly unfazed that she was naked. The woman was completely comfortable with her body, which surprised him. In his experience, most women weren't. Then again, when a woman looked as incredible as Ellie did, he supposed he shouldn't be surprised.

She shushed him. "Voices carry on the water. I'm checking to see who's at the inn. I only have a view of the edge of the parking lot from here. You go check." She pulled the T-shirt over her head.

"It's not like it will change anything, Ellie." He kept his eyes firmly on the ground. "Everyone knows we were out all night."

"Not necessarily. We can say we went for an early breakfast. But if Granny, Sadie, or Abby are there, we won't be able to fool them. Go." She waved him off.

He sighed and walked down to the water's edge. "We're good. The truck is the only vehicle in the parking lot." From the corner of his eye, he caught movement on the dock.

Joe waved. "Hey there, son. You kids have a nice, romantic night?"

* * *

"It's your fault," Nate told Chase as they replenished their trays with sandwiches in the kitchen six hours later.

Chase grinned. "I didn't tell you to stay out all night or to let Joe see you this morning." He popped a pink flower sandwich into his mouth.

"No, but you put the sleeping bag in there, and the wine." It was a lame argument. He had no one to blame but himself. And the woman currently serving tea to a table of six. Ellie looked up and their gazes met and held. She smiled at him. There was nothing flirtatious or sexy about her smile, but his body reacted as if she'd just promised him a night like the one they'd shared.

"Sorry to be the one to break it to you. But it had nothing to do with the sleeping bag and wine. You haven't taken your eyes off Ellie since Sadie and I arrived. You follow her every move, and she does the same with you. Then you both get these sappy looks on your faces and smile at each other. Face it, buddy. You're in love with her."

I'm not smiling, he started to say, but then he realized he was. *Damn it.* "Maybe you've been married too long to recognize the difference. It's lust, not love, bro." And just like that, Nate's conversation with Ellie about couples in love came back to him. The conversation they'd had seconds before they'd made love. Seconds before they'd had *sex*, he corrected his wayward brain, at the same time remembering what Ellie had said couples in love do. Exactly what his best friend said *they* were doing.

Chase patted him on the back. "Keep telling yourself that if it makes you feel better."

Sadie rushed over and grabbed the sandwich her husband was about to pop into his mouth. "Stop eating the sandwiches. We have another seating in twenty minutes."

Right, the one where Nate's family would take up half the dining room. He looked down at the kilt he'd been strong-armed into wearing by Abby. She'd had the *brilliant* idea that the staff at the inn should be dressed in Highland garb to pay tribute to the town's Scottish roots and name. Nate would never live this down. His brothers-in-law would tease him mercilessly. At least Chase would have to endure it too.

"Hey," Chase protested when Sadie popped the sandwich into her mouth. "How come you get to eat it and I don't?"

She swallowed, then grinned and patted her husband's cheek. "Because you've had four and I haven't had any."

And she knew this because she'd been sharing flirty glances with her husband the entire time she was waiting on tables. Nate and Ellie had been doing the same, only their glances weren't flirty. They were heated, fueled by the memory of last night.

Nate groaned. How could he have been so stupid?

Sadie frowned at him. "What's wrong?"

"Don't worry, honey. He'll be fine. He's just realized he's in love with Ellie."

"I'm not in love with her. I'm in..." Yeah, that's not something he'd say to her cousin. "I'm in like with her." And now he sounded like he was in grade school. He was beginning to wonder if he'd done permanent damage to his brain cells along with temporarily losing his mind last night.

Sadie's eyes danced with amusement. "I'm glad you *like* my cousin, Nate. She deserves someone who *likes* her as much as you seem to." She glanced at the trays they'd loaded with sandwiches. "You know, we should probably wrap those up and put them in the refrigerator. We'll need them for the next sitting. You can serve the trays of desserts instead." She pointed at the counter. "We have more in the fridge."

Nate had to figure out a way to be gone when his family arrived, or, at the very least, relieved of his serving duties and the kilt he was wearing. Ellie and Sadie looked cute in their uniforms of black T-shirts and plaid skirts. He and Chase just looked like idiots.

"Are Abby and Mallory on duty for the next shift?" he asked Sadie, as if Ellie hadn't already asked him to take on serving duties for all three seatings.

"I thought Ellie told you. The baby's fussy, so Abby can't make it. And Mallory and Gabe took the kids for a hike."

Since Ryder and Toby had spent the night at the Buchanans', Nate couldn't complain. They'd saved him having to explain where he and Ellie had been all night. Neither Joe nor the judge had bought their excuse that they'd taken off early that morning to check out the cabins. Although Joe had given Nate's idea to fix up the cabins with Ryder next week the thumbs-up.

Thinking about the older men, he asked, "What about Joe and the judge? They should be back from the grocery store by then. They left over an hour ago."

"If that's where they actually went, they would be," Sadie said. "They're playing poker at Granny's. She'll be here as soon as Michaela goes down for her nap. Somewhere around one thirty, I'd think. If you have something to do, I'm sure she'd be happy to fill in for you."

The last thing he wanted was Mrs. M anywhere near his family. "It's okay. You can tell Mrs. M to stay home with the baby."

"As much as she loves Michaela, there's no way she'd pass up the opportunity to meet your family. We might be able to get Hunter to fill in for you though."

"Don't worry about it. I'm good." No way was he leaving Mrs. M to her own devices.

"Great." Sadie skirted the counter to pick up a dessert tray. Chase joined her, and the two of them started whispering and giggling like a couple of lovesick teenagers.

"You realize everyone can see you," he said when he caught them sharing a kiss. He was about to tell them to get a room but was afraid they'd take him up on the suggestion and leave him on his own.

With a disgusted sigh, he retrieved the tray before Sadie dropped it and walked to the closest table. "Time for dessert, ladies. What's your pleasure?" He crouched by the table to give them a better view of the cupcakes, shortbread, and tarts on the tray.

"You are, laddie," the older woman on his left chortled. "How about a kiss to go with my cupcake?"

"How about two cupcakes inst—" He broke off when the woman on his right pushed back her chair, folding herself in half in an attempt to get a look under his kilt.

He grabbed the back of her leopard-print blouse to save her from taking a header out of her chair while pushing to his feet at the same time, balancing the dessert tray in his other hand. "I warned you what would happen the last time you tried to sneak a peek, Jeannie. No dessert for you."

"That's not fair. I didn't get so much as a little look." She pouted.

"He's a big strong lad, Jeannie. I doubt anything about him is *little*," the woman to her right said, giving Nate a lascivious grin while the rest of her tablemates, including Jeannie, broke up in peals of laughter.

Nate narrowed his eyes at them before picking up Jeannie's teacup and bringing it to his nose. His eyes burned from the overpowering smell of whiskey. He shook his head to clear it, then asked, "Which one of you is supplying the booze?"

All five of them reached into their purses and pulled out flasks. "I'll say one thing for you, you ladies know your whiskey. But you've also had enough, and you won't be driving home."

"We didn't plan to. We want a ride on your hog," Jeannie said.

"On my—"

"Are you ladies giving Nate a hard time again?" Ellie asked, coming to stand beside him.

"Just having a little fun with him, dear," Jeannie said, helping herself to two tarts. "We heard you've been having fun with him too."

"Um, yes. Nate's a lot of fun to work with," Ellie said, her cheeks turning pink.

"I'm sure he is, but that's not what I was talking—"

Her blush deepening, Ellie handed Nate the teapot. Then she took the tray of desserts from him, making room for it on the table. "There you go, ladies. Enjoy." She took him by the arm, steering him away from the table.

"Honestly, Grandpa is a bigger gossip than Granny." She looked around, no doubt seeing the same thing he was, that everyone was watching them. "Maybe it's for the best. We obviously won't have a hard time convincing anyone we're together."

Right, they were back to fake-dating. And this time, it was his own fault. He couldn't blame sleep deprivation or wanting a little fun. Granted, being with Ellie had been a hell of a lot of fun. So much *fun*, he was afraid she'd ruined him for any other woman. He'd spend the rest of his days living like a monk. All because he'd been jealous at the idea of Ellie spending time with another man. A first for him. He didn't have a jealous bone in his body.

"Is something wrong?" Ellie asked, placing a hand on his arm.

He ran a finger along the neck of his T-shirt, stretching it out. It felt like he was wearing a shirt two sizes too small and a tie that fit like a noose. He needed to put an end to this now. Before it was too late. But looking into Ellie's beautiful eyes, he couldn't say the words. "No. It's all good. But how about we hold off with the fake-dating until your ex arrives?"

She gave him a smile that seemed forced. "Sure. Whatever you want."

That smile had him backtracking. "At least until we get rid of my family."

She looked relieved, like that explained his sudden change of heart. "Oh, okay." She smiled then, a smile that was as warm and as beautiful as she was. And despite the voice in his head telling him he was an idiot for not putting an end to this now—and it was a voice that hadn't steered him wrong in the past—he returned her smile.

Only she was smiling at someone behind him, waving at them too. "Your family just arrived. I'll take them for a tour of the guest rooms first. You don't mind, do you?"

"Go for it," he said, gratified for the reprieve. Putting up with the teasing of Jeannie and her friends would be easier than putting up with his family's.

As Ellie hurried from his side, he figured he should at least turn around and acknowledge his family. Ellie was greeting his sisters and nieces like they were long-lost friends, while his five brothers-in-law were standing in the opening between the reception area and dining room with their phones raised, laughing and taking pictures. Of him. Standing there in a skirt and holding a teapot. He gave them the middle finger.

"Nate, I need more tea." A woman held up a teacup three tables over from Jeannie's.

The teapot was empty. "I'll be right with you." He sighed when four other women held their cups in the air. "With all of you."

Sadie and Chase waylaid him as he walked to the

kitchen. "We need to hurry everyone along," Sadie said. "People are arriving for the next seating."

"It's just my family. Ellie's taking them to see the guest rooms."

"A few others have just arrived."

Nate looked over his shoulder. Several women stood waiting where his brothers-in-law had been moments before. He glanced at Jeannie's table. "I can get rid of a few of them for you right now." By the time he'd driven each of them home on his bike, his family should be ready to head out. He shared his plan with Sadie and Chase without sharing the reason behind it.

"That's sweet of you to offer, Nate. But I have to pick up Granny anyway. I'll drop them off. Besides, I'm sure you want to spend time with your family." Before he could assure her he didn't, Sadie walked over to Jeannie's table.

Chase laughed. "Good try, buddy."

Twenty minutes later, Chase was no longer laughing as he helped serve Nate's family. They took up four tables. "It's not a skirt. It's a kilt," Nate heard Chase telling his boss and Nate's least favorite brother-in-law, who hadn't stopped teasing them since he sat down.

Which is why after saying hi, hugging and kissing every female member of his family, and enduring ten minutes of his sisters and nieces teasing and singing Ellie's praises, Nate stayed busy serving the other tables. But Ellie had pulled up a chair beside Val, and the two of them were involved in an animated conversation with his other sisters. As though she sensed his attention, Ellie looked at him and smiled. All five of his sisters did the same. He recognized those smiles and knew he was in serious trouble. Before he shot them a warning look in return, a commotion at the other end of the dining room drew his attention.

The older women at the table closest to the entrance were all aflutter, patting their chests and batting their eyes at a guy wearing a pink button-down, navy pants, and a pair of brown dress shoes that probably cost more than Nate made in a month. Ditto on the sunglasses that he removed, giving the older women a smile that indicated he was used to garnering attention wherever he went. Nate didn't see the appeal, but then again, he wasn't a woman.

Nate was about to replenish his empty sandwich tray when Ellie hurried over to him. She fisted her hands in his T-shirt and tipped her head back. "Kiss me," she said, sounding desperate.

"What's going on?"

"Spencer," she hissed. "He's not supposed to be here until Tuesday!"

"That's your ex?" He glanced back at the man half the women in the dining room were now staring at with their hearts in their eyes, including the female members of Nate's own family. But there was only one woman who held Spencer's attention, and that was Ellie.

"Yes! And I have no idea why he's here."

Nate knew exactly why her ex was here. *Tough luck, asshat*, he thought. No way was Nate about to let the guy think Ellie had been wasting away pining for him or that he had a chance in hell of winning her back.

Sliding an arm around Ellie's waist, Nate drew her tight against him and lowered his head to kiss her. It was a good kiss considering she was distracted and frantic, but it would take more than this kiss to convince her ex she was done with him. Thinking back to the romantic movies his sisters had subjected to him to, Nate bent Ellie low over his arm.

A small gasp escaped from her parted, kiss-swollen lips. Nate smiled down at her. "I'd never let you fall, Ellie."

She stared up at him, bringing her hand to cup the side of his face. "I already have."

Chapter Nineteen

♥

Oh yes, Ellie had fallen for Nate big-time. Somewhere over the course of the past few days, she'd gone from crushing on him to falling for him. Spending last night in the clearing with him under the stars had sent her over the edge. There was no going back now. She could no longer pretend that she wasn't in love with the man who'd bent her over his arm in a move straight out of a romantic movie. In front of his entire family. She wondered if he realized what he had done.

He would now, she thought at the whistling and clapping coming from his family's tables. Right on cue, his smile went from reassuringly sweet to outright panicked. Or maybe he'd just realized she wasn't talking about falling on the ground but falling for him. Either way, she imagined the result would be the same. She just hoped it didn't send him running for the hills.

"Baby brother, you're supposed to kiss her again," his sister Val called out.

"He must have missed that part of the movie," one of his other sisters said.

"Kiss her, Uncle Nate. Kiss her!" his nieces called in their singsong voices.

Nate's sun-bronzed cheeks reddened, whether from anger or embarrassment she wasn't sure, but he planted his hands on her waist, lifted her up, and put her over his shoulder. If he was making a run for the hills with her, she was totally on board with that. She wanted to be anywhere other than in the dining room with Spencer.

Ignoring their audience, who were now on their feet hooting and hollering, Nate stalked to the sliding glass door and threw it open. Feeling like she had to do something other than just hang off his back, Ellie lifted her head and offered a smile to their audience and a little wave. "We won't be long."

Nate sighed at the inappropriate comments that followed them onto the patio. Ellie noticed that the only person in the dining room who didn't seem to be enjoying the show was Spencer. He stood with his arms crossed, an irritated expression on his handsome face. She didn't think it had anything to do with her being with Nate. It was just that Spencer was used to being the center of attention.

Ellie tapped Nate on the back as he strode off the patio. "You can put me down now."

"Sorry." He slid her off his shoulder and set her on her feet. "I don't know what the hell came over me."

Ellie had a fairly good idea what had set him off, but instead of sharing her thoughts, she said, "I think you were just looking for the quickest escape route, and you didn't want to leave me behind."

He rubbed the back of his neck. "Yeah. Maybe. But I didn't do either of us any favors. I've just created more for them to gossip about."

"Well, that was kind of the point, wasn't it? No one will question that we're together now." Except Nate. To him, this was all an act.

"Especially my family." He glanced over his shoulder and shook his head. "Look at them."

His sisters and nieces had their faces pressed to the glass. When they saw Nate was looking at them, they made hearts with their fingers.

Ellie held back a laugh. She loved his family. She especially loved how much they loved Nate. "They're very sweet."

"*Sweet* isn't the word I'd use to describe them." He groaned. "Mrs. M is here. I was hoping Michaela wouldn't go down for her nap, and she'd be stuck at home."

Ellie's grandmother was smack-dab in the middle of Nate's family, introducing herself to his sisters and nieces. Obviously having the same thought, Ellie and Nate hurried to the patio door, opening it to say, "Don't shake her hand."

"Don't mind them," her grandmother said, and held up her hands. They were covered in red plaid gloves that matched her kilt. Sadie must have gotten her to wear them. Their grandmother couldn't tell fortunes when wearing gloves. Agnes looped her arms through two of Nate's sisters'. "Now don't you think autumn is a lovely time for a wedding?" she said, winking at Ellie and Nate.

Nate shut the door, turned, and strode off the patio.

"Where are you going?" Ellie called after him.

"For a ride."

"Okay, but don't you think you should change first?"

He shook his head. "Unlike what you, Jeannie, and her friends seem to think, I'm not commando under this thing. I have on bike shorts." His eyes narrowed at her. "What do you have on?"

"Unlike you, I went the traditional route," she teased in hopes of lightening his mood.

"Are you seriously telling me you have nothing on under your skirt?" He stalked back to her.

As he got up close and personal, she saw that his eyes were almost completely black. Maybe teasing him wasn't such a good idea, she thought, when, in response to the heat in his eyes, she felt a little warm herself. But it was better than him looking like he wanted to tear someone's head off. Now he just looked like he wanted to tear her skirt off, which she would have been on board with if they didn't have an audience.

Sadie opened the door and stepped onto the patio. Her eyes were wide, and she looked a little panicked. "Ellie, what are you doing out here?" Sadie glanced from her to Nate. "Am I interrupting something?"

"Yes," Nate said at the same time that Ellie said, "No."

"Ah, okay, I'll just leave you to it. But please don't be too long. Ellie, Spencer is here, and he wants to talk to you."

"Not happening," Nate said.

"Nate, I have to talk to him. There's too much riding on this."

"No, you don't," he said.

"Ellie's right, Nate. She has to talk to him. He's obviously here for a reason." The phone in Sadie's hand pinged. She glanced at the screen. "Abby's on her way."

"Tell her it's fine. She doesn't have to come. I've got this. I won't let everyone down. I promise." Ellie placed a hand on her stomach, which was churning at the thought of talking to Spencer for the first time in more than a year. Taking a calming breath, she reached for the patio door.

A heavy hand came down on her shoulder. She glanced back at Nate. His fierce *don't mess with me* expression was back on his face. If she wanted to ensure Highland Falls didn't lose its chance of being named Most Romantic Small Town in America because of her, the last thing she needed was Nate anywhere near Spencer.

She smiled, saying in her over-the-top cheerful voice, "Go take that ride. I'll be fine." His eyes moved down her body. "I was joking, Nate. I'm not commando," she murmured in hopes that Sadie, who was standing close to her, wouldn't hear.

"He thinks you're commando?" Sadie asked with a laugh. "No wonder he looks like that." Her cousin patted Nate's arm. "Trust me, Ellie would never...Okay, it's not that she would never go commando, because she has done it before."

"Sadie," Ellie grumbled.

"Well, you did. Someone dared you that one summer at the parade, and you were never one to pass up a dare. She even went skinny-dipping in the middle of the day. And then there was the time she—"

"All right, you're done now." Ellie opened the door and pushed Sadie inside ahead of her. "Honestly, Nate, I'll be fine. You deserve a break after having to fend off the ladies today."

"I'm not going anywhere." He lifted his chin to indicate that she should go inside.

"All right, but you have to promise you'll be on your best behavior. No growling or snarling or saying anything that makes Spencer fear for his life," she warned him.

He smiled.

"That is not comforting, Nate. You look like a wolf."

This time when he smiled there was a glint of amusement in his eyes. Then he bared his teeth and snapped them before leaning in to her and whispering a line from "Little Red Riding Hood" in her ear.

Her cheeks heated, and she lightly elbowed him in the stomach. "You're getting me back for teasing you about being commando, aren't you? Well, it worked. So we're even. Seriously though, Nate, as much as I'd love you to scare Spencer away, I need him to feel welcome and to sell him on Highland Falls. And I can't do that if I'm worried what you're going to say or do."

His gusty sigh warmed her ear. "Fine. I'll behave."

"Thank you." She opened the patio door and walked inside with Nate on her heels. "It would be helpful if you did your behaving over there." She pointed to the kitchen, well aware they were the focus of everyone's attention, including Spencer, who was sitting with a group of women at one of the tables.

It's now or never, Ellie thought, and she walked across the dining room without seeing if Nate was doing as she asked. Her throat suddenly dry, she swallowed a couple of times while surreptitiously wiping her sweaty palms on her kilt. As she approached the table, she forced a welcoming smile on her face.

Spencer stood—he was tall, but not nearly as tall as Nate—and moved to hug her. She took a step back and stuck out her hand instead. "Hi, Spencer."

He took her hand between both of his, casting an apprehensive glance behind her. Ellie barely bit back a groan. She glanced over her shoulder. Nate stood in front of the table directly across from them. His arms were folded over his massive chest, and his equally massive biceps flexed. Ellie gave him a *seriously?* look. He raised an eyebrow and gave her another of his wolfish smiles, which made her think of what he'd whispered in her ear. She shook her head with a laugh, and some of her nerves disappeared.

"Don't mind Nate. He's just overly protective."

"What about the rest of them?" He nodded behind her.

Once again, she glanced over her shoulder. Chase and Nate's brothers-in-law now stood with him, mirroring his stance. Knowing her grandmother, she'd filled his family in on who Spencer was. "They're harmless." At least compared to Nate they were.

"Good to know," he said just before he winced. Ellie was about to pull out her phone and text Nate when she realized he wasn't the reason for Spencer's wince. "Hello, Mrs. MacLeod. It's nice to see you again," he said when her grandmother joined them.

His voice was excruciatingly polite and decidedly cool. He'd met her grandmother twice. Once when they'd first started dating and a few months after they'd gotten engaged. Thanks to Ellie's mother, Spencer wasn't a fan of Agnes. He said she made him nervous.

His reaction to Agnes had been one of the reasons Ellie had never shared with him that she was psychic. She'd only read his mind once the entire time they were together. Hours after she'd caught him in bed with his costar, he'd begged Ellie to give him a second chance. He'd said he still loved her, but that's not what she saw when she read his mind. He was relieved he'd been caught.

Her grandmother smiled and offered her hand.

Spencer balked, looking a little green.

"You're a nervous Nellie, aren't you?" her grandmother said. "I have my gloves on, laddie. I can't tell your future."

"Sorry, of course." He gave her grandmother's hand a quick shake.

"We didn't expect you until Tuesday. Are the rest of your people coming early too?" her grandmother asked.

"No. I only learned that you were in town and running the inn yesterday, Ellie." He looked from her grandmother to Nate and then back to her. "Do you think we could talk somewhere privately?"

"There's an empty table over there." Her grandmother pointed at the one Nate, Chase, and his brothers-in-law were blocking.

"I, ah, was thinking a little more private than that," Spencer said.

"We can talk in my office, if you'd like," Ellie offered.

"Yes." He nodded. "That would be great."

"I have a feeling Ellie's beau would disagree. He's an agent with the NCSBI," her grandmother shared. Then she grinned. "He kills people for a living."

"That, um, doesn't surprise me," Spencer said.

Ellie rolled her eyes. "My office is this way," she said, leading Spencer from the dining room, sighing when she realized her grandmother was trailing after them. "Granny, I think Sadie could use a hand with the dessert trays."

Afraid someone, namely a very large and lethal someone, might decide to join them too, Ellie fished her phone from her bra and texted Nate. I'll be in the office with Spencer. I won't be long. There will be a desk between us, and there's a gun in the safe. I know how to use one, in case you're wondering.

Her phone pinged with a text from Nate. My gun is bigger than yours.

She snorted, then texted back. I know exactly how big your gun is and just how well you use it. She smiled at the sound of choked laughter coming from the dining room.

"So, you and this guy, is it serious?" Spencer asked.

"We haven't been together that long, but yes, I think it's headed that way." She hoped so at least. According to his sisters, the fact that Nate was still here spoke volumes.

"It looked pretty serious from what I saw."

Their plan had worked, then. Though from Spencer's expression, she wasn't sure how he felt about that. It would be easy enough for her to find out, but that wasn't something she would do. And surprisingly, she really didn't care how he felt. All she cared about was ensuring that their past didn't mess with Highland Falls' chances of winning the contest.

"Why did you come two days early, Spencer?" She opened the door to the office and ushered him inside.

"To see you," he said, taking a seat. "We didn't exactly part on the best of terms, and according to the itinerary my assistant sent me, we'll be spending quite a bit of time together on air. I didn't want it to be awkward, for either of us."

Abby was livestreaming the events on her channel.

"I may not be as good an actor as you, but I'm perfectly capable of putting on a show for the camera."

"I was hoping you wouldn't have to act, Ellie." He searched her face. "I missed you, you know. I missed us. We were good together, weren't we?"

"I don't know if we were, Spencer. If we had been good, you wouldn't have cheated on me."

"She didn't mean anything to me. It was a stupid mistake. I—"

Ellie raised a hand. "Please, that's not fair to either her or me."

"You're right. I'm sorry, sorrier than you'll ever know. I wish there was something I could say or do to make it up to you."

He'd just given her the opening Abby had been hoping for, but Ellie couldn't use it. "A heartfelt apology works. You never said sorry, you know."

"Of course I did."

"No, you didn't. You begged me for a second chance. Swore you'd never do it again. Blamed it on work, exhaustion, your costar coming on to you, and even on me for not dropping everything to be on location with you. But not once did you apologize, Spencer."

"Would it really have made a difference?"

"I don't know. It was over a year ago. But it doesn't matter anymore. We've moved on with our lives. I'm happy. Happier than I've been in a very long time."

"Happier than you were with me?"

That wasn't a question she'd asked herself. But thinking about it now, she realized that she was. And while Nate and her feelings for him certainly played into the contented, warm bubble of happiness that filled her these days, it was more than that. Her life was fuller here, more balanced. She was surrounded by people and a place that she loved.

He held up his hand. "Don't answer that. I'm not sure my ego could handle it."

She smiled. "I'm sure it would take more than that to wound your ego, Spencer."

"I'm glad you're happy. I really am. I just wish I'd made you as happy as you seem to be now." He leaned forward in the chair, reaching across the desk to take her hand in his. "I'm sorry for messing up. I'm sorry I hurt you, but mostly, I'm sorry I ruined us."

Chapter Twenty

♥

What do you think of this one?" Ellie asked as she walked into the kitchen, modeling another sundress for Nate. They'd moved up several stops on the tour of Main Street to today.

He looked up from cracking an egg and dropped it, shell and all, into the mixing bowl. She looked amazing. The purple floral sundress brought out the color in her eyes and hugged her curvy frame.

"Too short."

She looked down. "How can it be too short? It's longer than the last one. You can't even see my knees."

He'd forgotten that was what he'd said about the blue dress. "I meant the neckline is too low. I guess you could wear a sweater."

"It's seventy degrees out, and it's only nine in the morning." She tugged at the neckline. "Do you really think it's too low?" Her phone pinged. She pulled it out of her pocket and read the screen. "It doesn't matter anyway now. Spencer vetoed it."

"You modeled the dress for him too?" he said, and cracked another egg in the bowl, imagining it was Spencer's head.

She looked from the bowl to his face and grinned. "You're jealous, aren't you?"

"Of him? Please, the guy's an idiot. He's so in love with himself, he doesn't need a girlfriend; he just needs a mirror."

"He's not that bad," she said, her eyes sparkling with amusement. That dress really did make the color of her eyes stand out.

"Easy for you to say, Miss I Have a Headache and I'm Going to Get an Early Night. We were the ones stuck watching the first season of his *dramedy* on Netflix." By the time everyone had cleared out, it was close to seven. They'd ordered pizzas, which Mr. I Have to Be Careful with My Weight barely ate. Ryder, the judge, and Joe made up for the asshat's lack of appetite.

"You two gave me a headache with your male posturing. It was exhausting trying to keep the conversation in neutral territory. Plus, Spencer made me watch it three times when it first came out, and he has a habit of narrating the entire time."

She leaned in to Nate and picked a large piece of eggshell from the bowl, then used it to scoop out the smaller pieces. She didn't just look amazing, she smelled amazing too. And Spencer was going to be sniffing her all day, not him.

"Your perfume is a little strong. You should probably go wash it off."

"That's not what you said to me the other night."

He'd said a lot of things to her the other night that he shouldn't have. And he'd meant every one of them. "I'm not allergic to scent. Some people are." *Lame, Black. Really lame.*

She sighed. "So not only do I have to have another shower, I have to find something in my closet to match Spencer's white-on-white ensemble."

"He's wearing white pants?" he asked as he pulled a frying pan from the bottom cupboard.

"Yes, and he wants me to wear a white dress."

Nate almost dropped the frying pan onto the burner. "How can you not see that the guy is still in love with you?"

"Didn't you just say he's too in love with himself to be in love with anyone else? And what does a white dress have to...Oh, right, a wedding dress. I didn't think about that." She wrinkled her nose. "I overheard him talking to his partners at Happy Ever After Entertainment before the pizzas arrived last night. Spencer mentioned that we'd been engaged. Maybe they suggested he make more of our current relationship than there is for the publicity."

"And that doesn't bother you?" It sure as hell bothered him.

"It just depends on how far he goes, I guess." She tossed the shells in the compost bin under the sink and smiled at him. "And I can almost guarantee he won't take it too far because you'll be with me, and he's afraid of you."

"I can't go. I've got a conference call with the task force. And Ryder, Joe, the judge, and I are going to get started on the cabins today. We've got less than a week to get the work done. I don't want to leave you with another project to complete."

The sparkle left her eyes, and he felt like a jerk for reminding her he was leaving. And then he remembered what she'd said when he'd bent her over his arm in the middle of the dining room yesterday afternoon. She'd said she'd already fallen for him, and as much as he'd tried to convince himself he was misinterpreting the meaning of those words, he knew he hadn't. It was why he'd acted like an idiot.

The second those three little words came out of Ellie's mouth, big red *Danger* signs flashed a warning in his head. All he could think was that he had to get out of there. He had to hop on his bike and ride like the wind, putting as much distance between them as he could. Instead, he'd taken her with him. And that was something he refused to analyze.

His sisters had shared their thoughts about it before they'd left. According to them, they were booking the chapel for this time next year. They'd considered booking it for Christmas, but figured he'd need some time to come to terms with his impending loss of freedom. It felt like an eighty-pound weight was sitting on his chest, making it hard to breathe. He wondered if he was having a panic attack.

"Thanks. I appreciate you taking on the cabins." The smile she gave him was forced. "I should go get ready."

He reached for her as she turned to walk away. "Ellie, I'm sorry. I—"

Without meeting his eyes, she shrugged. "You don't

have anything to explain, Nate. It's not as if I expected you to stick around."

She'd hoped he would though. He could see it in her eyes. He watched her walk away, wishing he could say something that would make things right. But he wouldn't make her a promise he couldn't keep.

* * *

Nate stood on the patio, checking for messages on his phone. Ellie hadn't responded to the text he'd sent over an hour ago. He'd asked what she wanted him to make for dinner. He glanced at the time. It was six thirty. He'd thought she'd be back by now. He'd spent the better part of the afternoon watching for her from across the lake.

Flames shot up from the barbecue, and he put down his phone. The beef burgers would be as hard as rocks if he didn't get his mind off Ellie and put it where it belonged. He moved the burgers and lowered the heat. She wouldn't be happy he was serving Joe and the judge beef burgers, but he figured they deserved a treat. They'd put in a solid eight hours on the cabins with him and Ryder today.

Nate tested the centers of the burgers with the edge of the stainless-steel spatula. They were well done. He slid them onto the platter and turned off the grill. As he carried them inside, he was greeted by Ellie's laughter. He smiled. The woman had an incredible laugh, but that wasn't why he was smiling. He was glad she was finally home.

He put the platter of burgers on the kitchen counter

and walked into the entertainment room, expecting to see her. What he didn't expect was to see her on the big screen...with Spencer. Ryder had hooked up a laptop to the TV.

It looked like they were at the bookstore on Main Street. One of the four stops on today's tour. The last stop, if he remembered correctly.

"Burgers are ready," he said, unable to pull his eyes from the screen. Ellie and Spencer each held a book, taking turns reading the lines from *Romeo and Juliet*. They looked good together.

Joe patted the spot beside him on the couch. "Come sit for a minute. They're almost finished. We have a bet on whether Ellie will kiss him or not."

The eighty-pound weight was back, only this time it lay heavy in Nate's belly instead of on his chest. "I'll cover the burgers with foil so they don't get cold," he said, and walked away, bowing his head at the sound of Joe groaning in the entertainment room. The old man had lost his bet.

Fifteen minutes later, Nate scrapped his half-eaten burger into the garbage. His cell phone rang. It was Chase. "Hey. What's up?" He heard music and laughter in the background.

"Where are you?" Chase asked.

"Here. At the inn. Why?"

"You need to get over to Highland Brew ASAP."

"Why? What's going on?"

"Ellie and Spencer are here. They've already overtaken Abby and Hunter in the Most Romantic Couple in Highland Falls contest."

His gut twisted beneath the heavy weight. It was probably the kiss they'd shared at the bookstore that had put Ellie and Spencer over the top in the contest. "I'm not coming, Chase. I—"

"Crap. They're dancing."

An image of him and Ellie dancing under the moon at Chase and Sadie's wedding came to him. Ellie was smiling up at him. He didn't want her dancing with anyone but him. "I'll be there in fifteen minutes."

Nate walked into the crowded bar. He spotted Ellie and Spencer on the dance floor. They were in each other's arms. He recognized the song—Aloe Blacc and LeAnn Rimes's "I Do." It was their song. His and Ellie's. The last dance they'd shared that night before he got called away.

He pushed through the crowd to reach the dance floor and tapped Spencer on the shoulder. Nate didn't ask if he could cut in, he just stood there, staring at Ellie. Her hair was down, cascading over her shoulders in long, shiny blue-black waves. He remembered how that silky mane had felt sliding between his fingers the other night. The soft sounds she'd made. The way she'd looked at him with the moon and the stars in her beautiful eyes. She looked at him the same way now.

Spencer put up his hands and walked away.

"You were dancing with him to our song," Nate said as he took Ellie in his arms and drew her close. Closer than he should in the middle of a dance floor in Highland Falls, but he didn't care.

"You remembered." She smiled up at him and

looped her slender arms around his neck, closing what little distance there'd been left between them.

He bent his head, bringing his mouth to her ear. "I haven't forgotten a single moment of that night, Ellie." He rubbed his cheek against her hair, inhaling her perfume. He loved the soft, sexy fragrance, he loved the feel of her in his arms, he loved...everything about her.

"I'm sorry about this morning. I shouldn't have brought up me leaving right before you headed out. I should have waited until we could talk about it. Until I had a chance to explain."

She stiffened in his arms, moving her hands to his shoulders, putting some distance between them. "To explain what? That we'd had our fun but that our little fling was over?"

"No. That's not it. It wasn't a fling. I...care about you." When she went to step away from him, he framed her face with his hands. "Look at me. I've never felt the way I feel about you with any other woman, Ellie. Believe me, if I could give you what you want, what you deserve, I would."

"So that's it? You'll leave Sunday, and I'll never see you again?"

In his head he knew that a clean break would be the best for both of them. But he couldn't convince his heart. There were people here that he loved, not just Ellie. And that had been his first mistake, getting involved with someone whom the people he thought of as family loved too. "You'll see me again."

She pressed her lips together and shook her head.

"I can't do this. Not here." She moved away from him and hurried off the dance floor.

Nate ignored a frowning Chase and Hunter, who were waving him over to their table. He didn't want to talk right now. He walked to the bar and ordered a beer. He didn't want one, he just needed something to hold on to. Otherwise he might put his fist through a wall.

"Thanks," he said to the bartender when he handed him a bottle of beer and a frosted glass. Nate leaned against the bar, nudged the glass away, and twirled the bottle between his hands, thinking about how badly he'd messed up with Ellie. He wanted to make it right, but he didn't know how.

Spencer moved in beside him and ordered a beer. Nate slowly turned his head, giving the actor a *get out of my space or you'll regret it* look. He wanted nothing more than to rip the guy's head from his shoulders. Obviously, Spencer wasn't as good at reading body language as Ellie claimed because he didn't move.

"I don't want to fight with you," Spencer said.

Nate snorted. "I'd like to see you try."

"I wasn't talking about a physical fight. I'm not stupid." He picked at the label on the beer bottle, then glanced at Nate. "Maybe I am. You'll probably beat the crap out of me when I say what I have to say."

With his beer bottle, Nate gestured for him to go ahead at the same time as he glanced around the room. He spotted a clear path to the exit door nearest the river that flowed beside the brewery. If Spencer confessed that he was still in love with Ellie and wanted her back,

Nate was going to haul the guy through that door and toss him into the river.

"I played a police detective on my last series. I actually won an Emmy for the role."

Nate rolled his eyes. Of course all the guy wanted to talk about was himself.

Spencer sat there smiling for a minute as if recalling the memory of accepting his award. Then he said, "I take my roles seriously. I went on a few ride-alongs, spent a lot of time with our men and women in blue. I have a lot of respect for what they do, for what you do. But I also saw the kind of stress that goes with the job and what it does to their families, the people that they love." He picked at the label on his beer bottle again. Then he cleared his throat. "I don't want to see Ellie hurt. You guys won't work. You're not good for her, Nate."

Nate saluted him with his beer bottle. "That's the first intelligent thing you've said since I met you."

Spencer blew out a breath and went to clink his beer bottle against Nate's. "Thank God. I seriously thought you were going to beat the crap out of me."

Nate smacked his beer bottle against Spencer's, beer splashing onto the bar and the actor's white shirt. "You're no good for her either, so stay the hell away from her."

Spencer nodded, dabbing at the damp stain with a napkin. "I know, and you have no idea how much I regret what I did to her. I loved her." He glanced at Nate and held up his hand. "Don't punch me, but I still do. I'd do anything to get her back, but she's made it clear she's not interested."

"So why'd you cheat on her?"

"I was scared. Stupid, right? I had the most beautiful, incredible woman willing to marry me, and I threw
it all away because I started having doubts. I was on
location for six weeks in Paris without her. I'd go out
with the crew and my costars after the day's shoot.
Out for dinner or to a nightclub just to cut loose. It was
fun, a lot of fun. Those first few weeks, I made sure
I went back to the hotel early to avoid the temptation,
and trust me, there was a lot of temptation. But the
longer I was away from Ellie, the harder it became.
I started feeling like I was missing out, like maybe I
wasn't ready to settle down and lose my freedom." He
shook his head. "This past year, since Ellie and I broke
up, I've taken advantage of my freedom, and I can tell
you, it's not all it's cracked up to be." He went on
to tell Nate everything he missed about Ellie, all the
moments in their relationship that meant the most to
him, that he couldn't get out of his head—every single
one in excruciating detail.

And Nate didn't tell him to shut up or walk away,
or toss him in the river like he wanted to. He just sat
there listening in silence while a battle raged on inside
him. Maybe he'd been wrong about Spencer. Maybe
Spencer was the right man for Ellie after all.

Chapter Twenty-One

♥

W e could really use Nate right about now," Sadie said from where she stood on a ladder, attempting to tie the colorful *Welcome to Highland Falls* sign to a branch of a tree. The printer had forgotten to include Highland Falls' new tagline: *the small town where love is always in bloom*. But they'd made up for it by printing the slogan on the balloons decorating the trees.

The executives from Happy Ever After Entertainment were scheduled to arrive in the next hour. Ellie had agreed to host a ceilidh—a party with traditional Scottish songs and dances—to welcome them to the inn. It wouldn't be long before half the town showed up.

"Damn," Sadie said when her end of the sign fluttered to the ground. "Where is he?"

Ellie hadn't seen Nate since he'd crushed her hopes and dreams on the dance floor. One minute, she'd felt like she was dancing on air, like all her hopes and dreams were about to come true. He'd remembered the last song they'd danced to at the wedding. He'd called it their song, and she'd made the mistake of thinking that he'd listened to the lyrics and it was his way of declaring his feelings for her. Instead, seconds later, he'd brought her crashing down to earth in a blink of her star-filled eyes. Now he was avoiding her as much as she was avoiding him.

"Ryder said he's been on his phone for the last hour." Ellie stood across from Sadie on the other ladder, tying her end of the sign to the pole, the town's flag flapping above it in the light breeze off the lake. "Don't worry. I'll take care of your end," she told her cousin.

Ellie might as well get used to doing things on her own again. In a little more than five days, she wouldn't have Nate here helping her out. Ryder either.

She climbed down the ladder, wondering how she'd get through the next few days. She didn't know if she had it in her to smile and pretend everything was wonderful when all she wanted to do was sit down and cry, which was probably a better idea than trying to convince Nate to give them a second chance. As she knew from past experience, that would be about as productive as trying to read his mind.

She walked to her cousin's side, looking around to see what they had left to do. Ryder, Joe, and the judge had helped her and her friends set up this morning. Abby and Mallory had left forty minutes ago to pick up the donations from the local eateries in town, which were providing the food for today's event. Abby was also on a secret mission for Ellie. She was picking up several family-size packs of chocolate bars to replenish her stash.

"I know I promised not to bring it up again, but are you and Nate really okay?" Sadie asked.

"We're good. Honestly, we are," she added at Sadie's raised eyebrow.

Last night, when Sadie and their friends had followed her into the ladies' room at Highland Brew, Ellie had downplayed what had happened on the dance floor with Nate. She didn't want their family and friends to feel like they had to take sides. Nate had been nothing but honest with her. It wasn't his fault she'd fallen for him despite his warnings not to.

"Ellie, you've barely smiled or laughed all day. You sing and dance when you work, and you've been walking around like you have the weight of the world on your shoulders. So you can't expect me to believe everything is all right."

"I'm worried about Bri." It wasn't a lie. "She hasn't returned any of my calls, and they go straight to voice mail. This morning, I called my mother and Richard. They haven't returned my calls either."

"I wouldn't worry. Aunt Miranda probably called Bri and Richard the minute she stormed out of here Saturday, and you know how Bri is. She won't go against your mother. Just give it a few days. I'm sure she'll call you back."

Ellie nodded, gesturing for her cousin to come down off the ladder. "You're probably right. No doubt Richard banned Bri from talking to me." He'd done it before. "He'll be furious that we've blown the deal he put together." And her brother-in-law's temper was why Ellie couldn't completely push her worries about her sister away.

She was about to try calling Bri again when the door slammed. She turned to see Ryder storming from the inn with Toby loping after him. "Ryder, what's wrong?"

"I hate him. I hate him!" he cried—his face red and tearstained—before he took off running down the road without further explanation.

Nate. He had to be talking about Nate. Her grandfather and the judge ran out of the inn.

"Grandpa, what's going—"

"Don't worry, Ellie my love. We've got him," her grandfather said, and then both he and the judge headed down the road in the direction Ryder had gone, calling out his name.

"I've got this. You go talk to Nate," Sadie said.

As much as Ellie would like to continue avoiding Nate, she couldn't. "I won't be long," she said, and hurried across the lawn to the inn.

The inn was empty and quiet. Spencer had gone to pick up his partners at the airport in Asheville. She hadn't seen much of him today either.

Supposedly he'd spent the day in his room reading the script for the movie that they'd hopefully be filming in Highland Falls. She had a feeling it was his way of avoiding helping out at the inn. He'd always preferred giving orders to lending a hand. Then again, they couldn't expect him to pitch in on an event that was being held in his production company's honor.

Ellie hesitated as she reached the door to Nate's

room. It was slightly ajar. She saw his duffel bag sitting open on the end of the bed, and her chest tightened. He wasn't leaving Sunday. He was leaving now. It explained why Ryder was so angry and hurt. Nate was breaking his promise to him.

She knocked on the door. "Nate?"

"Yeah. Come on in, Ellie."

He walked out of the bathroom with his shaving kit in his hand. "You're leaving," she said, stating the obvious.

He glanced at her as he tossed the shaving kit into his bag. "I have to. I just got off a call with the task force. Word is my boss is pulling us off the case at the end of the week. I can't let that happen, Ellie. I have to find something that will change his mind."

"This isn't about me, Nate. It's about Ryder. You made a promise to him, to both him and Gina."

"I know I did." He sat on the side of the bed and scrubbed his face. "And I hate that I've hurt him. But there's nothing I can do about it. I owe it to Brodie to see this through."

"Are you sure this is about Brodie?"

"Come on, Ellie. I'm not leaving because of what's going on between us. I—"

"I didn't think you were. You made it clear last night that there was no us."

His expression softened, and she was afraid he'd say something sweet and kind in another attempt to let her down gently. If he did, she was all but certain the tears she'd managed to hold at bay all day would escape. "What I meant was, Are you sure what's driving you to solve this case is just about bringing these men to justice? The people who are directly responsible for Brodie's death are behind bars. You did that, Nate. You and Chase. You got justice for Brodie."

"It's not enough." His expression went from soft to fierce. "And how no one can see that pisses me off."

"Will it ever be enough, Nate? Once you find the head of this organization, once you bring them down, will that be enough? Or will you find someone else, no matter how tenuous the link to Brodie's case, to go after?"

Nate speared her with a look. He was furious that she'd challenged him, that much was obvious. But she didn't care. She was angry at him too. Angry that his obsessive need for revenge was ruling his life, his every decision. He couldn't even see the damage he was doing to Ryder.

"I don't have time for this," he said, and got off the bed.

"You better make time."

He fisted his hands on his hips. "Excuse me?"

She closed the distance between them, which was probably a bad idea because he towered over her and she had to tip her head back to look up at him. "I said you better make time. You're not leaving here until you work this out with Ryder."

"Yeah? How exactly are you planning to stop me, Ellie?" he asked in a low, rough voice she was familiar with.

"Not the way you think." Was she tempted to? Of course she was. Anytime she was in a room with him, this close to him, all she wanted to do was kiss him. But she didn't fool herself that anything she did would stop him from leaving.

His lips twitched. "No? So you don't want to kiss me?"

"No, I don't. At the moment, I'm more inclined to hit you than kiss you, Nate." She took a step back, narrowing her eyes at him when he grinned. "It's not funny. I'm serious. You're not leaving until you make this right with Ryder."

His expression sobered. "There's nothing I can say that'll make this right for Ryder. At least not now. He's too angry to listen."

"He's more hurt than angry, Nate. He looks up to you. He loves you. For him, it must feel like your job is more important to you than him."

"It's not just a job. Why can no one see that? This is about Brodie." He held up his hand. "Don't say it. I hear it enough from Chase. I don't need to hear it from you too." He dragged a hand down the side of his face. "This isn't just about me, you know. Ryder loves it here. He's gotten close to you, Joe, and the judge. Not to mention Toby. The kid loves that dog no matter how cool he plays it."

"And he's had fun with Mallory and Gabe's boys."

"I know, and I hate that I'm cutting his time short. But I don't—"

"I'll keep him. He can stay until Sunday. As long as Gina's okay with it." She held up her hand when he went to object. "He's no trouble, Nate. I enjoy having him around. Joe and the judge do too."

"If you're absolutely sure you're okay with it. You've got a lot on your plate right now."

"Like I said, I enjoy having him around. He's a big help, and honestly, Toby will be lost without him."

"I'll give Gina a call. I'm sure she'll be on board with it. You've probably saved me from her ripping me a new one, so thanks for that."

"Good. Now all you have to do is make up with Ryder."

"You didn't hear him. The kid wants nothing more to do with me." As much as Ryder tried to play it cool about his feelings for Toby, Nate did the same about his feelings for Ryder.

"That was just his hurt and anger talking. He'll be more open to listening to you when you tell him he doesn't have to leave. Stay for the ceilidh. Not all of it, just for a little while. Ryder's excited about it, and you can spend some time with him doing something fun."

He nodded, holding her gaze. "I meant what I said last night, Ellie. I wish things were different. I wish I could be the man you deserved."

"I wish you realized that you already are," she said, turning to hurry from the room before he saw the tears in her eyes.

Ellie didn't have time to indulge in tears or wishes that would never be fulfilled. The minute she rushed from Nate's room, she was swarmed by partygoers. They'd arrived earlier than expected. In the end it was probably a good thing that they had. Everyone pitched in to get the food on the table and organize the entertainment. As Spencer drove up to the inn with the other Happy Ever After executives, they were greeted by two men and two women playing the bagpipes. Then the dancers from a local troupe entertained them with a Highland fling.

"Join in, Ellie. You know you want to," her cousin Sadie yelled from where she and Michaela clapped on the outer edge of the circle.

Ellie laughed and shook her head. "Too much to do." She pointed to the tray of fizzy pink drinks in her hand. It was the signature cocktail for the event— Love Blooms.

"They'll wait," her grandmother said, handing the tray off to a man in the audience. He wasn't someone Ellie recognized. She thought he might be with the production company. He was a little too suave and debonair in his bespoke gray suit with a purple square in the pocket to be a local.

"Off you go now. Show them how it's done." Her grandmother gave her a little push. Before Ellie could demur, two of the teenage dancers grabbed her, one by each arm, and pulled her into the circle. The steps came back to her quickly as the fiddlers played "Devil in the Kitchen."

She'd learned to dance the Highland fling mostly so she could take part in the Highland Falls parade every summer. She'd had a crush on one of the boys in the band. If she wasn't mistaken, he was one of the fiddlers. He winked at her, confirming her suspicion. Ellie laughed, whirling, kicking, and high-stepping with the much younger women.

As she performed one last high step and twirl, she

met Nate's smiling eyes. He stood with Ryder, an arm
slung over the teenager's shoulders. She bowed in their
direction at the end of the performance, happy that Nate
had stayed. Ryder laughed, and Nate whistled before
turning to say something to the teenager. The laughter
faded from Ryder's face. His shoulders hunched, and
he shoved his hands in his pockets. Nate pulled him
in for a hug. Ellie turned away. He was leaving now.
She didn't want to say goodbye, especially with an
audience.

She approached the man holding the tray of drinks
and smiled. "Thanks so much," she said, but he didn't
seem to hear her.

She followed his gaze. He was staring at Nate and
Ryder. And maybe because she was feeling a little
emotional right then, his thoughts floated to her on
the warm spring breeze. He felt bad for Ryder losing
his father, but along with the sympathy was something
else. Guilt. Guilt and sorrow mixed with anger. His
emotions confused her. She was trying to make sense
of what he was feeling when his gaze moved to Nate
as he walked away. There was no guilt or sympathy in
the older man's mind now. The only emotion she read
was fear. Not for himself, but for someone else.

As though just realizing she was standing there,
the man offered her a polite smile and handed her
the tray.

"Thank you," she said, working to keep the nerves
from her voice. "I'm sorry to have you helping out
when the party was meant to welcome you and your
team to Highland Falls." She no longer believed this

man was with the production company, but she needed an opening to find out who he was. She dropped her barriers completely. After what she'd already read in his mind, she had no compunction about invading his privacy.

"It wasn't a problem, my dear." *But you have been, Elliana MacLeod. A very big problem indeed. To not only me but your mother.*

As the pieces of the puzzle slipped into place, Ellie's fingers trembled. The glasses clinked into one another, causing the fizzy pink liquid to slosh onto the tray. "I better pass these around. Enjoy the party." She tightened her grip on the tray and hurried away, searching for someone to hand off the drinks to. She spotted Spencer a few feet away. She handed him the tray. He looked from her to the drinks like he had no idea what she expected him to do with them. "Pass them out to the members of your team, please."

She didn't wait for a response. She took off at a run. She had to catch Nate before he left. As she rounded the front of the inn, she saw him talking to Chase, his duffel bag slung over his shoulder. Chase looked about as happy as Ellie was about Nate leaving.

"See if you can talk some sense into him," Chase said as he walked past her.

Nate shook his head, then offered her a half smile. "You didn't have to run over here. I wouldn't leave without saying goodbye."

She waved him off, glancing over her shoulder. "That's not why I was running. I need to talk to you. Did you see the man in the gray suit?"

He winced. "Yeah, I didn't want to say anything, but I'm pretty sure he's the developer your mother signed the agreement with. He's been casing the place since he got here. I have a meeting with the task force in forty-five minutes or I'd stick around, but Gabe and Chase are on it. They'll keep an eye on him, see what he's up to. But tell them immediately if he says anything to you or Joe."

"I know who he is, but I don't think the property is the only reason he's here." She took a deep breath, dreading what she had to do, but she had to tell him in case it was somehow connected to his case. In case it put Nate in danger.

"Ellie, what's wrong?"

"I have to tell you something, and I need you to believe me." Worrying her bottom lip between her teeth, she looked around, making sure they were alone. Then she blurted out her secret. "Nate, I'm psychic."

He stared at her. "Say again."

"I inherited my grandmother's gift, only mine is different than her's. I can read people's minds."

His lips twitched and he crossed his arms. "Read mine."

"I can't. You're the only one I can't read. But I don't have to, to know you think this is a joke. It's not, Nate."

"So why don't you do it all the time? You could make a fortune."

"Because I don't think of it as a gift. It's always been a curse to me. It's why my mother rejected me. I read her mind, Nate. That's how I found out Bri wasn't my father's daughter, and that's why my mother spent years trying to convince me I was mentally unstable. I'm not, in case you're wondering. I'm completely sane. But whether you believe me or not, you need to hear what he was thinking when he was staring at you and Ryder." She repeated the man's thoughts exactly as she'd read them. "I don't know how or why or what his involvement is, but I think he's somehow connected to your case. I'm almost positive he's also my sister's father."

"I don't know, Ellie. Are you sure you aren't just imagining that's what you... Sorry. I get that you believe in this sort of thing. It's just that I have a harder time with it. You know that. We've talked about it. But I'll look into it." At least he didn't laugh at her or outright reject her, but he was humoring her.

"I don't care that you're a skeptic and don't believe me. You need to look into him, Nate. Promise me that you will."

"I promise. Now I really do have to go." He moved in to give her a hug, but she stepped back and held out her hand.

"Goodbye, Nate. Be safe."

Chapter Twenty-Two

♥

Thanks a lot, Ellie," Ryder said from the doorway of her office.

She looked up from the computer. He was holding out his phone with the screen turned to her. She grinned at the picture of him doing the dishes this morning. "I couldn't resist. You looked so cute in the apron. And I know for a fact your mom loved it."

She'd sent the photo to Gina a couple of hours ago. They'd chatted for an hour after the party had ended last night. Five hours and twenty minutes after Nate had left. Yes, Ellie was that pathetic that she'd resorted to counting the minutes he'd been gone. She'd missed him making breakfast with her this morning too.

"What are you guys up to now?" she asked, closing the online banking app. The inn's account balance made for depressing reading.

"Me, Joe, and the judge are going to finish up one of the cabins today. Nate is expecting an update." He rolled his eyes but she didn't miss the happy twitch of his lips. "Gabe's going to bring the boys over after school to help out."

She smiled, pleased that Ryder's relationship with Nate hadn't suffered irreparable damage over the broken promise. She couldn't say the same for her relationship with Nate. Ryder was the only one of them receiving texts from him. Then again, in Nate's mind, they didn't have the kind of relationship that warranted daily texts or updates.

She imagined he felt like he'd dodged a bullet after learning her secret. But she didn't regret telling him. He needed to know what the developer had been thinking. What Nate did with the information was up to him. Part of her wondered if he'd do anything with it at all. Or would he simply write her off as one of the crazy people who had come forward to offer help on his previous cases?

It hurt to think that he would, and she had to work to keep the bright and cheerful tone in her voice. "I'll bring you guys a picnic lunch. We have a ton of food left over from the party."

"Thanks, Ellie. See you later." Ryder's smile disappeared when Spencer joined him at the doorway.

Ellie frowned, wondering at his odd reaction. He'd seemed to like Spencer. Maybe not so odd after all, Ellie thought, when Ryder leaned against the door like he had no intention of leaving. Apparently, in Ryder's mind, Ellie belonged to Nate, and Spencer was encroaching on his godfather's territory. Sweet but completely unnecessary. However, her and Nate's nonrelationship wasn't a subject she wanted to broach with Ryder at the moment.

"Hi, Spencer. Ryder, don't forget to take some pictures of Toby. I want to send them to my sister." Despite Bri being incommunicado, Ellie continued sending the pictures in hopes her sister would eventually respond. She'd yet to receive a reply to her latest texts to Richard and her mother.

Ellie had been tempted to confront her mother about what she'd read in the mind of Bri's father. Not about what had felt like a threat at the time—once her panic had subsided, and she'd had a chance to mull over the older man's thoughts, she'd realized his tone had been more amused than threatening. No, what she wanted to confront her mother about was the feeling that their affair was not in the past but ongoing.

Ryder gave Spencer a narrow-eyed look before pushing off the doorjamb. "Sure," he said, then sauntered away.

Ellie fought back a smile. Ryder had Nate's saunter down to a T. Though he couldn't quite pull off his scary look yet.

"Someone's in a mood today. I guess he's still mad at Nate for taking off," Spencer said, dropping into the chair across from her.

Honestly, she had no idea why she'd once thought Spencer was good at reading body language. But she wasn't about to correct him. Nate was the last person she wanted to talk about to Spencer.

"So"—he rubbed his hands together—"are you ready for the big day?"

There were several events for the production company today, including a presentation at the town hall.

"I wish I could, but I have things to do around here." Like cleaning rooms and doing laundry, and then making dinner for the Happy Ever After executives tonight. She'd nearly fainted when Spencer presented the menu to her this morning. It was her own fault for saying she'd be happy to make whatever they wanted. She'd had no idea they'd opt for a steak-and-lobster feast that included three different types of wine to go with each course.

"Come on, don't be a spoilsport. It won't be nearly as much fun without you by my side." He leaned forward and reached for her hand. "Please, for me."

She gave his hand a tepid squeeze before pulling it away. "I really can't, Spencer."

"If this is because of Nate, you don't have to worry. He knows how I feel about you. He gave me the all clear."

She stiffened. "The all clear? What exactly does that mean?"

"You know, he cleared the way for me to be with you. He stepped aside. Pretty decent of him, if you ask me."

"Apparently neither of you thought to ask me." Ellie was equal parts hurt and furious. Of all the high-handed, asinine things she'd ever heard of, this took the cake.

Either Spencer hadn't heard her or he decided her opinion didn't rate the same attention as his. "Then again, the writing was on the wall, I guess. He knows

I'm the better man. At least for you, I mean," he quickly amended, no doubt in response to her narrow-eyed stare. He didn't have to be an expert body language reader to know she was ticked.

"First of all, the only person who gets to say who's good for me is me."

"You don't think I'm good for you?"

"Spencer, where is this even coming from? Before Sunday, we hadn't talked in more than a year."

"I know, but we're so good together. It was like old times. We were completely in sync. Everyone saw it, Ellie. We're tied with Sadie and Chase for Most Romantic Couple in Highland Falls."

And Nate hadn't believed that the Love Blooms in Highland Falls campaign had the power to change hearts and minds. Why was she even thinking about him? He'd basically passed her off to another man.

"But it was all an act, Spencer. We were playing Romeo and Juliet. We were reading lines." She'd known it was a terrible idea, but she hadn't wanted to disappoint their audience.

"So you didn't feel it?"

"No. I didn't." She softened her tone at the hurt expression on his face. "I'm sorry, Spencer. I didn't know you still had feelings for me."

"And you don't have them for me, do you?" He searched her face. "Did you ever love me, Ellie?"

"Of course I did."

"I sometimes wondered if part of the reason you were attracted to me, at least in the beginning, was because your mother loved me. I know you guys didn't get along, but I could tell her approval meant a lot to you."

No matter how much she wanted to say there was no truth to his observation, she was afraid there might be. "I loved you for you, Spencer."

"And I blew it." He scrubbed his hands over his face. "I think it's best if I leave. It's probably not fair for me to judge the contest anyway. I'm not exactly impartial." As though sensing her panic, he smiled. "Don't worry, Ellie. If I'm an example of love blooming in Highland Falls, you guys have this in the bag. I just needed to find a woman who hadn't given her heart to another man. You love him, don't you?"

She had, but that was before she'd heard what he'd said to Spencer. "It doesn't matter how I feel. Nate has made his feelings for me perfectly clear."

"Sounds like you and I are in the same boat. Too bad we can't share it, Ellie." He came around the desk. "A hug for old times' sake?"

"Of course." She stood and hugged him. "Be happy, Spencer." And because she was feeling a little emotional right then, her barriers dropped...and she nearly slugged him. He'd already replaced her in his mind with a woman who was auditioning for the role opposite him in the romantic movie they'd be making in the small town that won the contest.

* * *

Nate sat behind his desk, debating whether to call Ellie. He'd been thinking about her all day. Instead, he called Chase. He glanced at the time on the computer screen. His best friend was probably home by now. Sadie and Michaela were his priority. Chase had work-life balance down to a science.

"Hey," Chase answered. "Hang on a minute. Talk to Michaela. Say hi to Uncle Nate, baby."

Nate took the phone from his ear and shook his head. He didn't have time for this. He sighed, bringing the phone back to his ear. He didn't want the kid to scream in his ear so he pitched his voice higher, as Ellie had suggested. "Hey, kid. What are you up to? Eating some of that organic crap your parents like to feed you?"

One of the other agents turned to stare at Nate as he walked by and ran into a desk.

Nate rolled his eyes. He didn't sound that weird. "You know, you should try pizza," he told Michaela. "Can you say *pizza*?" He heard a crash. "Kid, are you there? Please tell me you didn't jump out of your high chair while I was phone-sitting you."

In the background, he heard Chase and Sadie laughing hysterically. "Have you two had me on speaker the entire time? Hello, are you there?" he said when they didn't answer him.

"No, not the entire time," Chase said, a hint of laughter still in his voice. "She threw the phone on the floor. She was terrified. Her eyes practically bugged out of her head. Honestly, after hearing you talk in that voice, I don't blame her."

"Ellie told me...Never mind. Don't take me off speaker. I want to talk to Sadie too."

"Okay. What's up?" Chase asked.

He looked around and lowered his voice. "Has Ellie ever mentioned that she's psychic?"

Sadie gasped. "She told you?"

"Wait a minute. Ellie's psychic? How come no one told me?" Chase asked.

"Because Ellie doesn't want anyone to know," Sadie said. "I just found out last fall. As far as I know, my aunt Miranda is the only other person who knows. Granny probably knows too, but we haven't talked about it. And now both of you know."

"So you believe her?" he asked Sadie.

"Nathan Black, if you dare made her feel like she was crazy when she told you, I'll shoot you."

"Calm down, honey. I'm sure Nate wouldn't do that." Chase sighed when he didn't immediately respond. "I was wrong. He did."

"I didn't say she was crazy. I just said that I have a hard time buying into all that woo-woo crap. Come on, Chase. How often have any leads you've had from a so-called psychic ever panned out?"

"Never," he admitted with some obvious reluctance. "Sorry, honey. But it's true. Not that I don't believe Ellie is psychic. It's just that—"

Sadie interrupted her husband, "I don't know about the people you guys have dealt with in the past, but Ellie is the real deal. If it wasn't for her, I wouldn't have known your grandfather was trying to break us up, Chase."

The judge hadn't been happy when Chase announced he was leaving Washington and giving up a career-making promotion to live in Highland Falls with Sadie and the baby. But he'd eventually come around.

"So whatever my cousin told you, Nate, you can trust that she's not imagining things."

"What did she tell you?" Chase asked.

Nate shared with them what Ellie had told him about the man she believed was her sister's father.

"Wait a sec. Miranda had an affair with this guy? Bri's not Bryan's daughter?"

Nate grimaced. "Forget you heard that. I promised Ellie I wouldn't tell anyone. So that goes no further than us. Okay?"

"She told me too. I'm just a little surprised she told you, Nate."

"And I'm surprised you didn't tell me. We said no secrets, remember?" Chase said to his wife.

"It wasn't mine to tell. And Ellie just told me ten days ago," Sadie said. Then she shared with Chase how Ellie had found out and how her mother had been punishing her ever since. "My heart breaks thinking of what my aunt put Ellie through. And no one ever knew. She kept it to herself all these years."

"If you ask me, it's about time Ellie stops trying to protect everyone else. After everything her mother's done to her, Miranda deserves for her secret to come out." She deserved a lot worse than that, and Nate would be happy to make her pay.

"I agree with you, but that's just not who Ellie is. She'd protect her family with her life."

Sadie was right. Ellie didn't have a vindictive bone in her body. She was warm and kind and loving. The sweetest woman he'd ever met.

"So I guess we can all agree that Miranda deserves a special place in hell and that Ellie is the real deal," Chase said.

"Agreed," Nate said, even though he was still having a hard time wrapping his head around the idea that Ellie was psychic. "And now I have to sell it to the task force."

"I don't envy you that, buddy. But you're right, you do. Don't worry though. If you get pushback and you can't get them on board, we'll work the case together. I'm sure Gabe will want in too. Same goes for Elijah. My wife too, right, honey?"

Elijah and Sadie were the offspring of a world-class hacker and had inherited his mad skills. Only they used theirs for the greater good.

"Honey?" Chase said when his wife didn't respond. "What is it?"

"I just got a text from Ellie."

There was a brief pause. Then Chase groaned. "What were you thinking, Nate?"

"What did I do now?"

"According to Ellie, you told Spencer that you weren't interested in her and told him to go for it," Sadie said.

"I didn't tell him I wasn't interested in her, and I sure as hell didn't tell him to *go for it*."

"What did you tell him?" Sadie asked in a silky voice that he didn't trust.

"I might have said he deserved her more than I did."
Or maybe he'd just thought it.

"He cheated on her!"

"I know, but you didn't hear him talk about her.
The guy loves her. He knows he was an idiot, and he
regrets it."

"He's not the only idiot," Sadie muttered.

Nate didn't need anyone reminding him that he
was an idiot for letting the best thing that had ever
happened to him slip away. He'd spent the entire day
kicking himself in the ass. He'd also called himself a
lot worse than an idiot.

"So how did things end up with Spencer and Ellie?"
Nate asked, playing it cool, acting like his heart wasn't
practically pounding out of his chest.

"Why do you want to know, Nate?" There was that
silky voice again. "I thought you weren't interested.
It's okay, baby. Mommy and Daddy are finished talking to the idiot."

"Daddy wouldn't mind talking a little longer to the
idiot," Chase said, and the line clicked off speaker.
"Spencer left town."

Nate sagged in his chair. He'd been afraid Chase
was going to tell him that Ellie had forgiven Spencer
and was giving him a second chance. "Good. He
doesn't deserve her."

"He doesn't, but you do. And don't even think about
telling me you're not good enough for her. You're one
of the best men I know. No one gives a crap about your
past, Nate. You did what you had to do to survive."

"You don't think I blew my chance with her?

Chase?" he said when the seconds ticked by without a response from his best friend.

"If her text is anything to go by, you blew it big-time, buddy. But don't worry, we're all pulling for you. We'll help you find a way to win her back." Sadie said something in the background, and Chase sighed. "Agnes and I will."

Nate texted Ellie as soon as he'd disconnected from Chase. The text bounced back. She'd blocked him. He tried calling her. Nothing. No voice mail, no nothing. Chase was right. He'd blown it. But he didn't plan on giving up without a fight. He didn't care how long it took. Somehow he'd win her back.

Nate called a meeting of the task force. A few of the members grumbled at the short notice, but an hour later, they were gathered in the conference room.

"We have a new person of interest," he said, taping the photo of Dimitri Ivanov on the whiteboard. Nate hadn't had time to do a deep dive on the man, but he laid out what he had so far to the team.

"You said our guy would be playing close to home. Looks like you were right, bro," one of the DEA agents said.

Now came the hard part. "He's not our guy, but someone close to him is."

"What makes you think it's not him? He fits the profile. Midfifties, filthy rich, connected, and his development company provides cover for moving the product and laundering the money."

He repeated what Ellie had told him.

Several of the agents groaned. "A psychic? Come

on, Black. You don't believe that crap any more than we do."

"You're right. I'm as skeptical as the rest of you. We've been burned too many times. But not by her. She's legit. I'd stake my career on it."

"And so would I," Chase said as he walked into the conference room. He winked at Nate. "Your brother-in-law pulled some strings. Let's finish what we started."

Chapter Twenty-Three

♥

Ellie, come quick!" Ryder yelled from the reception area.

At the panic in Ryder's voice Ellie's heart beat double time in her chest, terrified that her grandfather or the judge had been hurt. She dropped the bedding she was about to load into the washing machine and ran. The door to the inn was flung open. Toby was beside himself, whining and barking on the porch. A taxi was parked in front of the inn. Ryder and the driver were helping a woman from the back seat.

"Bri!" Ellie ran down the porch steps. Her sister's head was swathed in a white gauze bandage, the right side of her face was swollen and bruised, and she had a cast from the top of her right thigh to her foot.

Her sister lifted her gaze to Ellie. "I should have listened to you." Bri's voice was little more than a hoarse whisper.

Ellie went to slam her barriers shut. She didn't want to see how her sister had ended up broken and bruised. As it was, she was struggling to keep it together for

Bri's sake. But she needed to know. She needed to know if Richard had done this to her sister. And the last thing she wanted to do was ask Bri to relive what had happened to her.

Ellie opened herself to her sister's thoughts. Bri was traumatized and in pain. So much pain. Ellie's fingers clenched into fists, her nails biting into her palms as she pushed past Bri's pain to reach the images that were coated in her sister's fear.

Bri and Richard were fighting. Her sister had been coming to the inn after all. When Richard learned that Bri planned to talk their mother into ending the agreement with the developer, he wouldn't let her leave, terrified that she'd jeopardize the deal. He grabbed her phone and threw it on the floor, then crushed it under his heel. Bri stared at him as if seeing him for the first time. She told him he needed help and that she was leaving him. His face contorted with fear and rage, he grabbed Bri by the shoulders, shaking her so hard that her head snapped back. She pushed him, and he slipped on her shattered phone, falling onto the glass table in the living room.

As the glass shattered around him, Bri ran for the door and wrenched it open. She sprinted for the bank of elevators at the end of the hall. She jabbed the Down button several times—*hurry, hurry*—but the elevator was stuck on the penthouse. She glanced over her shoulder. Richard was coming. She looked to her right. The stairs. She ran to the door and flung it open. Richard caught it before it could swing shut. He put out a hand to stop Bri, and she jerked away. The abrupt movement caused her to lose her balance on the concrete step.

Ellie shut down the images of Richard crying while holding her sister's broken body at the bottom of the flight of stairs. He might not have pushed her, but he was responsible for what had happened. "Ryder, honey, go hold on to Toby."

He nodded and handed Ellie the crutch she hadn't noticed in his hand. The driver held the other one. "Is it easier for you to use the crutches or to lean on me?" she asked her sister.

"I..." Bri lifted a shoulder helplessly.

"It's okay. You don't have to do anything or think about anything. We've got you now," she said, remembering how hard it had been for her grandfather right after his stroke. Of course, why hadn't she thought of that? "Sit for a minute. I'm going to get Grandpa's wheelchair, and I have a ramp for the stairs."

"You go and do what you have to," the driver said, helping Bri sit back down.

"What the devil has gotten into that dog?" her grandfather asked as he rounded the inn. He stopped in his tracks when he saw Bri, pressing a hand to his chest. "Mother of God, what happened to you, child?"

Bri started to cry, and Joe rushed to her side. "There, there, now. It'll be all right." He lifted his gaze to Ellie as he gently rubbed her sister's shoulder, searching her face for answers.

She shook her head. She couldn't tell him, not now. As soon as her sister was settled, she would.

By the time they got her sister tucked into Joe's

bed on the first floor, an hour had passed. The driver wouldn't leave until he'd seen for himself that Bri would be well taken care of. He'd picked her up at the hospital in Charlotte. If his suspicions were correct, her sister had checked herself out against the doctors' wishes.

"I got the impression she was afraid to stay there." He handed his card to Ellie as he slid behind the wheel. "I'd appreciate you letting me know how she's doing."

"Of course. Thank you for getting her to us safely."

He seemed to weigh his words before saying, "It's her husband who did this to her, you know."

"She told you that?" Ellie asked, surprised her private sister would tell a complete stranger.

"Not in so many words. But I was worried about her traveling this distance in her condition. I saw her wedding ring and suggested I call her husband for her, as she didn't have a cell phone. Her reaction gave her away."

The first thing Ellie did when she returned to her grandfather's room was check Bri's purse. There was no medication. "What are you looking for?" Joe asked from the chair by the window. He'd watched over her sleeping sister while Ellie saw off the cab driver. Ellie motioned for him to follow her into the hall. Pulling the door shut behind them, she told him the driver suspected Bri had checked herself out and the lack of medication confirmed it.

"You're calling Jace?" her grandfather asked when she pulled out her phone.

She nodded. Her brother would know what she should do.

"I'll put on a pot of tea and reheat the soup. Your sister will need something to eat when she wakes up."

"Ryder and the judge should eat something too. Have you seen them?"

"They took the dog for a walk. The three of them were shaken seeing the condition Bri is in. I probably didn't help when I raised my suspicions it was her no-good husband who'd done this to her. It was him, wasn't it, Ellie?"

She nodded. "I think so, Grandpa." He was upset as it was. She'd wait until they knew Bri was going to be all right to tell him the rest.

"And you'll be finding that out for sure, won't you?"

"I will," Ellie said as she opened the door to check on Bri. Her sister was still asleep so Ellie went to her office and called her brother. As soon as his steady, deep voice came over the line, Ellie broke down.

"Hey, Ellie. What's wrong?"

"Bri. It's Bri, Jace," she said through a sob. Once she'd pulled herself together, she told him about their sister's condition and who she suspected was to blame. She couldn't bring herself to tell her brother that she was psychic.

Jace swore, something he rarely did. "She needs to be under a doctor's care. What the hell was she thinking checking herself out? She's smarter than that."

"The driver thinks she was too scared to stay. I

haven't been able to reach her for days, Jace. I called Richard, texted him too, and he didn't respond." Now she knew why.

"Hang on a sec." Seconds later, she heard him talking to someone. It sounded like he was relaying Bri's medical condition. A few minutes later, he came back on the line. "Cal's taking over Bri's care. He'll be there within the hour."

"Cal, as in Cal Scott?" *Please don't let it be that Cal.* He was the last person her sister would want as her doctor. Cal and her brother were friends. They'd been joined at the hip when they were younger and Jace was in town. But what her brother didn't know was that Bri and Cal had dated for almost a year back in the day. Ellie didn't know why they'd broken up, but her sister had been heartbroken.

"Yeah. He's one of the best trauma surgeons I know. We're lucky to get him. He's the only one I trust to look after Bri."

"I didn't know he'd moved back to town," Ellie said. Her sister was going to kill her. "Jace, you didn't tell him we suspect that Bri's been abused, did you?"

"Of course I did. He has to know what he's dealing with."

"Ellie, we've got trouble," her grandfather said, leaning against the doorjamb, clearly out of breath.

"What's going on?" her brother asked.

"I don't know. Grandpa, what's wrong?" She put her brother on speaker so he could hear their grandfather's symptoms. "Are you feeling okay? You're not dizzy, are you?"

"I'm not having a damn stroke, if that's what you're worried about. I went out looking for Jonathan and the boy and spotted Richard coming up the road in his fancy SUV. I had to run here to beat him."

"Grandpa, go sit with Bri and lock the door," she said, and walked to the safe.

"Don't take the pistol, take the rifle." Her grandfather pointed at the gun case above the safe.

"Ellie. Elliana, don't you dare confront him with a gun. Call the cops," her brother yelled through the phone.

"They won't get here in time," Ellie and her grandfather said in unison as she took out the rifle and checked the chamber.

"Don't worry, Jace. Your sister knows what she's about. I taught her well." Joe picked up her phone. "We'll call you when it's over," she heard her grandfather say over her swearing brother.

Ellie hurried into the reception area, relieved that Richard hadn't made it inside. Opening the door, she strode onto the porch and raised the rifle. "Don't come one step closer," she said to the man rushing up the walkway.

She caught movement to her left on the road. It was the judge and Ryder returning from their walk. "Ryder, hold on to Toby," she called without taking her eyes off her sister's husband. "If you know what's good for you, you'll leave now," she told Richard.

He ignored her and kept coming. "You have no right to keep me from my wife. Step asi—"

Ellie widened her stance, sighted the gun, aiming

for the spot between his shoes, and pulled the trigger. Richard's eyes went wide, and he staggered backward. For a second Ellie thought she'd hit him. She didn't feel bad about that at all. But then she noticed the gouge in the paving stone, exactly where she'd been aiming.

"Next time, I won't miss." Once again, she loaded the chamber.

"You're crazy! Just like your mother said you were." He stabbed a finger at the door. "That's my wife you have in there, and you can't keep me away from her! Do you hear me?" he shouted, walking backward to his SUV. "I know people. People who will make you sorry you ever went up against me. You'll pay for this. Mark my words, you'll pay."

She opened her mind to his thoughts. The developer. Dimitri Ivanov. Richard was going to Bri's father for help. Except he didn't know the man was his wife's father. Which meant Richard wasn't blackmailing her mother. So had her mother been playing on Ellie's love for her sister and her father to get her to back down? Richard revved the engine and squealed out of the parking lot. Ellie didn't relax until his SUV disappeared down the road.

"That was totally badass, Ellie!" Ryder said, hanging on to Toby's leash with his eyes glued to his screen as they walked to the porch.

"I'd admonish you for your language, son, but I can't think of a better way to describe what we just witnessed. You, Ellie MacLeod, are a badass."

Hearing the word out of the judge's mouth made her laugh. "Thank you." She narrowed her eyes at Ryder, who was shaking his head, watching his screen with a mile-wide grin on his face. "Ryder, tell me you didn't film that."

He lifted a shoulder. "You took a picture of me wearing an apron and doing dishes, Ellie. What do you think?"

"It's not the—" She broke off as a black jeep peeled into the parking lot.

"Who's that?" Ryder asked, his eyes going wide when the man slammed out of the jeep. He was almost as big and as broad as Nate and dressed in green scrubs. He had a phone to his ear and a medical bag in his other hand, and he was shaking his head at Ellie. She had a fairly good idea who was on the other end.

"Dr. Caleb Scott. My brother sent him," she told Ryder, then smiled at the man walking up the steps. "Hi, Cal."

"Still the same rebel without a cause, I see." He held out the phone to her. "Your brother wants a word."

"Trust me, this time I had a cause," she said, taking the phone from him.

He took the gun from her and gave her a one-armed hug. "I know you did," he said, then strode into the inn. The judge, Ryder, and Toby followed him inside.

Ellie brought the phone to her ear. "I'm fine, Jace. Richard's gone." For how long, she didn't know. And she was worried that when he returned, he'd have friends. She had to get to Dimitri Ivanov, and she knew the one person who could. She cut off her brother midlecture. "I need to call Mom. I'll call you once Cal has finished examining Bri."

Ellie called her mother from Cal's phone in hopes she'd answer an unknown number. She did. "Mom, Bri's hurt. It's bad." She quickly explained her sister's condition and what had transpired between Richard and Bri. "You need to get here, and you need to get here as fast as you can."

"I'm twenty-five minutes away."

"How? How did you know to come here?"

"Your sister has me listed as her emergency contact. One of her nurses called as soon as they discovered Brianna was missing. The nurse told me, Elliana. She told me they suspected Richard was involved but that your sister said it was an accident."

"You knew she was in the hospital, and you didn't tell me?"

"I had no idea. I had no idea about anything." Her mother choked back a sob. "I should have listened to you, Elliana. I should have—"

"We can talk when you get here, Mom. The doctor's examining Bri. I need to be with her."

"Yes. Go to her."

Ellie disconnected and rushed into the inn, running down the hall to her grandfather's room. As she went to open the door, her grandfather, the judge, and Ryder hurried out. She could tell by their expressions that whatever was happening in that room wasn't good. Her grandfather handed Ellie her phone. "You need to call your parents."

She nodded, pressing her lips together to hold in a sob. What little composure she retained she nearly lost when she entered the room. Cal was on the phone.

"I have a code three at Mirror Lake Inn. Yeah, that's what I said. Hot response."

"Cal, what—"

He held up a finger and placed another call on the landline. "It's Cal. I need you to hold an OR open for me. Yeah. Is she still there? Good. Tell her I need her to assist."

"Cal, how bad is it?"

"I'm not going to lie to you, Ellie. Bri's slipped into a coma. I don't have her charts or images yet, but aside from her obvious injuries, I believe she has a fractured skull and internal injuries."

She swallowed a sob and knelt beside the bed, taking her sister's hand in hers. "Did we hurt her when we moved her, Cal? Did we make it worse?"

"The five-hour drive here didn't do her any favors. But I honestly have no idea how she walked out of that hospital on her own." He crouched beside the bed and took Bri's other hand in his, placing his fingers around Bri's slender wrist, monitoring her pulse. "She's tough, stubborn too. A fighter just like you. If anyone can pull through, it's your sister."

"Can you keep Richard, her husband, away from her at the hospital? You can't let him near her, Cal."

"I'll do what I can. But unless she brought charges against him, Ellie, we'll have a hard time keeping him away. If he brings lawyers into it, there won't be anything we can do to stop him."

But Ellie could. She could go to Dimitri Ivanov with her mother and show the man what Richard had done to his daughter. Ellie placed Cal's phone on the foot of the bed and then lifted her own, taking photos of her sister. She sent them to her mother.

"Ellie, the hospital in Charlotte will have taken a full set of images. I should have them within the hour."

She nodded. She couldn't tell him why she needed the photos. No one could know what she was going to do.

"Ellie, get out. Get out now."

"Why? Oh God, no," she cried when he started chest compressions. As Ellie stumbled from the room, she heard him say, "Come on, baby. Don't give up now."

"What is it? What's wrong?" her grandfather said when Ellie leaned against the wall outside the room, tears streaming down her cheeks.

She couldn't bring herself to tell him that Cal was trying to revive her sister. "Cal has to operate on Bri. The ambulance is on...Thank God," she cried at the sound of sirens. She ran down the hall to the reception area and opened the door. The ambulance was backed up to the porch. "She's in here." She waved the paramedics inside. Joe, Ryder, and the judge moved out of the way.

They stood huddled together in the reception area, waiting for the paramedics to come out of the room with Bri on a stretcher. It felt like an hour had passed but it couldn't have been more than ten minutes when they rushed past with her sister. Cal's long-legged strides ate up the distance between them, his entire focus on Bri.

As if he'd just remembered they were there, he stopped and turned. "I don't know how long she'll be in surgery. But prepare for a long night. I'll talk to you after it's over," he said, then jogged to the ambulance and jumped inside, closing the doors behind him.

"Grandpa, can you and Jonathan take Ryder and Toby to Mallory's? I'll meet you at the hospital. Mom's on her way. I have to wait for her."

"I'll drive," the judge said, taking the keys from her grandfather's shaking hand.

Ellie called Mallory and explained the situation. "Of course, bring him right over. He can stay the night. I'll go to the hospital as soon as Gabe comes home. Sometimes it helps to have a go-between. But Ellie, you couldn't ask for a better surgeon than Cal. Bri's going to pull through this."

She talked for a few minutes with Mallory. Then she disconnected and called her grandmother and Sadie. She had a feeling they were halfway out the door before she'd said goodbye. She hugged her grandfather and the judge as they left, promising to see them soon.

She stopped Ryder with a hand on his arm. "Are you okay staying with Mallory and Gabe?"

"Yeah, but I'd kind of like to be at the hospital for Joe and the judge. They might need me."

Ellie hugged him. "Has anyone told you lately what an amazing kid you are?"

"Yeah, you. Yesterday." He smiled. "So is it okay if I go to the hospital?"

"Of course. Just drop Toby off at Mallory and Gabe's. I'm sure the boys won't mind looking after him, and I don't want him staying here on his own."

Ellie's mother pulled into the parking lot fifteen

minutes after they'd left. Ellie had locked everything up tight, grateful that the executives from Happy Ever After Entertainment had left earlier that day. She ran to her mother's SUV.

"How is she, Ellie? How's Brianna?"

"She's in surgery, Mom."

Her mother nodded as she backed out of the parking lot, nearly taking out the inn's sign. She slammed on the brakes. They jerked to a stop, and her mother pressed her forehead against the steering wheel. "Maybe you should drive to the hospital, Elliana."

"We're not going to the hospital, Mom. Not yet."

"I don't understand. Why aren't we going to the hospital? We need to be there, Elliana. We need to be there for Brianna."

"Right now, there's nothing we can do at the hospital for Bri. She's safe where she is. Cal will make sure she pulls through this. I know he will. But Mom, they can't stop Richard. If he goes in there with a lawyer and says he wants Bri transferred to another hospital, they won't be able to stop him. He never told us she was hurt, Mom. Not a word. But Brianna's father, he can stop Richard. We're going to Dimitri Ivanov's."

Her mother stared at her. "How did you know? How did you know Dimitri was Bri's father?"

She told her mother about Dimitri showing up at the inn yesterday. "I don't think he'd let a man who would do this to his daughter near her, do you?" She held up her phone, pictures of her sister open on the screen.

Ellie felt like she was betraying her father. She knew how much he loved Bri. Knew he would do anything to protect her. But he didn't have the ability to control Richard. Dimitri Ivanov did.

Her mother covered her mouth. "No. No, he wouldn't," she whispered into her hand.

Chapter Twenty-Four

♥

Nate rubbed his eyes and reached for his cup of coffee. It was cold. "I'm getting too old for this," he said to Chase, who sat beside him at the table, looking annoyingly wide awake.

They'd worked twenty-four hours straight, and they weren't any closer to providing the evidence required for a search warrant of Dimitri Ivanov's vacation home and offices.

"Have you been taking a nap every time you leave the boardroom?"

Chase huffed a laugh. "No. I'm used to working on little to no sleep. Michaela barely slept when her molars were coming in. Wait until you have a kid—you'll see what I mean."

An image of Nate holding a baby girl who looked just like her mother, all big purple eyes and wavy black hair, came to mind, and instead of feeling panic tighten every muscle in his chest, he smiled. He got up from the table and tossed his cold coffee in the garbage. Obviously, he was sleep deprived.

"You want another cup?" he asked Chase, pouring the dark, sludgy brew into his own mug. He added two tablespoons of sugar.

"How can you drink that? It tastes like—" Both his and Chase's cell phones started pinging at the same time. "Something's up."

"Yeah, let's hope we finally caught a break." Nate retrieved his phone from the table. Not a break, not a break at all. "Sounds like Bri is in rough shape," he said, reading through the texts from Mrs. M and Ryder about Ellie's sister.

Chase nodded. "Sadie said they nearly lost her. They were just lucky that her cousin Jace called his friend to check on Bri."

Nate called Ellie, and just as his calls had over the past twenty-four hours, he couldn't get through to her.

Chase glanced at him. "Ellie still not taking your calls?"

"No, but she will now." He called Ryder. "Hey, buddy. You doing okay?" He listened as Ryder relayed what had happened. He sounded pretty shaken up. "I'm sure she'll pull through, buddy. She's in good hands." Ryder said the nurses had told them the same thing. Bri's surgeon was supposedly one of the best. Nate prayed that he was.

"I'm glad you're there for Ellie, Joe, and the judge. What do you mean she's not there? Where is she?" He glanced at Chase while listening to Ryder. Chase was on the phone with Sadie. He shook his head as if confirming what Ryder had just told Nate.

"No, I'm sure Ellie's fine. But I'll try and get a hold

of her now." How Nate was going to do that, he had no idea. Ryder was still talking, and what he'd just said shocked Nate. "She what? Yeah, send it to me now. I'll see you in a bit, buddy. Call me if you need me."

"Does Sadie have any idea where Ellie is?" Nate asked Chase when he'd disconnected from his wife.

"None. Supposedly she was waiting for her mother at the inn and they were going to the hospital together, but she hasn't shown up. Neither of them have."

That didn't make sense to Nate. "Her mother lives five hours away. Why wouldn't Ellie just meet her at the hospital?" Nate asked as he opened the video file Ryder had just sent him.

"According to Sadie, the hospital called Miranda when they discovered Bri was missing, and she left for Highland Falls as soon as she got the news. Sadie can't reach Ellie either. Nate, what is it?"

He turned the screen to Chase, a flood of adrenaline rushing through his veins. "I think I know where she is." As he raised the volume, he prayed his feelings for Ellie were messing with his objectivity and that he was overreacting. "Listen closely to what Richard says to her."

"Damn, and I thought Sadie was a good shot," Chase said as he viewed the video.

If Nate hadn't already been half in love with Ellie, seeing her standing on the porch expertly handling the rifle with a fierce expression on her beautiful face would have done it for him. Ryder was right. She was a total badass. He just wished the video ended there.

Chase leaned in, angling his head to listen. He

slowly raised his gaze to Nate. The look in his eyes took away any hope that Nate was wrong.

* * *

Ellie drove up the long, winding mountain road to Dimitri Ivanov's vacation home. They were in the middle of nowhere. She'd given her mother some time to pull herself together, but she couldn't afford to give her any more. They were less than ten minutes from their destination.

"Mom, there's something else you need to know." Ellie told her about Dimitri's reaction to Nate and Ryder. "I don't know how, but I think he's connected to the organization that supplied the drugs to the people responsible for Brodie's death."

Her mother shook her head. "No. He wouldn't be involved with drugs."

Ellie was a little surprised that her mother didn't scoff or belittle her for talking about her ability to read the man's mind. "Why do you say that?"

"Because he lost a daughter to drugs." Her mother twisted her purse straps around her fingers, then glanced at Ellie. "You said he was afraid of Nate, but not for himself?"

"Yes. Do you know who he's protecting?"

Her mother nodded. "His son, Adrian. He's the one who's blackmailing me, Elliana. Not Dimitri."

"Why didn't you tell Dimitri?"

"He doesn't know that Brianna is his daughter."

"If he doesn't know, how did his son find out?"

"His mother. Dimitri's wife. She died last year. He asked her for a divorce two months after our affair began."

"He loved you."

"He did," she said with a soft smile. "I loved him too, Elliana."

"Were you going to leave Dad?"

"Yes. Your father and I hadn't been happy for a long time. I know that's a terrible excuse. But I honestly didn't go looking for another man. I was content with my life. I had you and your brother, a job that I enjoyed, and in my own way, I loved your father."

"So why didn't you leave?"

"Dimitri's wife had grown suspicious, and she hired a private investigator. She threatened me, you, Jace, and your father. They weren't idle threats. Her family was involved in organized crime. Dimitri wasn't, if that's what you're thinking. He had nothing to do with his wife's family. He was a self-made man and very proud of his accomplishments."

"So you ended your affair with Dimitri to protect us?"

"Yes. But his wife still had us watched. That's how she discovered I was pregnant. Someone sent a photo of me grocery shopping when I was six months pregnant. I kept that and the threat that accompanied it in my safe-deposit box to be opened if anything happened to me."

Ellie reached for her mother's hand. "I'm so sorry, Mom. That must have been horrible for you."

"It's why I was terrified when you figured out your father wasn't Brianna's biological father. It's no excuse for the way I treated you, but for me, the threat never ended. Not until the day I read her obituary in the newspaper. That was the best night's sleep I had in…well, sometimes it feels like forever. But that ended last month when Richard introduced me to his clients. I knew the moment Adrian looked at me that he knew about his father, me, and Brianna. I think it's why he convinced Dimitri to let Richard handle the deal for them. He's his mother's son, playing all the angles."

Her mother's confession shone a new light on what she'd put Ellie through as a teenager. While she couldn't forget the pain she'd caused or how that had affected her life, Ellie thought, in time, she could forgive her. Maybe once all this was over they'd be able to rebuild their relationship. She didn't feel the same about her parents' marriage. But that wasn't something she could think about now. "Is Adrian still connected to his mother's family?"

"No. Dimitri didn't want them anywhere near his family or his business. He blamed them for his daughter's death. He believed they were involved with the drug trade and wanted no part of it. He divorced his wife months after their daughter died. He wouldn't…Wait. I just remembered something."

Her mother's cheeks pinked. "I met with Dimitri. Two days before our meeting at the inn with you. We were having coffee on the patio, and he was reading the newspaper. There was an article about a man who'd just been arrested for suspected drug trafficking. Dimitri flew into a rage, which isn't like him at all. He called Adrian, and he came right away. Dimitri threw the newspaper at his son and asked him to explain what his cousin was doing in North Carolina. He accused Adrian of working with him. Adrian swore he wasn't, but I think he might have been lying. Dimitri thought so too."

"I think I know the man you're talking about. Nate arrested him. But if they discovered his connection to Adrian and Dimitri, why didn't they bring them in for questioning?"

"According to what Adrian said to his father, his cousin wouldn't talk upon threat of death. Nate and the people he works with wouldn't make the connection on their own because the man has been living under an assumed identity for more than two decades. The family faked his death when the FBI were closing in on him for murder. The family also ensured his prints and DNA aren't in the system."

"Mom, I don't want to scare you. But people have been killed for knowing what you know."

Her mother shook her head. "Soon everyone will know. Dimitri's spent the last nine years since his daughter's death not only accumulating wealth and power but collecting evidence to bring his wife's family down. I think he's ready to make his move. He warned Adrian to steer clear of his mother's family or he'd find himself going down with them. What are you doing?" her mother asked when Ellie slowed down and pulled off the road a few yards from the Ivanov estate.

"Calling Nate. He needs to know what you just told me."

Nate picked up on the first ring. "Ellie, thank God."

A heated shiver raced down her spine in response to his deep, gravelly voice. A totally inappropriate response given the gravity of the situation, but she couldn't seem to help herself where Nate was concerned. She reminded herself why she'd been blocking his calls and his texts, and that shiver-inducing desire was replaced by a resolute determination to protect herself.

"Where are you?"

"It doesn't matter. I have information you need."

"If you're headed to Dimitri Ivanov's place, it sure as hell does matter. And if you ever block my calls or texts again, I'll—"

"I don't have time for this. Just listen to me," she said, and repeated what her mother had told her.

"Hang on. I'm putting you on speaker. Listen up, people," he said. Then he told Ellie to continue.

Several times he interrupted her with questions, some of which she had to put her mother on the phone to answer.

"Will that help?" Ellie asked once she was finished.

"You have no idea how much, babe. Thank your mother for me. Now do me a favor, turn your car around and head to the hospital."

"We can't. We have to make sure Richard doesn't go anywhere near Bri. Dimitri is the only one who can stop him."

"Ellie, you can make that happen, and so can your mother. Put me on speaker."

"Okay, you're on speaker."

"Mrs. MacLeod, if Ellie lodges a complaint of spousal abuse against Richard using evidence that she's obtained by using her psychic abilities, will you back her?"

"Yes. Yes, I will." Her mother reached for Ellie's hand and gave it a comforting squeeze. Ellie didn't realize why until a tear dropped onto their joined hands. It wasn't only that her mother was willing to acknowledge her abilities that made her emotional, but that Nate was too.

Her mother continued. "I will also lodge a complaint concerning an incident I witnessed a few months ago but that I allowed both my daughter and her husband to explain away."

"Gabe will meet you at the hospital and take your statements. Richard won't get anywhere near Bri. And if he's at the Ivanov estate when we arrive, which should be within the next thirty minutes, he'll be cooling his heels in jail for as long as we can legally hold him."

As Ellie pulled onto the long tree-lined driveway of the Ivanov estate in order to turn the car around, she spotted Richard's SUV. "He's there." In response to Nate swearing under his breath, she said, "We're leaving. I just had to turn—" A Range Rover pulled in behind her.

Her mother looked over her shoulder. "It's Adrian."

"Get the hell out of there now, Ellie!" Nate yelled through the open line.

"Quiet," she said, powering down her window. She stuck her head out, smiled, and pointed to the road.

"Sorry. Wrong address. If you back up, I'll get out of your way."

The man got out of his vehicle and walked over to her open window. "I'm sure my father would love to meet you, Ms. MacLeod. Miranda." He nodded at her mother, his lips curled in a sneer.

"And I'd love to meet your father too. But we'll have to discuss the sale of Mirror Lake Inn at another time, Mr. Ivanov. My sister had an accident, and she's undergoing surgery as we speak. We need to get to the hospital immediately."

"Funny you should mention that. It's why I'm here. My father is very upset that you wouldn't allow Richard to see his wife. But I'm sure we can clear this up. As soon as we do, you can be on your way to the hospital. Please, drive in." He moved his jacket aside. It wasn't an invitation. He had a gun.

Ellie did as he directed. She didn't have a choice. It wasn't like she could move his Range Rover out of the way, as she told Nate. "Don't worry, I'm armed." She ended the call, looking for somewhere to hide her phone. She didn't want Adrian to find out she'd been talking to Nate. She reached down and tucked it under the mat.

"You're armed?" her mother said, her eyes wide.

"Yes, and lucky for us, Grandpa taught me how to use a gun." She glanced at her mother. She'd lost all the color in her face. "It's going to be okay, Mom. Nate is coming, and you trust Dimitri, right? You don't think he'd let his son hurt you?"

"I trust Dimitri, but I don't trust Adrian. He hates me."

"We need to let Dimitri know what's going on," Ellie said as she drove up the tree-lined road at a snail's pace, buying time. "You need to call him. Put him on speaker and put your phone on the console."

As soon as the call connected, Ellie said, "Mr. Ivanov, this is Ellie MacLeod. My mother's with me. If Richard is with you, please pretend this is a business call."

"Jerome, I've been expecting your call."

"Thank you. I'm sorry to do this, to both you and my mother, but you have to know. My sister Bri is your daughter."

"Elliana!" her mother cried.

"I'm sorry, Mom. But he has a right to know. Don't blame my mother, Mr. Ivanov. The only reason she kept Bri a secret from you is that your wife terrorized her for more than twenty-seven years. And your son has picked up where she left off. He's blackmailing my mother to sell Mirror Lake Inn to you. He's also forcing us to meet with you now. I'm going to send you a photo. Don't show Richard. He's the reason Bri is in the hospital."

She parked the SUV beside Richard's. Adrian pulled in beside her. "I have to go. Your son's coming." She hit End. "Send him the photos, Mom, then delete the conversation and put your phone under the mat."

Chapter Twenty-Five

♥

Nate slammed his palms against the table when the line went dead. He was going to kill Adrian Ivanov with his bare hands, slowly and painfully.

"Ellie has a gun, and she knows how to use it," Chase said, clearly trying to reassure him. Except his best friend looked as worried about the situation as Nate.

"They'll take it from her as soon as she gets out of the car."

"Right. Of course they will. But Ellie has her superpower. She can read their minds. That's something they won't expect, and she can use it to her advantage. She's also smart and resourceful." Chase smiled, nodding at the door. "And she has us for backup."

An agent walked into the conference room, waving a warrant. "Saddle up, boys and girls. It's time to ride."

Everyone grabbed their gear that they had waiting for precisely this moment and headed for the door. Nate's boss blocked him.

"Where do you think you're going, Black? You're riding the desk. You can coordinate with your team over their comms."

"Boss, I have to go. They've got the woman who broke the case for us, Ellie MacLeod, and her mother."

"Did we not just have this conversation yesterday morning?"

"Yes, but this isn't about Brodie or the case. If Ellie wasn't there, and in danger, I'd gladly stay out of it." And he realized that was the absolute truth. He no longer needed to avenge Brodie's death or gain the absolution he'd believed it would grant him. But he'd move mountains to get to Ellie, and right now, his boss was the mountain. "Please, I can't sit here knowing she's in danger. I'm in love with her."

His boss smiled. "Then what are you waiting for? But Black," he called as Nate ran from the room, "do me a favor and don't kill anyone. The paperwork's a bitch."

* * *

Adrian took Ellie's gun as soon as she stepped from the SUV. "Do you always go armed to a social call, Ms. MacLeod?"

"Do you always blackmail a woman to get what you want, Mr. Ivanov?"

He blinked and then his eyes narrowed. "Miranda, I'm surprised you shared your dirty little secret with your daughter." Adrian tsked, but Ellie didn't think he was as cool as he pretended to be. His jaw was clenched, and his face had reddened.

Ellie prayed that Dimitri wouldn't take long to act on her warning.

"It's funny how it's always the woman's dirty little secret, isn't it, Mom?" She smiled at Adrian. "It takes two to make a baby. Didn't they teach you that in school?"

"You have a smart mouth. How would you like me to teach—"

"Miranda darling, I wasn't expecting you." Dimitri rushed out of the mansion and past his son, taking Ellie's mother in his arms. He kissed her forehead and then murmured something in her ear before tucking her against his side, wrapping a protective arm around her. He smiled at Ellie. "Finally we meet, Elliana. May I call you Elliana?"

"Ellie is fine. It's nice to meet you, Mr. Ivanov," she said, taking his proffered hand.

"Good. I am glad you don't hold my love for your mother against me."

"Papa, show some respect for me and Mama. You had an affair with this woman. Do you think it's fair that you rub it in my face?"

"Remember who you are talking to. Watch your mouth." Dimitri's eyes narrowed on the gun. "What's this? Put that away. I apologize for my son. He has no manners."

Careful, Dimitri, don't push too hard, Ellie thought.

"It's her gun. You're lucky I took it from her," Adrian told his father. "She could have shot you. How easily you forget what she did to Richard." He nodded at her mother. "She makes you weak. You let her manipulate you, Papa."

Richard came out of the mansion. "What's going—" He broke off, a relieved smile creasing his face when he spotted Ellie. He walked to Adrian and clapped him on the back. "Thank you. I knew I could count on you. Both of you." He moved to her mother. "Miranda—"

"Don't come near me," her mother said. "And you will not go near my daughter. Either of my daughters ever again."

Richard's mouth dropped open.

"Miranda darling, what is this about?" Dimitri asked.

Ellie didn't understand why he was pretending that he didn't know Bri was in hospital or that Richard was responsible for her being there, but she had to trust that he had a good reason for keeping it to himself. Just like he was keeping his knowledge of Bri's parentage to himself.

Her mother searched his face, probably wondering the same thing. "He's been abusing Brianna. She's in the hospital because of him."

"No, that's not true!" Richard whirled on Ellie. "This is your fault. You've been spreading your sick, vicious lies about me again."

"Come, we'll go into the house and discuss this calmly." Dimitri reached for Ellie's hand, drawing her toward him. He tucked her under his other arm.

Ellie wondered if this was why he hadn't said anything. He could better control the situation from inside his home.

Richard and Adrian stayed where they were, talking, low enough that they couldn't be heard.

"I'm sorry, Dimitri. I'm sorry I didn't tell you about Brianna and that Adrian was blackmailing me," her mother whispered. "I was afraid."

"We don't have time to discuss this now, but I am also sorry. Sorry that my ex-wife and my son terrorized you and that you didn't trust me to protect you. But I will protect you now, both of you. Your friend, Mr. Black, were you able to reach him?" he asked Ellie.

"Yes," she said, praying she wasn't making a mistake by sharing that with Dimitri. "He's on his way."

"How long before he arrives?" Dimitri asked.

"Twenty minutes." Nate had said thirty, but at least ten minutes had passed.

Dimitri nodded as he ushered them into a living room at the back of the house. "Good. So we must keep both my son and Richard here until they arrive. I want this over today." He looked around the room. "Please sit." He gestured at a large sectional by the window. "Sit at the far end, Ellie. From there, you should be able to see when Mr. Black arrives. You will signal me when he is here. Like so." He rubbed his right eyebrow. "If my back is to you, say your mother's name."

Ellie nodded and leaned to her left. She couldn't see all the way to the front door, but she could see a good part of the hallway leading to the back of the house.

Dimitri hurried to the bar in the corner, glancing to his left as he pressed a button. A drawer slid open, and he removed a gun. He slid it into the back of his waistband. He looked up as he smoothed his jacket over the gun, noting what must have been the surprise in Ellie's and her mother's eyes.

He gave them a sad smile. "The problem with wealth and power is someone always wants to take them from you. I have learned to be prepared for anything. My son joining forces with my sworn enemies, my ex-wife's family, that I wasn't prepared for."

At the sound of the front door closing, he raised his voice. "Miranda darling, you look like you could use a glass of wine."

Ellie saw Adrian and Richard's shadows on the wall only seconds before they appeared in the living room. Which meant she'd have very little time to warn Dimitri when Nate eventually arrived.

"Ah, there you are," Dimitri said. "What can I get you? The ladies and I are having a glass of wine. Will you join us?"

Adrian frowned, looking from Ellie to her mother to his father. His expression relaxed as he walked into the room. Dimitri's genial smile must have put him at ease. "I'll have a whiskey, Papa."

"I'll have the same, Dimitri. Thank you," Richard said.

"Ladies first." He brought Ellie and her mother each a glass of wine. "Taste it, Ellie, and be sure it's to your liking."

She brought the glass to her mouth and took a sip. "It's lovely, thank you."

"Now, your drinks, and then we shall talk. Please, sit. Take your papa's chair, Adrian. You can take the one beside him, Richard."

The seating arrangement placed both men at the far end of the living room.

Dimitri picked up a crystal decanter and poured three fingers of whiskey into each of the old-fashioned glasses as if the situation weren't fraught with danger.

"Why are you looking at my papa like that?" Adrian asked Ellie.

She shrugged. "Just curious. He's the man my mother fell in love with when she was married to my father. I guess I'm wondering why." Her mother sank lower on the sectional and Dimitri winced. She didn't mean to hurt them but she thought maybe the affair would give her and Adrian something to commiserate over. She needed to buy time. "Don't tell me you weren't curious when you met my—"

"Shut your mouth," Adrian snarled.

Okay, so that was a terrible idea.

Dimitri calmly walked over to where Adrian and Richard sat in the armchairs, set both whiskeys on the table between them, and then slapped his son across the face. "Do not ever speak to a woman that way again."

As his father turned to walk away, Ellie saw Adrian reach inside his jacket for his gun. "Dimitri!"

Ellie threw herself in front of her mother. Father and son had drawn on each other.

"What the hell are you waiting for, Richard?" Adrian yelled, and that's when Ellie realized Adrian must have given Richard her gun when they were talking outside, a gun he was now pointing directly at her.

But he was scared, so scared that she could clearly

read his mind. He'd never held a gun before, let alone shot someone. He wanted to though. He wanted nothing more than to get rid of her.

Her mother sobbed into her hands, terrified that she would lose the only man she had ever truly loved. She was scared for Ellie too. She loved her. *Focus*, Ellie told herself.

She had to get through to Richard. He hated her, but he did love her sister. However twisted that love might be. "Adrian's using you, Richard. He's been using you all along. You see what he's capable of, holding a gun on his own father because he's gotten in the way of his ambition. What do you think he would do to Bri? She's his sister, Richard."

"No, it can't be true." He lowered his gun. "Adrian—"

"It is true. Brianna is my daughter," Dimitri said. "Like you, Richard, I found out today. But my son... How long have you known, Adrian?"

"A week after Mama died," he spit the words at his father. Then his lips twisted in a semblance of a smile. "Too bad you'll never know her. I guess I have you to thank for that, Richard."

Ellie took her sobbing mother's hand. "Don't listen to him. Bri's not going to die, Mom. She's strong. She—"

"It's not my fault, Dimitri. I didn't push her. I didn't!" he said when Adrian laughed. But Richard was focused on Dimitri, who moved his gun between him and his son.

"Look at you, all protective Papa now." Adrian

sneered. "How far would you go to protect her, I wonder?"

"I would do anything to protect her."

"Good. Perhaps this won't have to end in bloodshed after all. I'm sure you ladies would also do anything to protect his bastard daughter, wouldn't you?"

Ellie wanted to yell at him for calling her sister a bastard, but she kept her mouth closed and nodded. Her mother did the same.

"And you, Richard, will you keep your mouth shut?"

He gave a jerky nod. "Yes, of course. I'll do anything you say."

"Your silence is all I want, and yours," Adrian said to Ellie and her mother. "As for you, Papa, you will sign everything over to me. Everything. We'll see if your lover still wants you when you have nothing."

Ellie thought she heard the creak of the front door opening. She'd moved to the other end of the sectional to protect her mother, so she could no longer see down the hall. She opened her mind. Nate and his team were here.

Dimitri's back was to her. "Miranda!" Ellie patted her mother's cheek, relieved when her mother closed her eyes and let her head drop forward as though she had fainted.

"I will not allow you to use my company to funnel drugs!" Dimitri roared, no doubt in an effort to keep his son's focus on him and cover the sounds of their rescuers' arrival. "You will have to kill me first."

"That can be arranged," Adrian said, aiming his gun at his father's head.

"You would shoot me, Adrian? Your own papa. Why?"

"She destroyed our family. You don't care about me anymore. You don't care about the company. You only care about her." Adrian rubbed the gun over his sweaty forehead. "I wanted to rip her family apart like she did ours, but instead, I brought you back together."

"And what is your excuse for going into business with your uncle behind my back?"

"You treat me like your flunky. He doesn't. He respects me."

"He doesn't respect you. He's using you to get to me!" Dimitri shouted as he raised his gun. "You underestimate me if you think I won't pull the trigger. You have betrayed me. You are in bed with your mother's family. You are in the drug trade."

A flash of movement outside caught her eye. It was Nate. He was half-hidden behind the patio's stone retaining wall, a rifle aimed at Adrian. She tore her gaze away, afraid she'd alert Adrian to his presence.

"FBI, drop your weapons!" a familiar voice yelled. It was Chase.

Adrian stared at his father. "You knew. You knew they were coming, didn't you?" He didn't wait for an answer, instead jumping to his feet.

"It's over, Son. Please drop your gun. I don't want to lose you. Please." Dimitri stepped back from Adrian and placed his gun on the floor. Richard did the same and then raised his hands in the air.

Adrian swung his gun toward Ellie. "Get up. Get up now or I'll shoot your mother." He took a step toward them. He was going to use her as a hostage. Ellie glanced at her gun on the floor by Richard's feet. Adrian must have sensed what she planned to do because he rushed forward, lunging for her arm.

A shot rang out, shattering the glass. Adrian dropped his gun and crumpled in a heap at her feet. Nate had shot him.

Agents rushed into the living room with their guns drawn. "Don't move," Chase said to Dimitri as he went to run to Adrian's side.

"Please. He is my son."

The French doors onto the patio opened, and Nate stepped inside. He was on his cell phone, ordering the paramedics inside. His eyes held hers as he walked toward her. She got up from the couch on shaky legs, moving around a moaning Adrian to throw herself at Nate. His arms went around her, and he held her close, his voice a low rumble as he gave orders to his team.

Once he was finished, he stepped back and put an arm around her shoulders, bringing her tight against his side. "Let's get you out of here." He glanced at her mother, who was attempting to go to Dimitri, an agent holding her back. "Mrs. MacLeod, let the agents do their job and come with me."

"But they're going to arrest him. He didn't do anything wrong. Elliana, tell him. Tell him he tried to protect us."

"It's true, Nate. He did." She told him everything that had transpired in the past thirty minutes. A muscle pulsed in his jaw as he looked down at Adrian. Nate had shot him just below the right shoulder. He looked like he wanted to shoot him again.

Two paramedics carrying a stretcher entered the living room, and Nate gently moved her out of the way. "Chase, let Mr. Ivanov go to the hospital with his son. We'll take his statement there."

"Thank you, Mr. Black. I will give you all the information you need to bring my wife's family's organization down. I am sorry for the loss of your friend. Had I known what was going on, I would have stopped it." He gave Ellie a wan smile. "I am sorry for the hurt that I have caused your family. I love your mother, but you have all suffered enough because of me. I will stay away from your family."

Ellie glanced at her mother, who sobbed quietly into her hands. "Thank you, Mr. Ivanov. But where you and my mother go from here is up to her, not me. All I ask is that you give my sister time to heal before telling her the truth."

"Thank you, Ellie. You are a kind woman." He glanced at Nate. "I hope you know how lucky you are, Mr. Black."

Nate looked down at her and smiled. "I do. I—" He broke off when Richard yelled at Chase, who was cuffing his hands behind his back.

Dimitri glanced over his shoulder. "Keep him away from my daughter, and from me." He strode off to catch up to the paramedics who were carrying his son from the house.

"Why are you arresting me? I didn't do anything wrong!" Richard sent a pleading look at Ellie. "Tell him! Tell him I need to go to the hospital to be with my wife."

"You're not going anywhere near my daughter," her mother said to Richard. Then she said to Chase, "I would like to file a complaint against this man."

"I'll be more than happy to take your statement at the hospital, Mrs. MacLeod." Chase handed Richard off to another agent. "Yours too, Ellie." He came over and gave her a hug. "Glad you're okay." He looked from her to Nate. "Why don't we give you guys some time alone?"

"Appreciate it," Nate said.

"Mrs. MacLeod, I'll take you to the hospital."

"Thank you," her mother said to Chase and then she took Ellie's hand in hers. "You are the bravest woman I know. You protected me when I've done nothing to deserve your protection. You have a gift, Elliana. You are a gift, and I'm sorry that I didn't treat you that way. I'd like to try and make it up to you. To be the mother you deserve, if you'll let me."

"I'd like that, Mom." She leaned in and kissed her mother's cheek.

Her mother smiled and then glanced at Nate. "I have a feeling it will take more than words for you to believe that I want to make things right with my daughter, Mr. Black. But I want to thank you for what you did today. I'll be forever grateful." She gave Elliana's arm a quick squeeze. "I'll see you at the hospital."

"She's right, you know," Nate said as her mother walked from the room with Chase. "You are an incredibly brave woman. I just wish you were a little less brave."

"I'm not that brave." She looked up at him. "If you hadn't come when you did. If you hadn't shot Adrian, I—"

"Don't. Don't remind me. I can't think about that right now. Maybe in a couple days, we can talk about it. I was terrified I was going to lose you. I—" He glanced around the room. "I know the place is swarming with agents, but Ellie, I really need to kiss you."

"I don't think that's a good idea. I'm still mad at you."

"I'm the one who should be mad at you. You shut me out. Blocked my texts and my calls, and you put your life on the line. You scared ten years of my life off me."

"You walked away from me, from us."

"For less than twenty-four hours, and I never stopped thinking about you. Not once, Ellie."

"You basically passed me off to another man, Nate."

"Okay, that was stupid. I messed up. But it's only because I wanted...I wanted to give you everything that you deserved, and I wasn't sure I was the man who could give that to you."

"And now you do?"

He stepped away from her. "Read my mind, Ellie."

"I can't. I told you before. You're the only person I can't read, Nate."

"Try."

She let down her barriers and opened her mind to his. *I deserve every beautiful, badass inch of you, Ellie*

MacLeod. I love you. I think I've loved you since the first day I kissed you.. If you don't let me love you, let me kiss you, I don't know if I'll survive.

She threw her arms around his neck and murmured against his lips. "I love you too. I've loved you since the first day I kissed you. Kiss me, and don't ever let me go."

Chapter Twenty-Six

♥

Two months later

Ellie put the finishing touches on her painting, pleased with how it had turned out. The turquoise-blue water shimmered and the vibrant pink flowers she'd added along the shoreline popped. But the focal point was the cabins in the background.

She planned to give the painting to Ryder on opening day of Second Chance Camp. If everything went according to plan, they'd be welcoming campers at the beginning of August. Nate and the board of directors of the charity founded in Brodie's name, with some input from Ryder, were using the money to start the camp for at-risk youth in Brodie's memory. It was a beautiful tribute to a man who'd done so much for the struggling young people in his community.

Ellie turned from her painting to focus on the men and women sitting behind their easels on the lawn. "Just remember, the goal isn't for your paintings to look like mine. This is your interpretation of today's theme—love in bloom," she said as she walked along the third row, going over her lines in her head.

She chuckled as she'd been directed to by Spencer when she came to stand behind him and his leading lady, a pretty blonde with adorable dimples. They were sharing an easel and pretending to paint. At Spencer's request, Ellie had painted the landscape for them last night. "You two have done a wonderful job capturing our theme on canvas. I'm sorry we didn't have enough easels to go around, but I have a feeling this worked out just as it was meant to."

"I couldn't agree with you more, ma'am," Spencer said in a thick Southern drawl. "Love hasn't only bloomed on our canvas."

It wasn't easy, but Ellie managed to hold back an eye roll at the cheesy line.

"Oh, Dallas," his leading lady said, resting her head on his shoulder. "You make my heart sing."

Ellie was afraid she was going to laugh out loud and moved to the row in front of them. As she got a look at the last painter's canvas, the gurgle of laughter in her throat dissolved. "Painting the background black was an inspired choice," she whispered near her sister's ear so it looked like she was studying the painting and not talking. "The flowers will really stand out."

Bri had agreed to take part in today's scene for one reason and one reason only. They'd promised she could skip her physical therapy session. Two months into her recovery, her sister was doing better than expected. At least physically.

Her sister snorted at the idea of her painting flowers. Spencer cleared his throat. The participants weren't supposed to talk or make any noise unless they'd been given lines. Her grandfather had lost his chance to be in the scene when he burped.

Ellie's mother, who was sitting beside Bri, tapped a finger to the side of her head. She wanted Ellie to read her mind. Ellie sighed inwardly. It was her own fault. She was the one who'd come up with the idea.

Ellie stared into her mother's eyes. *I'm worried about your sister. She's not herself. I don't know who she is anymore. Maybe you should call her doctor.*

Calling Cal would not improve her sister's mood. She'd refused to go to him since they'd had an argument—a loud one—two weeks ago. Ellie didn't know what their fight had been about. But she had a feeling it was personal and not doctor-patient related. However, that wasn't something she could say to her mother at the moment, so she gave her an almost imperceptible nod.

She also couldn't tell her mother that part of Bri's struggle was knowing that Dimitri was her father. Her mother had decided it wasn't fair to keep the truth from Bri, and she was tired of living a lie. She wasn't back with Dimitri though. She was spending as much time as she could with Bri and Ellie while at the same time trying to make amends to Ellie's father. Ellie didn't know if her parents' relationship would recover, but she appreciated the effort her mother was making.

"Forget the flowers. I want to paint him," Jeannie said, pointing her paintbrush at the bare-chested man rowing across the lake. Two of Jeannie's friends wolf-whistled, standing up to wave at Nate.

Ellie pressed her lips together. They were in trouble now.

"Cut!" Spencer yelled, getting up from his chair. He walked to Ellie and put his hands on her shoulders. "I know this has been a tiring couple of weeks for you but could you work up a little enthusiasm? Maybe smile instead of staring everyone down?"

"I wasn't staring anyone down." Maybe she had been. Spencer had no idea how exhausting it was with everyone trying to get her to read their minds. "But I'm not the one who messed up the scene. It was Jeannie and her friends."

"I know. My assistant is taking care of that now." He nodded at the man trying to coax Jeannie and her friends off their chairs.

Good luck with that, Ellie thought.

Spencer continued. "Although it would be helpful if Nate put on a T-shirt before he decided to row over. But I was about to call 'cut' ten seconds ago because of your face. It's a very beautiful face, but it was a frowny face," Spencer said with a wink. "Just remind yourself that once we put this scene to bed, we film the final scene tonight. That should make you smile. And if that doesn't work, think of all the money you'll rake in once the movie releases. Everyone will want to stay at Mirror Lake Inn."

"You're right. I'll do better. And I really do appreciate you including the inn in the title and in so many of the scenes." Spencer had titled the movie *Love Blooms at Mirror Lake Inn*.

"Take your paws off my woman, *Dallas*," Nate said

as he strolled toward them, wiping his sweaty forehead with his T-shirt.

Ellie rolled her eyes. Nate thought Spencer's character's name was hilarious and teased him about it every chance he got, which was pretty much all the time. The cast and crew were staying at the inn and at the cabins.

"Honestly, Nate, would you put some clothes on?" Spencer said. "You're distracting my cast and crew."

Nate made a face and looked down at himself. He had absolutely no idea how incredibly hot he looked right now with his sweat-slicked bronzed body and all that sexy ink. "It's almost eighty degrees out. We don't all have people following us around with fans to keep us cool."

"Har har. I'll give you guys two minutes and not a second more," Spencer said, and then walked off to talk to one of the cameramen.

"Whatever you're thinking of saying to him, don't," Ellie told Nate. "The extras in this scene are stressing him out."

"I don't want to waste our two minutes on him anyway." He pulled her against him.

"You're all sweaty. You're going to stain my top."

"You didn't mind last night." He tapped his finger against the side of his head.

"No way. I know exactly what you're thinking about, and I don't need that image in my mind while we're filming this scene. And I was naked last night. I didn't have to worry about stains."

"You're killing me, babe." He tapped his lips. "Just lay a quick one on me."

Their quick one must have gone over the two-minute mark because Spencer yelled, "Cut!"

"I'm not going to miss them when they pack up tomorrow morning," Nate said. "It'll be nice to get back to normal."

"It's been a lot of work but it's been fun too. Everyone is excited about tonight. You should wrap up over at the cabins soon. Your family will be here in a couple of hours. Ryder and Gina too."

Ryder, Gina, and Toby arrived every weekend to help get the cabins into shape. Ellie hadn't had the heart to separate Ryder and Toby. They would have been lost without each other. No matter how cool Ryder tried to play it. He missed Joe and the judge too. Ellie had a feeling the teenager would be spending his summers on Mirror Lake just like she once had.

"One more roof to go. But don't worry, I wouldn't miss tonight for anything. Just one thing: as of now, stay out of my head, beautiful."

"Now you've got me curious. Do you have a surprise for me? Nate, what are you planning?" she called as he walked to the sliding glass doors.

He glanced over his shoulder and waggled his eyebrows at her.

"Places, people," Spencer yelled, waving over a woman.

She took her place in front of Ellie's painting with the clapper board. "Scene five, take one hundred and forty-three," the woman said wearily, clacking the boards together.

It took three more tries before they got the scene right. Spencer had asked everyone to return at nine o'clock to film the last scene of the movie. The man was demanding, but, according to the cast and crew, an excellent director. He was also happy they'd chosen Highland Falls as the winning location. The other night at Highland Brew, he'd announced that Happy Ever After Entertainment would be filming there again, which had guaranteed he was man of the hour.

* * *

"Are you decent?" her cousin asked through the door of Ellie's room.

"Come on in. You have great timing," Ellie said when Sadie walked into the room, turning to point at her back. "I need help with my zipper."

"I love that dress," Sadie said, closing the door behind her.

"Really? I wasn't sure if I should wear it, but Nate practically insisted that I did." She glanced over her shoulder at her cousin as she zipped her up. "Don't you find that a bit odd?"

"No. Why?"

"I wore it for my tour of Main Street with Spencer. I didn't think Nate would want a reminder of that day."

"Yes, but don't forget your romantic dance with Nate. Every woman in the bar that night was practically swooning."

"Have you forgotten how our dance ended?"

"No, but I have a theory that's when Nate finally realized he was head over heels in love with you."

Ellie laughed. "And ran terrified into the night. After he gave Spencer the all clear to date me."

Sadie grinned. "That'll be a story to tell your kids."

"Don't say that to Nate. He'd probably have a panic attack thinking I was trying to tie him down."

"I'm guessing you haven't seen the plaque over your door," Sadie said.

Ellie opened the door and stepped into the hall. Over the door to her room was a wooden plaque that read *Ellie and Nate*. Ellie pressed her hands to her chest, incredibly touched. For a man who was allergic to commitment, that sign said a lot. "So that was his surprise." Except she found it a little odd that he didn't want to do the reveal himself. "He was honestly ticked that Spencer and I finished higher in the most romantic couple contest than Nate and I did."

Sadie and Chase had actually won and had their own guest room named after them down the hall, but Spencer and Ellie had come a close second. She and Nate had finished seventh.

Sadie laughed. "I know. Chase told me he grumbled about it for a week. Oh well, he got his revenge. He got you."

"He did. And speaking of Nate, have you seen him? I haven't seen him since he rowed over earlier." She went to the window and searched the gathering crowd. "There's no way I'll be able to spot him. He's probably with his family, Ryder, and Gina."

"We should get going anyway. You know what a stickler Spencer is for being on time," her cousin said.

As they walked down the stairs to the reception area, Ellie came to a standstill. "Sadie, look."

The dining room had been transformed. The tables were dressed with pink linen tablecloths and gorgeous floral displays graced each one while fairy lights lit up the entire room.

"Wow. It looks like love really is in bloom at Mirror Lake Inn. The Happy Ever After set designers are amazing. I'm totally stealing this idea," Ellie said.

"If you think this is amazing, wait until you see what they've done outside."

Sadie was right. The set designers had outdone themselves. "I don't want them to take any of this down. It's so romantic."

"I think that's the point. This is the big romantic scene. The one where the couple finally realizes that they can't live without each other."

"I hope Nate doesn't laugh. You know how he is about love and romance. Spencer wants to wrap this up in one take."

"Places, people!" Spencer yelled.

"He's wearing his white suit. The one he wore with me on the tour." Ellie spun around. "I have to change."

"You're not going anywhere, beautiful. I love you in that dress," Nate said from behind her.

Ellie turned and he held out his hand. "Are you sure, Nate? It'll just take me a couple minutes to change. There's so many people, no one will even notice."

"Never been surer of anything in my life." He walked her to the dance floor.

She tugged on his hand. "Nate, you're going to ruin Dallas and Deena's big moment."

"Relax, babe. Spencer wants the couples who finaled in the Highland Falls contest to dance with them."

Ellie bit back a laugh. "Honey, I hate to tell you, but I don't think seventh place equates to finaling."

"We got robbed. You and Spencer weren't even a couple," he said as he took her into his arms.

"But we have a room named after us and that's all that counts, right?" She looped her arms around his neck and stretched up on her toes to kiss him. "I loved my surprise. Thank you."

"I hope you do," he said, his eyes amused.

She was about to ask him what he was up to when Spencer called for quiet and then laid out what he expected from the extras. He directed the couples to move toward the edges of the dance floor once the song began. He looked at Ellie and Nate and said, "I think you two will love our song."

"Three, two, one," he said, and then he led his leading lady onto the dance floor to the first strains of Aloe Blacc and LeAnn Rimes's "I Do" coming over the speakers.

"He stole our song," Nate muttered.

"Shh," Ellie whispered, struggling not to laugh. "Move toward the side. You're blocking the camera's view of them."

"Good," Nate said. Then his eyes went wide. "And now he's stealing my move!"

Spencer had bent his leading lady over his arm, staring lovingly into her eyes.

"Honey, it's not exactly your move," Ellie said. "I must have seen it in at least five movies."

"I'd never let you fall, Deena," Spencer said.

Deena cupped the side of his face. "I already have."

Ellie looked from the couple to Nate. "They totally stole our lines!"

Spencer and his leading lady straightened, and arm in arm they bowed to the audience. "Since we took some creative liberties with one of Highland Falls' couples' most romantic moments, we thought it only fair we play their song for them again." Spencer motioned to his sound woman. "You've got the floor, Ellie and Nate," he said as "I Do" began to play.

"There's a reason I wanted you to wear that dress again, Ellie. I wanted a do-over. I messed up that night. I wanted a second chance to make it right," Nate said, looking into her eyes as they swayed to the music in the middle of the dance floor.

"You don't have anything to make up for, Nate. But I love that you wanted to do this for me. It's very romantic and a memory I'll cherish."

"I hope so." He stopped dancing and removed her hand from around his neck, holding it as he went down on one knee in front of her.

A sob escaped from between her parted lips and she covered her mouth as he removed a blue velvet box from his pocket, opening it to reveal a gorgeous engagement ring.

"Ellie MacLeod, I promise to cherish you and to do

everything in my power to make you happy. I promise to love you for the rest of your life. Will you do me the honor of marrying me?"

"Oh, Nate, nothing would make me happier than marrying you," Ellie said, smiling through her tears.

"And that's a wrap!" Spencer yelled over their cheering family and friends.

Recipes from the Mirror Lake Inn

I hate to be the bearer of bad news, but if you were hoping to make a reservation for afternoon tea at the Mirror Lake Inn, you'll be waiting a long time. The inn's phone hasn't stopped ringing since the movie came out, and their website crashes every second day with the number of people trying to make reservations at the inn and for afternoon tea.

The last time I checked, they were booked through December 2024. But with a little coaxing, Ellie agreed to share some of their recipes with you. Imagine my surprise when I discovered that the inn's recipes were almost identical to the recipes my Scottish granny passed down to me. 😌

And here are three of my granny's tips for making scones:

Tip #1: Don't overwork the dough.

Tip #2: Don't take your butter, buttermilk, cream, or egg out of the refrigerator before you're ready to use them.

Tip #3: Don't twist the dough when cutting it into shapes.

CURRANT SCONES

A classic and one of our favorites. We serve with Devonshire cream and strawberry jam, the same as they do at the inn. If you can't find Devonshire cream at your local grocery store, you can use whipping cream instead. We don't add sugar or vanilla when we whip the cream to stiff peaks, but feel free to do so if you like it sweet. Serve Devonshire cream and jam with strawberry scones as well as with lavender scones. Lemon curd and Devonshire cream are extra yummy with lavender scones.

- 2 cups flour (plus extra for dusting hands and countertop)
- ⅓ cup sugar
- 2 tsp. baking powder
- ⅓ cup cold butter
- 1 cup currants
- ½ cup buttermilk
- 1 large egg
- ½ tsp. vanilla
- 1 egg white whisked with ½ tsp. water or cream to make a wash (optional)

Before you get started, preheat the oven to 400 degrees and line a baking sheet with parchment paper.

In a large bowl, whisk flour, sugar, and baking powder together. Cut cold butter into small pieces over the flour mixture. With your fingers, or you can use a pastry cutter or two knives if you prefer, combine the mixture until the butter resembles pea-size crumbs. In a separate bowl, whisk together currants, buttermilk, egg, and vanilla. Pour into the flour mixture and stir (I use a wooden spoon) to combine.

Gather the dough into a ball—it will be sticky—and place onto a lightly floured countertop. With lightly floured hands, knead dough until smooth—a minute or two at most. With your hands, pat dough into a ½-inch-thick round. You can then brush with egg white wash, but you don't have to. Lightly flour a round cookie cutter and cut out the scones. You should get 10–12 scones from this recipe.

Transfer scones to a parchment-lined baking sheet and pop into the freezer for 10–15 minutes. Bake for 20–25 minutes until scones are golden brown, depending on how hot your oven is. (Mine take 22 minutes to bake, but it's always a good idea to check after 18 minutes.) Transfer baked scones to a wire rack to cool. Serve right away or cool completely and place in an airtight container. Scones will keep for four days in the refrigerator, two months in the freezer.

STRAWBERRY AND CREAM SCONES

- 2¼ cups flour (plus extra for dusting hands and countertop)
- ⅓ cup sugar
- 2 tsp. baking powder
- ⅓ cup cold butter
- 1 cup fresh strawberries, quartered
- ⅓ cup cream

- 1 large egg
- ½ tsp. vanilla
- 1 egg white mixed with ½ tsp. water or cream to make a wash (optional)

Before you get started, preheat the oven to 400 degrees and line a baking sheet with parchment paper.

In a large bowl, whisk flour, sugar, and baking powder together. Cut cold butter into small pieces over the flour mixture. With your fingers, or you can use a pastry cutter or two knives if you'd prefer, combine the mixture until the butter resembles pea-size crumbs. Gently fold strawberries into the flour mixture. In a separate bowl, whisk together cream, egg, and vanilla. Pour into the flour mixture and stir (I use a wooden spoon) to combine.

Gather the dough into a ball—it will be sticky—and place onto a lightly floured countertop. With lightly floured hands, gently knead dough until smooth, being careful not to squish the strawberries—a minute or two at most. With your hands, pat dough into a ½-inch-thick round. You can then brush with the egg white wash, but it's fine if you prefer not to. Lightly flour a round cookie cutter and cut out the scones. You should get 10–12 scones from this recipe.

Transfer the scones to a parchment-lined baking sheet and pop into the freezer for 10–15 minutes. Bake for 20–25 minutes until scones are golden brown, depending on how hot your oven is. (Mine take 22 minutes to bake, but it's always a good idea to check after 18 minutes.) Transfer the baked scones to a wire rack to cool. Serve right away or cool completely and place in an airtight container. Scones will keep for four days in the refrigerator, two months in the freezer.

LAVENDER SCONES

- 2 cups flour (plus extra for dusting hands and countertop)
- ⅓ cup sugar
- 2 tsp. baking powder
- 2 tsp. grated lemon peel
- 2 tsp. culinary lavender (the inn gets organic dried lavender from the mayor, but I order mine off Amazon)
- ⅓ cup cold butter
- ½ cup buttermilk
- 1 large egg
- ½ tsp. vanilla
- 1 egg white mixed with ½ tsp water or cream to make a wash (optional)

Before you get started, preheat the oven to 400 degrees and line a baking sheet with parchment paper.

In a large bowl, whisk flour, sugar, baking powder, grated lemon peel, and lavender together. Cut cold butter into small pieces over the flour mixture. With your fingers, or you can use a pastry cutter or two knives if you'd prefer, combine the mixture until the butter resembles pea-size crumbs. In a separate bowl, whisk together buttermilk, egg, and vanilla. Pour into the flour mixture and stir (I use a wooden spoon) to combine.

Gather the dough into a ball—it will be sticky—and place onto a lightly floured countertop. With lightly floured hands, knead dough until smooth—a minute or two at most. With your hands, pat dough into a ½-inch-thick round. You can then brush with the egg white wash, but you don't have to. Lightly flour a round cookie cutter and cut out the scones. You should get 10–12 scones from this recipe.

Transfer the scones to the parchment-lined baking sheet and pop into the freezer for 10–15 minutes. Bake for 20–25 minutes until scones are golden brown, depending on how hot your oven is. (Mine take 22 minutes to bake, but it's always a good idea to check after 18 minutes.) Transfer the baked scones to a wire rack to cool. Serve right away or cool completely and place in an airtight container. Scones will keep for four days in the refrigerator, two months in the freezer.

LAVENDER SHORTBREAD

- 1 cup butter
- ½ cup sugar
- 2 tsp. culinary lavender
- 2 cups flour
- 1 cup semisweet or milk chocolate chips (optional)

Before you get started, preheat the oven to 325 degrees and line baking sheet(s) with parchment.

In a large bowl, cream the butter and sugar until light and fluffy. In a separate bowl, stir the lavender into the flour. Slowly add the flour mixture to the creamed butter and sugar, using a wooden spoon to combine into a ball. Place dough onto a lightly floured countertop and gently knead for five minutes. Don't overwork. Once done, separate dough into two pieces and place each piece in plastic wrap, rolling into two logs approximately seven inches long. Refrigerate the wrapped logs for two hours. Cut the chilled dough into ½-inch rounds with a sharp knife. Transfer the disks onto the parchment-lined baking sheet(s), spacing at least 2 inches apart. Bake for 15–20 minutes until edges are golden, depending on how hot your oven is. Remove from oven and let cool for 10 minutes before transferring to a wire rack. The recipe should make 12–14 cookies.

Once the cookies are cool, you can dip ends into melted semisweet chocolate chips or milk chocolate chips. Coat one-third of each cookie with melted chocolate. We prefer milk chocolate.

AFTERNOON TEA SANDWICHES

We're a big fan of tea sandwiches in our house. We serve them at birthdays and showers. Bites of Bliss makes the sandwich bread for the inn, but I have to order mine from the local bakery. You might also be able to find sandwich bread at your local grocery store. I order brown sandwich loaves and white, as well as loaves dyed pink and sometimes blue.

Here are some of the most popular fillings at the inn and at my house. The amounts vary depending on how many sandwiches you're making and your personal taste preference, so you may want to adjust. You can also make double- or triple-decker sandwiches, using two or three of the fillings. If you go with a single filling, you can use cookie cutters to cut into shapes. Sandwiches can also be cut into rectangles, squares, or triangles. Once you have the fillings made, cut off bread crusts and use softened butter to butter bread.

Salmon

- 1 6-oz can of salmon
- 1 tbsp. lemon juice
- ¼–½ cup Miracle Whip or mayonnaise
- 2 green onions, chopped fine
- Pinch of salt and pepper
- Combine all ingredients and spread evenly on bread.

Tuna

- 1-oz can of tuna
- 1 tbsp. lemon juice
- ¼–½ cup Miracle Whip or mayonnaise
- 2 green onions, chopped fine
- Pinch of salt and pepper

Combine all ingredients and spread evenly on bread.

Egg

- 4 hard-boiled eggs, mashed
- ¼–½ cup Miracle Whip or mayonnaise
- 1 tsp. Dijon mustard
- 2 green onions, chopped fine
- Pinch of salt and pepper

Combine all ingredients and spread evenly on bread.

Chicken

- 3 boneless chicken breasts, boiled and chilled, either pulled apart or grated
- ¼–½ cup Miracle Whip or mayonnaise
- 2 tbsp. cranberry sauce
- 2 tsp. Dijon mustard
- 2 sprigs watercress, chopped

Combine all ingredients and spread evenly on bread.

Ham

- 3 cups grated ham (my mother-in-law uses canned ham, but I'm not a fan of the jelly, so I buy a smoked ham and grate it)
- ¼–½ cup Miracle Whip or mayonnaise
- 2 tbsp. green relish (or to taste)

Combine all ingredients and spread evenly on bread.

ROLLED SANDWICHES

We usually gather together to make these sandwiches the night before. They need enough filling to hold them together. We wrap the finished sandwiches with plastic wrap, cover with damp tea towels, and leave in the refrigerator until we're ready to serve the next day.

Banana and peanut butter—Cut crusts off bread and lightly roll with a rolling pin to flatten. Add softened butter to peanut butter to easily spread it onto the bread. Cut a whole banana to fit on the short end of the bread and then roll.

Gherkins and cream cheese—Cut crusts off bread and lightly roll with a rolling pin to flatten. Add softened butter to cream cheese to easily spread it onto the bread. Line gherkins on the short end of the bread and then roll.

Green olives and cream cheese—Cut crusts off bread and lightly roll with a rolling pin to flatten. Add softened butter to cream cheese to easily spread it onto the bread. Line the green olives on the short end of the bread and then roll.

Red cherries and cream cheese—Cut crusts off bread and lightly roll with a rolling pin to flatten. Add softened butter to cream cheese to easily spread it onto the bread. Line red cherries on the short end of the bread and then roll.

About the Author

Debbie Mason is the *USA Today* bestselling author of the Christmas, Colorado; Harmony Harbor; and Highland Falls series. The first book in her Christmas, Colorado, series, *The Trouble with Christmas*, was the inspiration for the Hallmark movie *Welcome to Christmas*. Her books have been praised by *RT Book Reviews* for their "likable characters, clever dialogue, and juicy plots." When Debbie isn't writing, she enjoys spending time with her family in Ottawa, Canada.

You can learn more at:
AuthorDebbieMason.com
Twitter @AuthorDebMason
Facebook.com/DebbieMasonBooks
Instagram @AuthorDebMason

Can't get enough of that small-town charm? Forever has you covered with these heartwarming contemporary romances!

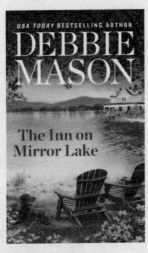

THE INN ON MIRROR LAKE
by Debbie Mason

Elliana MacLeod has come home to whip the Mirror Lake Inn into tip-top shape so her mother won't sell the beloved family business. And now that Highland Falls is vying to be named the Most Romantic Small Town in America, she can't refuse any offer of help—even if it's from the gorgeous law enforcement officer next door. But Nathan Black has made it abundantly clear they're friends, and nothing more. Little do they know the town matchmakers are out to prove them wrong.

FALLING FOR YOU
by Barb Curtis

Faith Rotolo is shocked to inherit a historic mansion in quaint Sapphire Springs. But her new home needs some major fixing up. Too bad the handsome local contractor, Rob Milan, is spoiling her daydreams with the harsh realities of the project...and his grouchy personality. But as they work together, their spirited clashes wind up sparking a powerful attraction. As work nears completion, will she and Rob realize that they deserve a fresh start too?

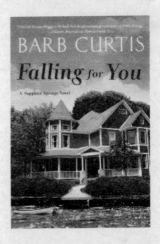

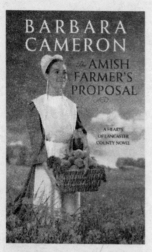

THE AMISH FARMER'S PROPOSAL
by Barbara Cameron

When Amish dairy farmer Abe Stoltzfus tumbles from his roof, he's lucky his longtime friend Lavinia Fisher is there to help. He secretly hoped to propose to her, but now, with his injuries, his dairy farm in danger, and his harvest at stake, Abe worries he'll only be a burden. But as he heals with Lavinia's gentle support and unflagging optimism, the two grow even closer. Will she be able to convince him that real love doesn't need perfect timing?

AUNT IVY'S COTTAGE
by Kristin Harper

When Zoey returns to Dune Island, she's shocked to find her elderly Aunt Ivy being pushed into a nursing home by a cousin. As the family clashes, Zoey meets Nick, the local lighthouse keeper with ocean-blue eyes and a warm laugh. With Nick as her ally, Zoey is determined to keep Aunt Ivy free. But when they discover a secret that threatens to upend Ivy's life, will they still be able to ensure her final years are filled with happiness...and maybe find love with each other along the way?

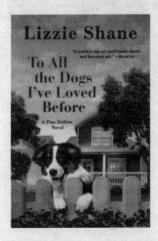

**COMING HOME TO
SEASHELL HARBOR
by Miranda Liasson**

After a *very* public breakup, Hadley Wells is returning home to get back on her feet. But Seashell Harbor has trouble of its own. An injury forced her ex-boyfriend Tony Cammareri into early retirement, and the former NFL pro is making waves with a splashy new restaurant. They're on opposing sides of a decision over the town's future, but as their rivalry intensifies, they must decide what's worth fighting for—and what it truly means to be happy. Includes a bonus story by Jeannie Chin!

**SUMMER BY THE SEA
by Jenny Hale**

Faith can never forget the summer she found her first love—or how her younger sister, Casey, stole the man of her dreams. They've been estranged ever since. But at the request of their grandmother, Faith agrees to spend the summer with Casey at the beach where their feud began. While Faith is ready to forget—if not forgive—old hurts, she's *not* ready for her unexpected chemistry with their neighbor, Jake Buchanan. But for a truly unforgettable summer, she'll need to open her heart.

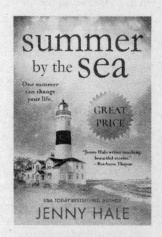